NIGHT TRAVELER

CARTER McKNIGHT

HELLA BOOKS

New York London Sydney

ISBN 978-0-9863957-5-8

Rev. 1.17

ACKNOWLEDGMENTS

To those kind folks who generously contributed their time, advice, and advocacy to this enterprise—you know who you are—a heartfelt thank you.

Cover by Steven Novak (http://novakillustration.com), whose artistic sensibility is second to none.

"Skepticism, like chastity, should not be relinquished too readily."

—*George Santayana*

NIGHT TRAVELER

1

Flashing red and blue lights up ahead gave the night sky a festive glow visible from a mile away. Emergency vehicles, and it would take a fleet of them to create a display like that. Whatever was going on up there had to be serious. A multi-vehicle accident, perhaps.

Dan Crocetti tapped the motor coach's brake to disengage the cruise control and let the big rig slow to a cautious thirty-five, thankful traffic was sparse at a quarter to nine.

"*Destination on right in one-half mile,*" the GPS said.

The destination was the Plush Horse RV Park, located a half-mile north of Brookings on U.S. Route 101, Oregon's scenic coast highway.

Crocetti yawned, so widely his jaw creaked like a hinge that needed oil. His eyelids felt like sandpaper, 100-grit. The day's drive, after a late start from his brother's place in Pendleton, had been long and tiring. What he should have done was stop at Chinook Winds Casino in Lincoln City, which allowed over-night camping, and grab six or seven hours of sack time before continuing on.

No matter, the Plush Horse was directly ahead. Check-in and parking the rig wouldn't take long and then he could fall into his soft bed without even bothering to hook up services or deploy the slideouts. With any luck, whatever was going on up ahead wouldn't delay that plan much.

In the morning he would continue south along the coast to Los Angeles, with stops in San Francisco and Monterey. From L.A. he planned to get on Route 66 and follow the historic highway—what remained of it—to its terminus in Chicago. He had fantasized about it back when he was on the job. The fantasies of course included Alison, who had shared the dream. God, he missed that woman.

"*Destination on right in one-quarter mile,*" the GPS said.

He could see the RV park's sign up ahead, illuminated by flashing red and blue light from the empty police cruiser parked underneath.

He slowed and turned into the entrance. Inside the park he counted ten more cruisers, all painting the night red and blue. The place was crawling with city, state, and county cops. A sheriff's deputy walked toward him, holding up his hand palm-out. He looked aggravated.

Crocetti stopped the coach and opened his side window. "Evening."

The deputy had wire-rim glasses and a pockmarked face. "Sir, you can't come in here. This is a crime scene. Someone's supposed to be at the entrance, keeping people out."

Crocetti produced his retired police officer's shield and I.D. "So what happened—somebody got murdered?"

The deputy gave him a thin smile. "You could say that."

"Just a second." Crocetti switched off the idling engine, grabbed his cane, and disembarked, as he'd taken to calling it. Before he could ask the deputy for details, a heavyset man in a gray suit walked up to them. The florid face was familiar, but Crocetti couldn't recall where he'd seen him before. Then it clicked: They'd sat next to each other at the Oregon Peace Officers Association awards banquet in Salem three years ago, shortly before Crocetti retired. Hopple, that was his name. A decent fellow.

"I thought that was you, Crocetti. What the hell you doing clear down here?"

Crocetti shook Hopple's hand. "On my way south, planned to spend the night here."

Hopple pointed to Crocetti's leg. "How's the knee?"

"Three surgeries and I figure it's about as good as it's going to get, given how bad the slug tore it up. The doctor wanted another crack at it, but I told him to take a hike."

"Well, you picked a great place to camp. A real beaut."

"How so?"

"We got us a double murder here."

Crocetti indicated the fleet of police cruisers, marked and unmarked, with a sweeping gesture. "All these cops, seems like overkill, even for a doubleheader. So who got whacked, the president and first lady?"

Hopple pointed at a motor coach with vivid red, gold, and bronze graphics adorning its side. "A couple from Redding named Ostrow, headed for Spokane to visit their daughter. When they didn't check out by noon like they said they were going to, the park manager came knocking. No answer, and their Mini Cooper was still hitched up. The manager waited a while and gave it another shot, with the same result. The third time, he tried the door and found it unlocked. So he pulled it open and called out to them. Then he noticed Mrs. Ostrow on the sofa. Her skin was white as a marble statue, and she was wearing a negligee. He found Mr. Ostrow in the bedroom, naked as a jaybird and just as white. The manager got out of there and called nine one one. That was three and a half hours ago."

"Sounds like a run-of-the-mill double homicide so far."

Hopple grunted. "So far. But come with me." He started toward the murdered couple's coach. "The C.S.U. team should be finished."

The coach had a temporary license sticker on the windshield, so it was almost brand new. Built on a Prevost chassis, it had taken a big bite out of a couple million bucks. Crocetti's rig, also a Prevost, was seven years old and cost him only two hundred and fifty thou. He'd bought it from an old guy in Cascade Locks who had parked and covered it after his wife died. Low mileage, a new generator, and new tires all around. And its depreciation curve had leveled off considerably.

"You ruled out murder-suicide?" Crocetti asked him.

"Sure did."

"So how did they die?"

"Massive blood loss."

"From knife wounds?"

Hopple's face was impassive. "Not exactly."

"What, then?"

"You tell me."

A lanky plainclothes cop stepped down from the victims' motor coach, an odd look on his face.

"Hey, Feldenstein," Hopple said, "you look a little green around the gills."

The man looked at Hopple and indicated the coach's open doorway with his thumb. "All yours."

"After you," Hopple said to Crocetti.

Crocetti climbed the metal steps and entered the coach. The palatial interior made his coach seem almost utilitarian, although it suited him perfectly. He didn't need or want a parquet floor, marble countertops, paneling with intricate inlaid designs, gleaming gold fixtures, leather furniture the color of eggshells, or indirect lighting all around the ceiling's perimeter. Different strokes.

The interior also had a peculiar smell. Mingled with the plasticky new-RV odor was a faint but pungent odor of decay, like rotting meat. The source couldn't be the victims; they hadn't been dead long enough. Dead bodies would need weeks to create a stench like that.

Supine on the leather sofa, Mrs. Ostrow looked to be in her sixties. Her skin had a pallor only exsanguination, a total loss of blood, could provide. Her makeup, perfectly coiffed silver hair, and blue negligee gave the impression she had been entertaining a lover. Strangest of all, the expression on her face. Not pain, fear, or horror. It was ecstasy.

Hopple pointed. "Those look like knife wounds to you?"

On the side of her neck, over the carotid artery, were two round holes about two inches apart. No blood around the holes. No blood anywhere.

"Puncture wounds." Crocetti said. "About what you'd get with a sharp, round implement the diameter of a pencil, the thick kind, like grade school kids use. Holes that size you'd have geysers of blood. So where is it?"

"Beats the hell out of me."

"It'd be nearly impossible to drain that much blood into a container without leaving some evidence of it behind."

"Almost makes you believe in vampires."

"I believe in psychopaths. Only a psycho would go to this much trouble to make it look like the vics were killed by a friggin' vampire."

"Then you don't think it's necessary to drive wooden stakes through the vics' hearts so they don't join the legion of the undead?" Hopple's falsetto laugh echoed off the inlaid walls.

Crocetti snorted. "Let's have a look at the husband."

While making their way back to the bedroom, Crocetti poked his head into the bathroom. The glassed-in shower was spacious enough for a poker game. He checked the drain for blood. He couldn't see any, but that didn't mean much.

On the king-size bed, Mr. Ostrow came close to matching the white sheets. His neck had acquired two large holes, and his face wore the same ecstatic expression as his wife's. The sheet was still damp with the semen he'd ejaculated.

"I'd bet money they were drugged," Crocetti said.

Hopple nodded. "Probably so high they didn't know what was happening to them."

"Think I'll stick around for the M.E.'s report." It wasn't like he was on a schedule. If he got to L.A. two days later than he'd planned, so what? It was a damned intriguing case. And he missed the job. Missed it a lot.

"Sure, you might as well hang around and see how this shakes out," Hopple said. "I could use your input."

Another yawn forced its way out of Crocetti's mouth. Somehow he'd forgotten how bone-tired he was. That used to happen on the job when things heated up. He turned to Hopple. "Any problem with parking my rig here?"

"Shouldn't be," Hopple said. "I'll square it with the park manager. Hey, looks like the meat wagon has arrived. What say we get out of their way?"

As the medical examiner's team filed in through the front door, he and Hopple left via the back door. Outside, he took several deep breaths, glad to leave the peculiar smell behind.

"There's the manager now," Hopple said. "Be right back." He returned a few minutes later. "He said pick out a spot."

Crocetti had a choice of three pull-through parking spots. He picked a space away from the trees, to keep his coach's roof as free of debris as possible. After the coach's auto leveler did its thing, he decided to hook up the power, water, and sewer after all. The black water tank needed to be dumped, but that could wait until tomorrow. He deployed the slide-outs, a matter of pressing buttons. He was washing his hands at the kitchen sink with antibacterial soap when someone knocked. He limped over to the door sans cane.

It was Hopple. "Busy?"

"Come on in for a minute, but I'm fading fast. Long drive."

Hopple stepped inside and looked around, nodding. "Nice setup, Crocetti. And they say cops got no taste."

"As long as you're here, maybe you can enlighten me as to the reason for the huge police response to the murder scene. It's bizarre as hell due to the pseudo-vampire angle, but it's still just a double murder."

Hopple perched a haunch on the sofa's broad arm, a cat-ate-the-canary expression on his face.

"Okay, Hopple, out with it. What the hell's going on here?"

"It's like this. Over the past two months there have been three other murders in Oregon RV parks—in Tillamook, Lakeview, and La Grande—all with the same M.O."

"Jesus. And they're keeping a lid on it?"

"You got it. Can't have the public panicking."

Smart move. Reports of bloodless bodies with holes in their necks would churn up hysteria in superstitious people ready to believe a vampire was on the loose.

But he had a theory how the killer had pulled it off.

2

Crocetti parked his red Honda Fit on the street in front of Meecham Funeral Home and beep-locked it with the dongle. It was only the second time he'd driven the little car since buying it in Portland. The coach didn't even notice when it was hitched behind, docilely following. The deal sealer: It had more than enough room for his 6-foot-2-inch, 205-pound frame. The Fit. It did indeed.

Meecham's ornate front entrance would have done credit to a church. Using his coat sleeve on the handle, he pulled one of the heavily lacquered doors open and went in. The rose-colored carpet in the foyer had a foam pad underneath several inches thick, it felt like. In the sepulcral silence a flowery-sweet smell floated on indoor air currents.

A tall, silver-haired gentleman in a dark suit appeared, looking like a mortician from central casting. He nodded at Crocetti and then walked past him and out the front door. Either the man didn't work there or Meecham's had the worst customer service in the world.

"Can I help you, sir?" The contralto voice belonged to a woman with hair dyed a shade of auburn that did not occur in nature. Other signs of a desperate battle with age: Lipstick transgressed her lip boundary to a degree that bordered on comical and drawn-on eyebrows expressed perpetual surprise. "I'm Erlene Meecham. How may we be of service?"

Shaking her proffered hand couldn't be avoided. "Dan Crocetti, Mrs. Meecham. I'm here to get some information."

"You have lost a loved one, Mr. Crocetti?"

"I have, but not lately. I'm working with the Brookings police on a confidential matter. In an advisory capacity."

"Oh." Her smile vanished. "What sort of information do you need?"

"Can you describe for me the process you use to remove blood from a body?"

"Of course. We use an industry-standard procedure. Two incisions are made on the deceased, one in a vein, the other in a major artery, usually the carotid. Then an arterial tube is inserted into the artery, and a pump called a Porti-Boy pushes the blood out of the open vein, replacing it with embalming fluid."

"So the blood is pushed out rather than sucked out?"

"Correct." Disappointment must have shown on his face, because she said, "Not the answer you were expecting?"

"I was hoping you used some sort of suction device to remove the blood."

"Well . . . I have seen suction devices at equipment shows, designed to remove fluids from the abdomen. I'm sure they would remove blood as well."

"Are they portable?"

"I guess so. The ones I saw weren't all that large."

"The instrument that's actually inserted into the body, can you describe it?"

"A cannula—a stainless-steel tube about five millimeters in diameter with a razor-sharp slanted tip."

"Mrs. Meecham, you've been very helpful. Thank you."

Back in the car he got a bottle of hand sanitizer from the glove box and squirted a dollop in his palm. The astringent odor was a welcome change from the cloyingly sweet smell of the funeral home. After distributing the sanitizer on his hands he smeared some on the door handle, the glove box button, and the steering wheel where he'd touched it getting in. Then he started the car and pulled away from the curb.

It had been forty years since he'd last been in Brookings, and he hardly recognized it. The formerly bustling downtown was now on life support, taken over by antique stores, craft shops, seedy real estate offices, gift shops, and secondhand stores. It was now indistinguishable from tens of thousands of other small towns that had been totally overwhelmed by Walmart, Carl's Junior, Best Western, Burger King, 7-Eleven, Applebees, Holiday Inn, McDonald's, Rite-Aid, Taco Bell, Subway, Starbucks, and Ace Hardware. Before long the U.S. would be a coast-to-coast strip mall, all traces of uniqueness and individuality erased.

His spirits rose when he found an old-time barber shop on Hillside Avenue, half a block from the main drag. He was past due for a haircut, so he parked in front and went in. Lloyd's Barber Shop had a selection of magazines for customers to read, including stacks of old *Mechanix Illustrated*. He picked up a couple of issues dated 1958 and sat down in the chair.

The barber, on the short side with a shiny pate, peered at him through trifocals. "Just a trim?"

"If you please," Crocetti said. "You must be Lloyd."

"No, I'm just running the shop while Lloyd's away. He's been gone a year now. Name's Charlie." He draped a white nylon barber's cape around Crocetti's neck and switched on his electric clippers, and then he launched into a tirade about gypsies. Gypsies, he said, had broken into his garage. "Busted the lock with a crowbar and made off with three hundred bucks' worth of power tools, the thieving bastards."

"How do you know it was gypsies that did it?"

"My neighbor Gus seen 'em running away carrying the tools."

"Did you report it to police?"

"Yes, for all the good it'll do."

"Lot of gypsies in this area?"

"Not usually. This bunch showed up a few weeks ago, don't know where they came from. They're called travelers. Wish they'd travel to somewhere else."

"How do they get around?"

"They all got RVs, a couple dozen of 'em. Travel in a cara-van and camp on public land. I hear tell they're camped east of town."

"I don't know much about gypsies," Crocetti said, "other than what I've learned from movies and TV shows."

"Alls I know is, they're thieving sons of bitches. Okay, all set." He removed the barber's cape with a flourish and shook off the hair trimmings with a snap.

Crocetti inspected the haircut in the mirror. "Nice job, Charlie. How much do I owe you?"

"Six seventy-five."

Crocetti took out a ten-spot and handed it to him. "Keep the change. And I hope you get your tools back."

Driving away after using hand sanitizer, he wished he had talked Charlie out of a couple issues of *Mechanix Illustrated*. He liked old magazines, and those were so ancient, any germs they harbored would have long since died.

On the way to the Plush Horse he stopped at a Union 76 station and bought a map of Oregon. It cost $8.95, literally highway robbery.

In the coach, after a trip to the bathroom, he opened up the map and spread it out on the table. He got some round stickers from the desk, red ones. Brookings, Tillamook, Lake-view, and La Grande received a sticker. The next step was to find out the order of the killings. Maybe it would show a predictable pattern of travel.

Charlie the barber had said the gypsies were camped on public land east of town. Crocetti's finger traveled to the southern end of the Rogue-Siskiyou National Forest, the only public land that filled the bill.

Perhaps if he got a chance he'd run out there and have a look. Might be interesting to see a gypsy RV caravan.

3

He met Hopple for lunch at a restaurant named the Flying Gull. North of town, right next to the Best Western. "Best steaks in Brookings," according to Hopple.

A smiling young woman filled their water glasses before Crocetti had a chance to inspect his. Not a problem—he'd order a bottle of beer. The cutlery passed inspection.

After they ordered, Crocetti excused himself to wash his hands. He awarded the restroom a cleanliness rating of ten. Meaning spotless. He washed his hands thoroughly. For good measure he used a dab of hand sanitizer from the travel-size bottle he carried in the right-front pocket of his pants. A couple of folded paper towels neutralized any biological threat the door handle posed.

Back at the table he asked Hopple if he'd heard anything from the medical examiner yet.

"Matter of fact," Hopple said, "I did. You won't believe it."

"Try me."

Hopple took a sip of water and leaned forward. "This is going to spin your head around. The M.E. found traces of two substances in the victims—an anesthetic and a very potent anticoagulant. But no drugs."

"Interesting."

"It gets more interesting. The anticoagulant he found has a very appropriate name. It's called—drumroll—*draculin*."

"I call bullshit."

"Swear to God, that's its name. Some Venezuelan scientist identified and named it."

"Did the M.E. say if this draculin can be easily obtained?"

Hopple shook his head. "Why don't you ask him?"

"I'll Google it first. But I'll be surprised if it's not available somewhere, ditto with the anesthetic. Find the source, find the killer."

Hopple grinned. "I saved the juiciest bit until last. The scientist, care to guess where he discovered draculin and the anesthetic?"

"No idea."

"Vampire bats." His grin widened.

"Which means the killer is meticulous about details. He's after total realism."

"Okay, let me ask you something. Have you considered the possibility, however crazy it sounds, that he's a real—"

Crocetti held up his hand. "The answer is no, I haven't. I'm a lapsed Catholic who believes in science. Everything has a sane and logical explanation, one that does not involve the supernatural."

The server placed his steak in front of him. He picked up his knife and cut into it. Bloody juice oozed from the red meat. He'd ordered the steak rare, as he usually did, but it wasn't appetizing now. He signaled the server. "Could I get this done a bit more, please? So it's pink inside instead of red?"

"Surely," she said and took it away.

She returned with it five minutes later, done to perfection. Hopple was right. It was the tenderest, tastiest steak he'd had in a long time.

"I'm curious," Hopple said between bites. "What kind of fuel mileage do you get in that big bus of yours?"

"It averages ten. The best it's ever gotten is twelve. My brother's a top-notch mechanic, a genius with diesel engines. He worked his magic on it. My rig doesn't have a humongous diesel, but it's big enough."

"Ten miles per gallon. Must be hard on your wallet."

"What I save in food and lodging more than makes up for it. And I get to sleep in my own bed every night."

Fuel consumption wasn't an issue for him. He had sold the house in Portland, which he'd owned outright, for $850,000, and after buying the motor coach he invested the balance in dividend-paying stocks, bonds, and funds that netted him a bit over nine hundred a month. Throw in another four grand a month from his FPDR disability pension and he was sitting pretty. His father made it to eighty-five, his mother eighty-nine, so he figured he had at least a decade of RV travel ahead of him, probably more. Long enough to see everything worth seeing in the States and Canada.

Hopple leaned back in his chair. "Dessert?"

"Not me, I'm too full as it is." He took out his notepad. "What was the sequence of the killings, the order of the towns he hit?"

"Let's see, now ... Lakeview was first, Tillamook second, La Grande third, and here last. Why?"

"Just curious. Next question. Have you had any trouble with gypsies?"

Hopple shrugged. "Just a few reports of pilferage."

"I heard they're camped on public land east of town."

"Yeah, you take South Bank Chetco River Road, then head east on Mount Emily Road. They're out about five or six miles. Why the interest in gypsies?"

"The barber yapped about them the whole time he was cutting my hair."

"Hey, maybe a gypsy fortuneteller can tell us where the vampire killer will strike next."

Crocetti gave him a courtesy laugh.

The server brought the check and Crocetti handed her a debit card. "I've got this."

"Muchas gracias," Hopple said.

Outside the Flying Gull, Crocetti loosened his belt a notch.

"Later, partner," Hopple said, "And watch your neck." He laughed all the way to his car. A real card.

4

A Google search for draculin turned up some articles about Venezuelan scientist Rafael Apitz-Castro and how he had discovered the anesthetic and anticoagulant in vampire bats' saliva. But no links to outlets for the substances, commercial or otherwise. So where did the killer score the stuff?

The map of Oregon still covered the table. He numbered the stickers in the order Hopple had said, and then he used a ruler and a red felt-tip pen to draw lines from Lakeview to Tillamook to La Grande to Brookings. Geometrically, the lines formed a lopsided figure eight with a flat top and open bottom. Not a logical route, which made it hard to predict where the psycho would strike next. So far the towns he'd chosen were all small burgs in far-flung corners of the state. And all were close to national forests.

Public land.

Whenever two things overlapped, his cop antennae went up. In this case the area of overlap was public land—gypsies camped on it and all the killings took place near it. Hard to ignore something like that. Tomorrow he'd jump in the little Honda and take a drive east of town and have a look.

He heard voices outside. Across the way, three couples stood talking. One of the men pointed at the Ostrows' coach. Crocetti grabbed his cane and hustled outside as fast as his bum knee allowed.

"Hi, folks," he said as he neared the group.

Their conversation halted and they turned toward him. "Hello," one of the women said.

"Name's Dan," he said. "Pulled in last night. That's mine there." He pointed to his coach with the cane.

"Nice rig," one of the men said.

Crocetti pointed at the Ostrow's coach. "Not as nice as that one, though."

"That there's a new one," the man said. "What a shame."

A woman with permed hair dyed an unnatural shade of red said, "Did you hear what happened to its owners, Dan?"

"Yes . . . but I didn't hear all the details. Maybe you can fill me in."

"They were *murdered*," she said, her eyes glistening. "The park manager saw the bodies. He said their skin was white as alabaster and they had—get this—*smiles* on their faces. Is that weird or what?"

"Did the manager say how they were killed?"

"No, he didn't look that close, he was so freaked out."

So he hadn't seen the holes in the victims' necks, which was just as well. He probably would have had a stroke. "Did anybody in the park see or hear anything?"

"Me and Dodie, we went around asking people," the red-headed woman said, indicating the rail-thin woman next to her, "and nobody seen or heard nothing."

"Nothing," Dodie echoed.

"Except for what the guy in the fiver told us," the red-head said, pointing at a fifth wheel as large as any of the coaches. "Hey, speak of the devil."

A smiling man wearing a Hawaiian shirt and cargo shorts with sandals and white socks walked toward them. The bird-like legs below his shorts made a startling contrast with his barrel chest and big gut. He nodded to the group. "Y'all hear any news about the murders?"

"Not a thing," a third woman said in a whiskey tenor.

"This here's Dan," the redhead said. "Tell him what you told us."

"Sure ... I got up during the night to take a piss—sorry, ladies—and I heard a rig start up." Bird Legs had a thick southern accent—Georgia, Alabama, Arkansas, perhaps Mississippi. "So I looked out and saw the all-black coach that was parked on the other side of them folks that got killed. I watched it leave, and then I went back to bed. That was three fifteen. Kind of an odd time to head out, seems to me."

"An all-black Class A," Crocetti said. "Notice anything else about it—make, model, length?"

"Didn't notice the make, but it looked a lot like that one." He indicated the Ostrows' coach. "Other than the paint."

"Was it towing a vehicle?"

"Nope. But one other thing ... I automatically look at RVs' plates to see what state they come from, and its license plate was white, pretty much, with dark letters. I didn't have my glasses on, so I can't tell you any more than that."

Crocetti turned to the three couples. "Anyone else notice that rig when it was parked there?"

They all shook their heads.

"The thing is," Bird Legs said, "what with its black paint and dark windows, it wasn't what you'd call eye-catching. Fact of the matter, it was prackly invisible next to the dead folks' rig."

"Did you tell the police about it?"

"I started to, but the young cop I was talking to asked if I'd excuse him a minute, but he never did come back. So I said to hell with it."

Typical. Sometimes in the pandemonium at crime scenes things were forgotten or overlooked. Bird Leg's story suggested the killer drove a motor coach. The vampire RVer.

Crocetti told them it certainly was fascinating stuff, all right. He nodded to them and headed for his coach to use the bathroom. Damned prostate. Afterward he'd head over to the manager's office and pay him for another three nights (at a steep forty-five bucks per) and try to pry some information about the black coach out of him. In particular, its plate number and when it arrived at the Plush Horse.

The manager was a stocky, ruddy-faced fellow in khaki pants and matching shirt with red suspenders. "I don't got any of that information," he said. "That rig musta come in after nine. After hours we operate on the honor system—folks is s'posed to check in the next morning, register and pay for the space. Guess he changed his mind about staying."

Or he'd concluded his business at the park.

Through the office window, a hundred yards away, the Ostrow's coach stood silent, its festive graphics belying the horror that had taken place within.

"My two cents," the manager said, "them poor folks was killed by gypsies."

"Think so?"

"Damn straight I do. Wherever gypsies show up, trouble ain't far behind. I gave the police an earful about them, too."

"I'm sure you did. Listen, you have a good day."

On the way back to his rig he gave a rock the size of a robin's egg a hell of a kick with his good leg and sent it skittering across the asphalt to strike the fence encircling the empty swimming pool. He had counted on seeing the park registration info. Without it, tracking down the black coach wouldn't be easy.

His cell phone trilled just as he stepped aboard his coach. It was Hopple. "I ran into the medical examiner today," he said, "and I asked him how someone would go about obtaining draculin. Know what he said?"

"I got a feeling you're going to tell me."

"He said it's impossible to get, unless you happen to have the know-how and specialized equipment to collect it from vampire bat saliva."

Crocetti sighed heavily. "That jibes with what I learned from my Google search. Too bad."

"Think our vampire's a scientist?"

"I don't know what to think. He's getting the stuff somewhere, though."

The alternative, that the draculin and the anesthetic came from the killer's saliva, was too absurd to even consider.

5

Crocetti paused with the door half open. He pulled it shut and went over to the desk and removed two items from the bottom drawer: a Colt .38 with the bluing worn off in places and a well-used leather shoulder holster. He took off his jacket and slipped into the shoulder rig and holstered the Colt. Three years since he'd felt that familiar weight against his ribs. He put on the jacket, grabbed the cane, and left the coach. Correction: disembarked from the coach.

With the fastidious care new cars inspire, he let the Fit warm up for a full two minutes before he put it in gear. He turned right on 101 and punched it so the logging truck in his rearview mirror wouldn't run the hell over him. The little Honda obliged with acceleration snappy enough to make him grin. After the fifteen-ton coach, driving the nimble car felt as though he'd swapped a battleship for a speedboat.

He crossed the bridge over the Chetco River and took a left on South Bank Chetco River Road, which wound alongside the river. He pushed it on twists and turns, even squealing the tires on a few curves. It brought back memories of more carefree days, flying through the twisties on the Oregon side of the Columbia Gorge in a Porsche 356. Dumbest thing he ever did, selling that car. The week before, a 356C, a pristine '65 like his, brought $105,000 at Barrett-Jackson. He had let his go for $3900 shortly after he joined the force.

He almost missed the sign that announced, "Rogue River-Siskiyou National Forest." A mile past the sign he came upon their encampment, an assortment of RVs—Class A coaches of various sizes, Class B van conversions, Class C cab-over vans, fifth-wheels, and Airstream trailers—parked in a semicircle, most of them fairly new. The gypsies weren't hurting for dough. No black coach in sight, though.

He parked next to a cluster of cars—all small and easily towed behind a motor home—and got out. Birds in nearby trees announced his arrival. A light breeze carried pungent forest smells, triggering memories of backpacking with his father a lifetime ago. "Miss you, Pop," he said aloud.

A crunch of gravel behind him jarred him back to the present. He turned around. A group of young men ranging in age from late teens to early twenties were walking toward him. For a welcoming committee they certainly didn't look very friendly.

"Morning," he called out to them.

They stopped four feet away. A tall kid with a simian face who looked like he might be a weightlifting fanatic stepped forward. "What do you want, mister?"

Crocetti sighed. He'd dealt with hundreds of young punks. Let them see any uncertainty and you were done for. "What makes you think I want something?"

"Why are you here?"

"It's public land." Crocetti indicated the surrounding forest with a gesture. "I'm a public."

"You're a cop."

Crocetti shook his head. "Private citizen."

"Then what's that bulge under your coat?" The kid had sharp eyes.

"The case for my sunglasses. What's it to you?"

"So you're a private citizen. Just came here to gawk at the gypsies?"

"Nope. But I wouldn't mind speaking with a few gypsies."

"We are Roma. Or Romani. We consider 'gypsy' a slur."

"So noted. No offense intended."

"Listen, Mr. Private Citizen, why don't you get back in your car and get the h—"

"Dimitri!"

Monkey Face flinched. His buddies moved aside to make room for an old woman in a purple jogging suit and Adidas—not exactly stereotypical gypsy regalia—her iron gray hair pulled back into a single braid that fell past her waist.

She glared at the group of young men, her hands on her hips. "That is no way to treat our visitor," she said. Her heavy accent was eastern European, perhaps Hungarian or Czech. "You boys run along now." She watched them go and then turned to Crocetti. "I have been expecting you."

After a flummoxed pause he said, "Is that so?"

"Come with me."

He followed her to a Class C motor home. They sat outside in folding chairs under the shade of an awning, and she served him tea in delicate (and sparkling clean) china. He regarded her over the cup's rim as he sipped the tea. Set in the deeply lined face, her dark eyes were intense. She must have been a striking beauty in her younger days.

"What did you mean, you'd been expecting me?"

She smiled. "The tarot cards told me."

"Right." He couldn't keep the sarcasm out of his tone.

"You do not believe in tarot?"

"I don't really know much about it." Or anything about it. The truth was, he hated woo-woo crap like that.

"The tarot cards said you would be coming. They revealed other things about you."

"Such as?"

"You are widowed and have one child, a daughter. Now you are a traveler. Like us."

He took a sip of tea. How in hell could she possibly have guessed those things?

"You have intense curiosity, a ravenous hunger to know."

On target again.

"I must warn you." Her eyes bored into his. "You are in great danger."

"How so?"

She looked off into the distance. "Your abiding curiosity will lead you to an ancient evil."

Right. An ancient evil. The worst kind. "Well," he said with a deadpan expression, "that's . . . very interesting."

"A wise man would heed the warning."

"This ancient evil—maybe you can give me a description to help me recognize it?"

She refilled his cup. "You will know it when you see it."

"Well then, I'll be on the lookout for evil. Ancient and otherwise." He blew on the tea. "Thanks for the warning."

"What you do with it is up to you."

Time to switch gears. "One of the reasons I came out here was to look over the camping situation. I have a motor coach that's currently parked at the Plush Horse RV Park north of town. Heard of it?"

"I have heard that a terrible thing happened there."

"Yes, a terrible thing. Night before last a man and woman were murdered in their motor home."

"How do you and the others think they were killed?"

Strange way to put it. Not, How were they killed?

"A madman stabbed them to death. A psycho."

"They lost all their blood?"

"That's right."

"And their necks each had two holes?"

"Yes, as a matter of fact."

Dark eyes bored into him. "It was the work of a nosferatu. A vampire. We call him the Night Traveler."

"Is that so?" Sweet Jesus, more vampire crap. The insanity seemed to be catching.

"There can be no doubt."

"Please don't take this the wrong way, but I don't believe in vampires."

"It is not necessary that you believe in a thing for it to exist."

"I have a more down-to-earth theory—the killer wants people to *think* he's a vampire. He's got a screw loose."

"You will learn the truth soon enough." She refilled their cups. "Did you come here hoping to find your killer among the Roma?"

"Not really. I'm trying to locate a black motor coach that might be camped somewhere around here."

"The Night Traveler's. This is the last place he would be."

"Why is that?"

She set her cup down. "He fears the Roma."

"Why?"

"We possess knowledge that can destroy him."

A gypsy curse, no doubt. RVs, automobiles, and jogging suits aside, the old gal clung to superstitious nonsense as though she were living in the twelfth century.

"Any idea where and when he'll strike next?"

"I cannot predict where, only when. After feeding he finds a secluded hiding place to digest his meal. A fortnight later he emerges to hunt fresh prey. So twelve days from today he will kill again."

Just for the sake of argument, assume she was right. After each killfest he'd hole up for two weeks at someplace secluded, where a forty-foot motor home could be concealed. Remote areas such as national forests and other public land would fill the bill nicely. Oregon alone had over thirty million acres of national forests and BLM land. Add Washington and Idaho and the total would climb to over a hundred million acres of public land. He'd have access to plenty of hiding places.

Monkey Face walked by, flexing his muscles and glowering at him.

The old gal shooed him away with a withering look.

Crocetti drank the last of his tea and set the cup down. "You handle those young guys like a drill sergeant."

She smiled. "I am a *phuri dai*, the senior woman in our *kumpanias*, our clan. To those boys, I am like a drill sergeant."

He declined her offer of more tea and told her he had to get back. "But I'm honored to have met with a phuri dai, and I appreciate the information. You've given me a lot to think about." And laugh about, he almost said.

As though she'd read his mind, she said, "For your sake, I hope you have taken my warning seriously."

"Perhaps we can talk again?"

She smiled "Perhaps."

Enigmatic. It was one of the words that Royer, his partner the last ten years on the job, had learned from the *Expand Your Vocabulary* booklet he carried around in his jacket pocket. Crocetti couldn't escape having his vocabulary expanded also, by osmosis. Enigmatic meant mysterious. The old gal had a corner on that.

"Thank you for the tea." He got up, nodded to her, and set off toward the car. On the way he made a detour into the woods and emptied his tea-swollen bladder behind a pine.

Driving back at a leisurely pace, he sifted through the things she had told him. Most of it was bullshit, of course. But how had she known that the Ostrows had holes in their necks and their blood had been drained? She damned sure hadn't learned it from a deck of tarot cards. A sheriff's deputy or someone in the coroners's office must have leaked the information and she got hold of it somehow.

He was in "great danger" from an "ancient evil," she'd warned. The Night Traveler. That was the bullshit part. But she had been dead right about one thing—his insatiable curiosity. Currently, it was trying to work out why she hadn't told him everything. She'd held back. The hunch was based on instinct honed by talking to thousands of bystanders, witnesses, victims, and perpetrators. Curiosity wouldn't let him rest until he wormed it out of her, all of it. That could wait a day or two, to give him a chance to nose around a bit more.

A frisson of excitement passed through him, just like it used to when he was on the job.

6

Hopple pulled up in a dust-coated black Chevy Malibu as Crocetti was getting out of the Honda. He unlocked the coach and held the door open for Hopple to enter first. After closing the door behind him, Crocetti went to the fridge for a couple of Pabst Blue Ribbons and handed one to Hopple.

"Well," Hopple said after a swig of his beer, "how'd it go with the gypsies—find out anything?"

"I learned a few things, not much. Unless you count the warning from a Roma—that's what they prefer to be called—an old gal who turned out to a be clan leader."

"What kind of warning?"

So Crocetti recounted the whole conversation. After he finished, Hopple grinned "See? What'd I tell you, partner? We got us a vampire for a perp."

"Yeah, sure. And I suppose his buddy the werewolf helped him?"

"Wouldn't surprise me a bit," Hopple said.

"On a more terrestrial note, do you happen to know the dates of the other murders?"

Hopple took out his notebook and thumbed through it. "Here we are. Lakeview was on June nineteenth, Tillamook July third, La Grande July eighteenth, and of course Brookings August first. Why?"

Crocetti jotted down the dates. "Just more curiosity."

"You working on a theory, Crocetti?"

"Yeah, but so far it's only half-baked. If I come up with anything solid you'll be the first to know."

Hopple finished off his beer and set the bottle on the counter. "Listen, this has been entertaining as hell, but the main reason I dropped by was to invite you over to the house for dinner tomorrow night. Meg's planning to make her world-renowned spaghetti, and there will be garlic bread and crab salad. Real crab, not the fake stuff."

"I'd be delighted. What time?"

"We'll eat at six, so get there a bit early and we'll have a beer or three before dinner."

"I'll bring a bottle of red wine."

Hopple got to his feet. "Sounds good, partner. Gotta take off now, try to get caught up on my paperwork. Some of us still got to do an honest day's work." He laughed as he shut the door behind him. The guy was a scream.

Crocetti went over to the calendar on the wall above the desk and with a red pen placed an X on each date Hopple had given him. Then he counted the days between them. "I'll be damned," he said. Give or take a day, there were two weeks between each one.

He opened another beer and sat down at the desk to think. What else had the old gal been right about? Maybe he really was in danger if he persisted in investigating the murders. Even if he were, it damn sure wasn't from a vampire or any other supernatural creature. The only ancient evil was inside people's craniums, a fact that had been demonstrated to him again and again when he was on the job. He picked up the red pen and marked an X on August 15th, the date the killer would strike next. Hypothetically, anyway.

His phone rang. The screen indicated the caller was his daughter. He answered it with a tap. "Gina. I was planning to give you a call later on. How are things up there in Yakima?"

"Hot. It hit ninety today. How's California?"

"Actually, I'm still in Oregon. Brookings."

"Seriously? I figured you'd be in L.A. by now."

"Yeah, well, I got sidetracked. I'm giving the local police a hand with something." No point in going into details.

"Well, that doesn't surprise me, actually. I know how you miss the job. Just be careful."

"Paul and the kids okay?"

"Everybody's fine. Last week Paul Junior got his driver's license and Peter earned a scouting merit badge."

"Tell them their grandpa's proud of them."

"Dad, I realized this morning." Her voice quavered. "Mom's been gone four years today and I . . . and I . . ."

"I miss her, too, Gina," he said, his own voice thickening.

Four years. It didn't seem possible. After the pancreatic cancer took Alison, all the days merged into a cheerless gray sameness. He immersed himself in the job for a year and it kept him on the rails until he retired. Sometimes only barely, it felt like at the time.

"Such a shame you guys didn't get to travel together in your motor home. She had so looked forward to it. But she's with you in spirit."

"I'm sure she is." He didn't say more, afraid he couldn't keep it together.

"Well, glad you're okay. Now I have to drop Peter and his friend off at the mall to see the new *Star Wars*. Love you."

"Love you back, honey. Talk to you soon."

He laid the phone down and picked up the framed photo of Alison on the desk, taken a year or so before she got sick. She had hated it. She'd hated every photo ever taken of her. But he loved it. He'd snapped it on a lazy Sunday afternoon at the Sandy River. That day she'd worn a vertically striped one-piece that showed off her figure, although it couldn't be seen in the head-and-shoulders shot. He'd taken a half-dozen shots of her that day, many of them full length. She had hated those, too.

But that face. It was the face of a woman much younger than her fifty-six years. He loved the intelligence and humor in her blue eyes, loved her slight overbite, loved the shape of her mouth . . .

He reached across the desk for a tissue and wiped his eyes and blew his nose with a honk. B-flat major.

Damn it all, anyway.

His eyes focused on the calendar on the wall. On August fifteenth the vampire wannabe would come out of hiding in search of prey. He opened a desk drawer and got the map of Oregon. After it was open on the desktop he checked for access roads into Rogue-Siskiyou National Forest. He counted fewer than a dozen. The roads capable of accommodating a forty-foot motor home, fewer still. But a considerable investment of time would be required to investigate all of them.

Perhaps forest rangers monitored vehicle traffic on access roads. It was worth a call to the Forestry Service office to find out. For that matter, maybe a ranger had noticed a black coach boondocking on national forest land. Crocetti snapped his fingers. Somewhere he'd heard that public land had a fourteen-day limit on dry camping. Perfect for the killer's requirements. Enforcement would surely require rangers to know who's camping where and how long they'd been there. It should have occurred to him before.

He opened the freezer and grabbed a Budget Gourmet, fettuccine Alfredo. A far cry from gourmet fare despite the name, it was actually pretty tasty. He microwaved it for the required time and garnished it with garlic salt and Parmesan. His beverage of choice: a Pabst. In a glass. There was something uncivilized about drinking from a bottle with a meal.

While he ate, he read the *Oregonian* he'd picked up on the way back from the Romas' campsite. A headline on page four, below the fold, caught his eye: "Redding Couple Murdered in Brookings." The article reported that the Ostrows had been brutally murdered at the Plush Horse. (Talk about bad publicity!) Nothing in the article about holes in their necks or missing blood. No suspect or motive has been identified as yet, but the investigation is ongoing, a police spokesman said.

As for his investigation, it was also ongoing. Next up, a call to the U.S. Forestry Service ... or maybe an in-person visit to the local office would be better.

7

The U.S. Department of Forestry maintained an office in Brookings on Chetco Lane. Crocetti swore when he saw the full parking lot. Hard to believe the Forestry Service did that much business. He caught a break when a pickup on the end backed out. He slid into the space, narrowly beating a faded green van to it. The van's driver, a guy in a baseball cap and three-day beard, shot him a dirty look. Tough luck.

The building directory indicated that the Forestry Service shared the building with other government offices, which explained the packed parking lot. The only person inside the office was a uniformed woman in her late forties, perhaps, named, according to the plaque on her desk, Kelly Buchanan. Chin-length hair, blond with highlights. Vivid blue eyes. She got up, revealing a trim figure. "Can I help you?"

"I'm hoping you can," he said. "My name's Dan Crocetti. I'm trying to find someone who's dry camping in the Rogue-Siskiyou National Forest in an RV."

"Do you know the approximate area where they might be, Mr. Crocetti?"

"No, but I think it's fairly close to Brookings."

"Thousands of acres of national forest are fairly close to Brookings."

"He's driving a forty-foot motor home. He'd need to be able to get the rig in and out."

"So accessibility's a factor. All right, that narrows it down a little."

"It's my understanding there's a fourteen-day limit on camping in national forests."

"Correct."

"So, in order to enforce that, you'd need to keep tabs on where people are camping and how long they stay."

"Ideally."

"Not actually?"

"Try sporadically. Congress pared our budget to the bone, making drastic personnel cuts necessary. We could use six more rangers in this district. That's about what it would take to fully enforce the fourteen-day stay."

Another reason to hate the current pack of jackals in D.C. "Shame on Congress. Seems public land is a low priority with those folks."

"As a federal employee, I can't comment on that."

"No need. I'll do the honors. Anyway, I had hopes one of your rangers saw him."

"It's possible that one of the guys who survived the cut-back did. I'll be glad to ask around. What's your friend's name and a description of his RV?"

"We're not friends and I don't know his name. But his motor home is a forty-footer, like I said. Fairly new. And it's all black, with dark-tinted windows."

"If you don't mind my asking—why are you trying to find this individual?"

"It's likely he murdered a couple from Redding."

"So you're a law enforcement officer?"

"Retired. Thirty years with the Portland Police Bureau." Feeling silly, he produced his retired officer's shield and I.D.

She leaned over and examined them. "How long have you been retired, Detective Sergeant?"

"Three years."

"Kind of an unusual retirement, chasing a killer."

"I'm lending my homicide expertise to the Brookings Police. Special consultant." Known only to Hopple.

"My late husband was a policeman. In Sacramento. A six-teen-year-old car thief shot him dead."

"I'm sorry."

"Me, too. Daryl was a wonderful guy and a good cop. He's been gone four years."

"Four years," he repeated. "My Alison died four years ago, too. Cancer."

After that they were at a loss for words. When the silence turned awkward he meandered over to the huge map on the wall and pretended to study it.

"It's almost five," she said. "Want to go have a beer?"

It caught him by surprise. Even more surprising, he really did want to go have a beer with her. "Sure, I—oh, wait. I can't tonight. Some friends invited me over to their house for dinner. Rain check?"

"Sure."

He picked up one of her cards and slipped it into his shirt pocket. "I'll call you tomorrow."

"All right, Dan Crocetti."

"Be talking to you, Kelly Buchanan."

He smiled all the way to his car. Then his smile vanished. A deep scratch in the red paint ran the length of the driver's door. Whoever did it wanted to be sure he saw it.

"Son of a bitch," he said aloud. He felt sick to his stomach.

The guy in the faded green van, it had to be him. Pissed off at losing the parking space, he'd defaced the brand-new car as revenge. Crocetti clenched and unclenched his hands, wishing he could have caught the punk in the act.

He got in and sat there a minute, eyes closed and breathing deeply, before he started the car.

"Come in, Dan. Alex is out back getting the table ready. We're eating on the deck."

"Nice to see you again, Meg." He handed her the Merlot. At twenty-one fifty a bottle, it had better pour itself and wash the glasses afterward.

She led him through the house to the deck. Hopple saw him and grinned. "Hey, partner. Glad you could make it. Get you a beer?"

"Sure."

"I'll get it," Meg said. She returned thirty seconds later and handed him a frosty green bottle.

"Heineken," Crocetti said. "You'll spoil me."

"Nothing but the best," Hopple said. "Hey, how did your visit to the Forestry Service pan out?"

"A bust. They don't have enough manpower, so coverage is spotty at best."

"Too bad. It was worth a shot, though."

"I guess. But when I got back to my car I found that some asshole had keyed it. There's a big scratch on the door of my new car."

"Man, that's sickening."

"I'm fairly sure it was a guy in a van, pissed off that I beat him to a parking space."

"I hate keyers. You don't mess with a man's automobile."

"Or a woman's," Meg said, setting a wooden bowl heaped with salad on the table.

"Know what?" Hopple said. "That building probably has exterior security cameras. You should call them tomorrow."

Crocetti smiled. "Tomorrow I'm going to have a beer with Kelly Buchanan, forest ranger and office manager. I'll ask her about it then."

"You dog," Hopple said, leering. "In town three days and you already got a date lined up."

"It was her suggestion, actually."

Meg halted, holding a platter piled high with garlic bread. "What's she like, Dan?"

"Yeah," Hopple said. "She a dish?"

"Attractive enough. And she seems intelligent, pleasant, and sane. Sanity is high on my list of desirable qualities."

Hopple chuckled. "Picky, picky."

"If I may change the subject, I'd like to get that door fixed. Can you recommend a shop in Brookings?"

"Try Saderman Body and Paint, on Pacific Avenue. They repainted the hood of a Cadillac that belonged to a sheriff's deputy I know. It came out perfect."

"Okay, thanks." Seeing the car's door perfect again would untie the knot in his gut that had formed when his disbelieving eyes first fell upon the scratch.

"All right, you guys," Meg said, "dinner is ready."

He sat down and reached for a linen napkin. Dishes, cutlery, and drinking glass passed his stealthy inspection. A dollop of hand sanitizer from the bottle in his front pocket—discreetly, under the table—and he was ready to dine.

"Just wait until you taste the spaghetti," Hopple said. "The sauce is her grandmother's recipe. Straight from the Old Country."

Crocetti looked at the blond, blue-eyed woman across the table. "I'd never have guessed you're Italian."

"My maiden name was Funicello. No relation to Annette."

"That's for sure," Hopple said, hands cupped over his chest.

Meg sighed, shaking her head slowly.

Crocetti ladled thick sauce over his pasta. "It sure smells great, Meg."

The spaghetti's flavor more than lived up to the promise of its aroma. He had two helpings. Then he laid his fork down and patted his belly. "You've foundered me, Meg."

"Glad you enjoyed it."

He finished his Merlot, which, he had to admit, was excellent, even though he rarely drank wine. When Meg began clearing the table, he hopped up and gave her a hand. That seemed to amuse Hopple.

"You'll make some lucky woman a wonderful little wife, Crocetti."

"Pay him no mind, Dan," she said. "Alex could have been the prototype for Archie Bunker."

Hopple shrugged and struck a match to light his cigar.

As a couple, they had an interesting dynamic.

But he was glad they'd invited him over. It took his mind off bloodless bodies and psychos who think they're vampires.

8

He phoned Kelly Buchanan first thing the next morning instead of taking a chance on waiting until after five over beers to find out if the Forestry Service's building had exterior security cameras. No telling how long they saved the videos.

"Yes," she said, "there are several cameras outside, but I don't know anything about them. You could ask the South Coast Protective Association down a few doors from our office. That equipment's their responsibility."

"Okay, I'll drive over and talk to them. Afterward we can firm up a time for our beer date. See you in a few." He winced as he tapped the End Call button.

Beer date. He couldn't come up with a more casual phrase in time. *Get together for a beer*, that would have been better. Because it positively was not a date, just two people hanging out. Something to do.

A half hour later he turned into the Forest Service parking lot and found the same end space available. He parked and avoided looking at the scratch as he closed the door. Walking toward the building, he noted the placement of exterior cameras and was pleased to see one mounted at the building's corner, perfectly placed to cover the parking space.

Kelly got up from her desk when he walked in. "Hi," she said. "I'll take you down to the SCPA office. Come with me."

He followed her, trying not to lag behind too much.

"I'm sorry," she said, waiting for him. "I wasn't thinking." She indicated his cane. "That happen on the job?"

He nodded. "Took a slug in the knee a month before I retired. The shooter was aiming at my chest, so I guess I'm lucky."

She held the SCPA's door open for him and then followed him in, as he'd hoped she would.

"Hi, Rhonda," she said to a doughy woman standing at a filing cabinet. "This is Dan Crocetti. Something happened to his car in the parking lot while he was in my office yesterday. He wants to know if one of the outside cameras caught the incident on video."

Rhonda had the look of a woman tired, frustrated, or both. She closed a file door and sighed. "What time yesterday, and where were you parked?"

"Between four thirty and five," Crocetti said. "I parked in an end space, the one closest to the street."

Sigh. "That would be Camera One." She walked over to a computer terminal on the counter and woke the monitor with a key press. "Ollie's in charge of the camera system, but he called in sick today. I will give it a try, but no guarantees." She placed a plump hand over the mouse.

Three sighs later the screen split into quadrants, each displaying a camera view in real time. The top-left quadrant was labeled "Camera 1," and it provided a clear view of his car.

Another click and the quadrant expanded to fill the screen. The current date and time were superimposed at the bottom. Several more clicks and the video blurred. At the top of the screen it said, "REW 32x," rewinding at thirty-two times normal speed. He watched the date and time decrement rapidly, much too quickly to follow. But somehow she managed to nail it. Beginner's luck.

"Here we go. Yesterday, four forty-nine p.m. She pointed at the screen. "Is that your car?"

"Yeah, that's it. Can you run it back to when I arrived?"

Another sigh. "I'll try."

She overshot the mark by only forty seconds. Onscreen, a pickup occupied the space. Its owner appeared and got in. As it began backing out, his car entered the picture—as did the van, from the other direction. The van couldn't match the little Honda's maneuverability, and the contest for the space was over in seconds.

"See that?" Kelly said, pointing. "He flipped you off."

"Yeah, he was steamed." Crocetti wrote down the van's license plate number, clearly visible in the frame. "Let's see what happens next."

He watched himself get out of the car and walk out of the frame, toward the building. Two minutes later a guy in a dark T-shirt and baseball cap appeared and looked all around before he sidled up next to the Fit. Holding something—keys, presumably—he scratched the door along its entire length. Then he sauntered away, out of the frame.

"Well," Crocetti said, "there you have it." He turned to Rhonda. "Can you fast forward to the point where I return to the car?"

"I think so," she said. "I'm starting to get the hang of it."

The picture blurred again, with "FF 8X" across the top. She stopped it at 4:57 p.m. and resumed normal playback. They didn't have long to wait. He appeared onscreen, with as much bounce in his step as the cane allowed. As he reached for the door handle he froze in place, staring. Then his shoulders slumped.

Watching the video, the shock and outrage he'd felt then resonated in him again, and he clenched his jaw. "How can I get a copy of this, Rhonda?"

She sighed. "That's above my pay grade. Ollie will be back on Monday, hopefully. I'll ask him to do it then."

"How long do you save the videos?"

"Ollie configured the system to save them for a week. That's what he told me, anyway."

"Good, plenty of time." Crocetti removed a silver USB flash drive from his pocket and handed it to her. "Please have him put it on that."

"You're sure he'll know what to do with this?" She held it with thumb and forefinger, as though it were a dirty sock.

"He should. Please tell him I only need the segment from four thirty to five o'clock." Crocetti took a card from his pocket and gave it to her. "Here's my phone number. He can give me a call if he has any questions or when it's ready to pick up."

She sighed and nodded.

"And Rhonda . . . you did great. You operated that camera software like a pro."

"Yes," Kelly said. "She sure did."

Rhonda's thin lips curled into a pleased smile.

He thanked her profusely and held the door open for Kelly. As they walked back to the Forestry Service office she asked him, "Now that you'll have a video of that jerk keying your car, what are you going to do?"

"Run his van's plate, find out who he is and where he lives. A local cop's a friend of mine. We'll pay the fellow a visit, exchange pleasantries."

"At the very least, that jerk ought to pay to have your door fixed."

"At the very least, Kelly."

"So we're Kelly and Dan now?"

"Unless you prefer Ms. Buchanan."

"Kelly's fine."

"Still want to grab a beer after work?"

"Sure, only . . ."

"Only what?"

"I want to be sure you're clear about something, Dan—it's not a date, just two people having a beer together."

After a moment's surprise he gave a nod. "Agreed."

"Then how about we meet up at the Pine Cone Tavern at, say, quarter after five? Assuming you're okay with being seen with a woman in uniform."

"Sure, if you don't mind being seen with a gimp. See you there at five fifteen." He gave her a parting nod.

Next stop, Saderman Body & Paint.

He pulled up in front of an open bay door and shut off the engine. A stocky guy swaggered out, wiping his hands on a shop rag. He wore a sullen expression and blue work clothes with "John" embroidered in a white oval sewn over the shirt pocket.

"Howdy," Crocetti said as he got out.

Saderman gave him a curt nod. "What can I do for you?"

Crocetti pointed to the door. "I need that fixed."

Saderman ran a finger along the scratch and grunted. "Too deep to buff out. It'll need to be repainted."

"I figured as much. How much will it cost?"

"I'll have to repaint the entire door, so I'd say ... five hundred. Your insurance oughta cover it."

"True, but I'm not going to make a claim. I'll just pay it out of pocket." And then squeeze the money from the punk who keyed it.

"Suit yourself. Tell you what. I'll give you a fifty-dollar discount, since you're paying cash."

"I appreciate that. I've been told you do excellent work. Would you happen to have any examples of it I can take a quick look at?"

He pointed to a pearl-white Lexus parked in front of a closed bay door. "Have a look-see at the trunk lid. Some kids egged it and the acid ate into the surface. Had to repaint it."

Crocetti inspected the trunk lid closely, looking for even the slightest flaw. He couldn't see any. "Very nice."

"After I paint several base coats, I clear-coat it and then bake it for an hour. Just like the factory."

"So when can you do it and how long will it take?"

He scratched his chin. "I can start on it early next week. I'll need it three days."

"Fine, I'll drop it off Monday morning and rent another car while this one's in the shop."

Driving away, Crocetti whistled a merry tune. Soon his pride and joy would be perfect once again. Then he could look at it without the sinking feeling he used to get as a kid when his toys got damaged.

9

It was twenty after five when he parked in a diagonal space in front of the Pine Cone Tavern, a rustic building on Brookings' main drag, half a block from the Redwood Cinema. Inside, the Pine Cone had a retro, funky vibe. An empty bandstand advertised live music on weekends ("Rock out to the music of Prime Cut"). He was checking out the pool tables when Kelly walked in. She spotted him and came over.

"Sorry I'm late," she said. "Been here long?"

"Just got here myself. Where do you want to sit?"

She waved hello to the bartender and pointed to an empty table against the wall. Crocetti followed her to it and, after ignoring the urge to pull out a chair for her, sat down. The previous occupants' empty glasses had lipstick on the rims.

A slender young woman with a tray collected the glasses and wiped the tabletop. "What can I get for you two, Kelly?"

"Hi, Beth. I'll have an IPA."

"Same for me," Crocetti said.

After she left, Kelly sat back and covered a yawn with her hand. "Pardon me."

"Tough day?"

Her laugh had an edge of irony. "Anymore, it seems like they're all tough days. One of our rangers quit. No notice, not even a phone call. Just skipped out."

"Mighty nice of him."

"Yeah. Retirement is sounding better and better."

"You don't look old enough to retire, Kelly."

"I'll be fifty-nine in December."

"No kidding? I'd guessed late forties."

"You really know how to cheer a girl up. So how old are you, Dan?"

"Sixty-three."

"Really? I'd guessed early fifties. You have all your hair."

They were laughing when Beth the waitress set their beers down in front of them. "That's what we like to see," she said. "Happy customers."

They clinked their glasses together and sampled the IPA. Kelly pointed out the Pine Cone's wide selection of Oregon craft brews.

He noticed two men jockeying a video poker machine through the door on a hand truck. They looked familiar. One of them had a simian face and bulging muscles.

"See those two guys, Kelly? They're Roma. Gypsies. I had a run-in with them the other day."

"With gypsies? How did that come about?"

"It's a long story."

"I've got time if you do."

He mulled it over as he watched Monkey Face and his pal set up the video poker machine. After they plugged it in, the screen displayed a royal flush on a green background, with red and yellow text urging customers to try their luck.

If he told Kelly the story it wouldn't make sense unless he included details about the Ostrows' murders, details kept tightly under wraps. "Kelly, I'm going to ask you a rude question. Do you have loose lips?"

The question made her smile. "Daryl used to discuss confidential police business with me all the time, and I never breathed a word to a single, solitary soul. I was a cop's wife. I can keep a secret."

So over a fresh round of beers he began recounting the story, starting with his arrival at the Plush Horse. He didn't omit any details and included theories and suppositions.

From time to time as she listened, Kelly would tilt her head to the side. The mannerism gave Crocetti a pang of sweet sadness. Alison used to do the same thing.

"And now," he said, wrapping up the story, "I'm trying to track down the black coach and a source for the draculin." He drained the last of his beer and set the glass to the side.

"Quite a tale," she said. "Sounds like a late-night horror movie."

"*Curse of the Vampire Wannabe*."

"According to your theory, the killer used a suction device to drain the victims' blood. Okay, I can buy that. But how do you explain the ecstasy on their faces?"

"I can't explain it, Kelly. Doesn't mean there isn't a logical explanation."

"I guess not, but it's weird. And then there's the draculin. Come on. I mean . . . *draculin*? Tell me that's not weird, too."

He shrugged. "That's why the psycho used it, probably."

"I'm fascinated by your description of the old gypsy—oops, Roma—old Roma woman."

"Ah yes, the phuri dai. Talk about strange."

"But she knew you're a widower with a daughter and all about the murders."

"True. Again, there has to be a logical explanation."

"Have you considered the possibility that she's telling you the truth and your quarry's a real vampire?"

He laughed at that, one short bark. "Not even for a second. I just can't accept supernatural nonsense. My rational nature won't let me. How about you?"

"No, not really. But I'm not as adamant about it as you are. I guess I have an open mind."

"Mine isn't closed, so much as pragmatic."

"Think your vampire wears a cape?" A hint of a smile played on her lips.

"You're joking, but I wouldn't put it past him. After all, he's striving for verisimilitude."

She looked at him sharply. "You're full of surprises, Dan."

"Think so?"

"I never met a cop who was even aware of the existence of the word 'verisimilitude,' let alone used it in a sentence."

"Until now." Thanks to Royer's booklet.

Beth the waitress stopped at their table and asked if they were ready for another round.

Kelly shook her head. "Two's my limit. Another one for you, Dan?"

"Not on an empty stomach. Speaking of which, I smell food. Feel like grabbing a bite?"

"Sure, if we can go Dutch."

There it was again. She wanted to be sure he understood that she was an independent woman. He was glad he'd had the good sense not to pull her chair out for her. "Agreed."

"The Pine Cone has killer pizza. We could split one. You like pizza?"

He laughed. "I'm Italian. My mama put tomato sauce in my baby bottle instead of milk."

To Beth, who'd been standing there smiling, Kelly said, "Bring us a large Supreme, please." She turned back to him. "We can take home what we don't eat."

After Beth left with their order, he sat back in his chair. "So did you and Daryl have any kids?"

"Twin boys, Parker and Taylor. They're musicians. They call themselves the Buchanan Brothers. Based in Nashville, but they're out on tour for their record label much of the time. Their sixth album just dropped, to use their lingo."

"I'll be damned. I saw your boys on Kimmel a while back. Their harmonies reminded me of the Everly Brothers. You must be very proud."

"Yes. Only ... I sure wish I could see them more often than once or twice a year." She sighed.

"I hear you. I feel the same way about Gina. But kids grow up, have their own lives."

"I know. And that's the way it is." Her eyes glistened.

"We haven't been put out to pasture yet, Kelly."

"We're not spring chickens."

"But we're not winter chickens yet."

She smiled at him. He liked her dimples and how her eyes crinkled at the corners when she smiled. Her eyes were a different shade of blue than Alison's, almost an azure, and her mouth seemed always on the verge of an ironic smile. The light gray in her hair blended with the original ash blond, and the effect was like a salon color weave. And her figure—damn few fifty-nine-year-olds had a shape like that.

He looked away, hoping she hadn't noticed his inspection. His apparent interest would not be welcome. Besides, he had no business looking. Alison had been the love of his life, his one and only love.

Their pizza arrived, and it lived up to Kelly's billing. He wolfed down two big slices in short order.

Kelly, still working on her first slice, seemed amused. "I take it the pizza meets with your approval?"

He answered by reaching for a third slice.

They managed to finish half the pizza, but he'd pounded down most of it. The remaining half they divided between them, wrapped in foil. Also divided equally: the bill and tip.

He smiled at her. "Ready?"

On the way out he stopped to look at a sticker on the side of the video poker machine. "Rom Concessions, LLC" it said. It explained how the Roma could afford their expensive motor homes and trailers.

Outside, feeling strangely awkward, he turned to her. "I had a good time, Kelly."

Her dimples deepened. "Me, too."

"You've got my card." Putting the ball in her court.

She climbed into a white Toyota Rav4, backed it out, and waved before she drove off.

He tossed the cane in the car and stood there watching her drive away. And hoping she'd call. Not that he was becoming enamored of her. She was pleasant company, someone to run around with. No reason why a guy shouldn't have a platonic relationship with a woman. No reason in the world.

10

Sitting at the dinette in his bathrobe, coffee in front of him, Crocetti woke the laptop and searched for license plates at Google. He found a site that had side-by-side thumbnails of license plates for every state in the Union.

Bird Legs had described the black coach's license plate as "white, pretty much, with dark letters." The "pretty much" qualification suggested that the plate might be light colored rather than white. Furthermore, dark blue or even red could be mistaken for black in poor light. Scanning the thumbnails, he counted twenty-five plates—half the total—that loosely fit the description. Too many to be useful. He bookmarked the site for further reference.

He took a sip of his coffee and then typed "vampire" in Google's search box. Almost before his finger left the *enter* button the screen filled with links. "About 243,000,000 results (0.71 seconds)," Google reported.

"That ought to be enough," he said aloud.

Specifically, he was after information about people who either pretended to be vampires or believed they actually were vampires. Both groups were of course genuine crackpots.

After over an hour sifting through a mountain of stuff about vampire movies, TV shows, novels, and online games, he finally turned up some useful information.

He learned about a rare medical condition called *prophyria*, an irregularity in the production of heme, an iron-rich pigment in blood. People who had acute prophyria were highly sensitive to sunlight, suffered from delirium, and craved blood to correct the imbalance. They had reddish mouths and teeth, caused by erratic levels of the heme pigment. The disease was hereditary, leading to concentrations of prophyria in certain geographical areas throughout history.

Interesting. But no mention of prophyria sufferers biting people's necks, injecting them with anesthetic and anticoagulant, and putting rapturous smiles on their mugs.

He read about the vampire subculture, a phenomenon spawned by Goth culture. A cult-like movement of mostly young people obsessed with vampirism, its followers went to great lengths to look and act the part. Hard-core devotees often had prosthetic fangs permanently installed. Some of them even went so far as to sleep in coffins and drink blood.

Wackjob stuff, but it was just pretend, an extreme rebellion against conformity. They didn't believe they actually were vampires or kill people and feed on their blood. Not unless they were shithouse-rat crazy.

Finally, since the killer seemed to be taking great pains to faithfully imitate a vampire, Crocetti researched vampire folklore. Supposedly, the creatures were immortal, but they had weaknesses: They could be destroyed by a stake through the heart, fire, beheading, and sunlight, and they shunned crucifixes, holy water, and garlic. Vampires didn't cast a reflection, and they had superhuman strength.

According to some sources, vampires possessed hypnotic control over their victims, and their bite was an erotic experience. That piqued Crocetti's interest. It neatly explained the Ostrows' orgasmic expressions. Too bad it was total fantasy.

He closed the laptop and then stood and stretched.

On Monday he'd have another chat with the phuri dai and see if he could pry the rest of the story out of her.

II

On a clear, bright Monday morning he dropped off the car at Saderman's and hopped in the rental, a burgundy Chevy Volt he had arranged to have waiting for him there. He'd been wanting to try out a hybrid for some time, and the Volt did not disappoint. It was smooth, silent, and luxurious. Too big to tow behind the coach, though.

Furthermore, it didn't handle curves with the Fit's nimble aplomb, which became clear on the winding road out to the Romas' campsite. But the heavier Volt's cushier suspension provided a smoother ride when the pavement ended. He parked next to the Romas' towed vehicles and got out.

No welcoming committee this time, he was relieved to see. He retraced his steps. The old woman, this time wearing a turquoise jogging suit, was sitting outside sipping her tea. Across the table were an empty cup and saucer.

"Ah," she said, one of her enigmatic smiles on her lips, "I've been waiting for you." She nodded at the empty chair and filled his cup with tea.

He sat down. "Tarot tell you I'd be dropping by today?"

She shook her head. "It was just a feeling."

He blew on his tea. "I've been thinking about the things you told me the other day." He took an exploratory sip. Still too hot. "I was hoping I could ask you a few more questions."

She smiled. "Your curiosity . . . it is like an itch, yes?"

"Yes," he said. "Like an itch."

"What is it you would like to know?"

He watched a hummingbird investigate a blue wildflower nearby before zipping off, and then he locked eyes with her. "I listen to my hunches. I've got a feeling you do, too. The last time we spoke you told me a great many things, but I have a hunch you didn't tell me everything. I think you know more than you let on about the . . . person who killed that couple." He sat back, arms folded.

"You were given what you needed," she said.

Her condescending attitude was beginning to bug hell out of him. Measuring his words carefully, he said, "Two innocent people are lying on slabs in the morgue and the killer is still at large. I need to know what you know."

Her dark eyes bored into him for a slow three-count before she answered. "His name is Viktor Kardos. He is from Romania, as are we. He was born in Bucharest in eighteen aught seven, the son of a Romanian prince. When he was thirty-seven years old he traveled to the Carpathian Alps and there he became a nosferatu, a creature of the night."

"Born in eighteen oh seven, you said." Crocetti did a quick calculation. "That would make him over two centuries old. Two hundred and ten, to be exact."

"That is correct." Crocetti's skepticism must have shown on his face, because she sighed and added, "I was reluctant to tell you more. I am beginning to regret it already."

"I'm sorry. Please go on."

She glared at him several seconds before continuing. "For decades Kardos fed on the blood of peasants in Europe. In eighteen eighty-seven he came to this country on a Dutch steamship named *Het Moedig*. The crossing took ten days. By the time it docked in New York three crew members had died under mysterious circumstances.

"He found good hunting in America, a task made easier by its people's lack of belief in vampires. Over the next century he moved steadily westward, leaving bloodless bodies in his wake. And now he is here."

"Explain something to me," Crocetti said. "Kardos arranged passage for a transatlantic crossing and, I assume, for lodging once he got here. In the present day he purchased a motor home, which would require a driver's license, insurance, and regular maintenance. Seems to me conducting such business would be practically impossible for a vampire, a creature that comes out only at night." Answer that one, gypsy lady.

"Vast wealth can open many doors. And Kardos has the power to bend people to his will and then make them forget all they have seen and done."

"Hypnotic control," Crocetti said.

"Yes."

"He doesn't cast a reflection and avoids garlic, holy water, and crucifixes, right?"

"You have been educating yourself. That is good."

"What about superhuman strength?"

"He has the strength of ten men, enough to lift a car with one hand. No man can stand against him."

"You told me he avoids the Roma because you know how to destroy him. Did you mean a stake through his heart or decapitation?"

"Neither. One must get close to him to use those methods. Too dangerous. There is another way. As you are aware, he must have darkness. He cannot abide the light of day."

Crocetti nodded. "He avoids direct sunlight."

"Yes, it is deadly for him. So we would destroy him with a portable sun. Ultraviolet."

It made sense. UV was a primary component of sunlight. He hadn't been expecting a high-tech solution from the Roma. But it wouldn't affect a pretend vampire in the slightest.

She smiled. "Have all your questions been answered?"

"All but one. I've heard that a vampire's bite is an erotic experience. The expressions on the murdered couple's faces would seem to bear that out. True or false?"

She pushed her empty cup aside and leaned back. "It has been said that the bite of a vampire is like a thousand orgasms. No one has ever survived to confirm it, though."

"Can you think of anything else I should be aware of?"

"I have told you everything I know about the Night Traveler. I hope it does not get you killed. You must take care."

"I will." He got to his feet. "And thank you. You've been very helpful." He felt her dark eyes on his back as he walked away.

First thing after he got back he'd run some searches on Viktor Kardos. The B.S. about him being over two hundred years old aside, he had to be in a few databases. Background checks, including a criminal background check, were only mouse clicks away. It was a foregone conclusion that Kardos had left a trail of some kind—criminal, financial, or social.

Finding it might prove to be a challenge, however.

He closed the laptop and sighed in a way that inflated his cheeks. The database searches he had run—criminal records, state DMVs, Social Security, INS, passport, Intelius—had returned a big, fat zero.

As though Viktor Kardos did not exist.

Unless she was the best liar in the world, the old woman hadn't made him up. Obviously, Kardos was using a phony name and bogus documentation.

12

Kelly phoned him the next day, waking him from a mid-afternoon nap. Not that he minded; he was glad to hear her voice.

"I have some news," she said. "Remember me mentioning that one of our rangers quit without notice?"

"Sure."

"When we couldn't get hold of him we assumed he had skipped town, but his girlfriend hadn't seen him in almost a week and she was frantic. He lived in an apartment over on Fir Street, and she convinced the manager to open the door. He wasn't there, but his stuff was. All of it, even his razor and toothbrush."

"Mighty strange."

"That's what his girlfriend thought. She filled out a missing-person report at the police station."

"What was he driving?"

"That's the other thing. One of our pickups is missing. Slipped under the motor pool's radar. We filled out a stolen-vehicle report."

Crocetti thought for a moment. "Was your ranger assigned a certain area in which to do his rangering?"

"He was, but it's a huge area. Our guys have a lot of forest to cover. Especially lately, when we're so shorthanded."

"I don't suppose you have a helicopter at your disposal?"

She answered with a laugh.

"Well, let me know if he turns up. Change of subject. I drove out and talked to the phuri dai again yesterday."

"Really? What did she say?"

"I'd rather tell you in person. If you're not busy tomorrow, would you like to come over for dinner? I make a fair lasagna, or so I've been told."

"Well . . . sure. That would be nice."

"Say, six o'clock?"

"Works for me. I'll have time to change out of my uniform. But I forgot the name of the RV park you're at."

"The Plush Horse, on the highway north of town. I'm in B loop. Look for a burgundy car connected to a charging cable. I'm driving it while my Honda's in the shop having its door repainted."

She said okay, she'd see him tomorrow at six.

So he'd better head on over to Safeway and get what he would need to make the lasagna. And a light dessert. Maybe he should pick up new place mats and napkins while he was at it and try to impress Kelly a little.

After tossing and turning for two hours, Crocetti threw back the covers and reached for his robe. Sighing, he trudged out to the kitchen and filled a cup with milk. Thirty seconds in the microwave warmed it to just the right temperature.

Cup in hand, he wandered over to the calendar on the wall. On August 15th the vampire wannabe would emerge from his hidey hole in search of new victims. Tomorrow was the 10th. That didn't leave much time to find him.

As he sipped the warm milk he pondered why he'd gotten so wrapped up in this case. He was retired, for chrissake, and Route 66 and its kitschy roadside attractions were waiting. A leisurely two-day's drive would put him in L.A. Hell, he could even lay over a day and visit Disneyland. It would be interesting to see how much it had changed since he was there with his folks fifty years ago.

Sure. He could hook up the car and be on his way south before daybreak without so much as a glance in the rear-view mirror. Who could blame him?

Only the man in the mirror.

He'd been one of the Portland Police Bureau's top homicide detectives, clearing over two hundred cases—a number of which were fairly high-profile—over a thirty-year career. His tenacity, insatiable curiosity, and almost obsessive attention to detail, coupled with serious study of criminal psychology, made him a formidable investigator. A shame to let all that hard-won skill and expertise go to waste.

So Route 66 and Disneyland could wait a while. He had a more pressing matter to take care of first: tracking down this so-called vampire and collaring the crazy son of a bitch.

He washed the cup and put it away. After he climbed back into bed, he managed to stay awake maybe two minutes.

13

He had just taken the lasagna out of the oven when he heard a knock at the door. The microwave's digital clock showed six o'clock on the nose. He set the sizzling lasagna on the counter, lowered the volume on Freddy Hubbard's *First Light* (an oldie but a goody, like him), and answered the door. To the smiling woman standing there he said, "Welcome to my humble abode."

Kelly climbed into the coach and handed him a bottle of red wine. Then she stood in the living room looking around her. She had changed to olive slacks and a cream-colored blouse, both perfectly tailored for her figure. On her feet, sensible but stylish flats. Her side-parted chin-length hair was swept back on one side and fastened with a clip, and her makeup accentuated her eyes.

He'd considered dressing up a bit but thought better of it. Now he wished he had. "You clean up well, Kelly," he said, regretting the dumb comment the instant it left his mouth.

She didn't seem to notice. "I'd heard these motor homes were plush, but I had no idea. It's like a luxury apartment on wheels."

"Compared to some, mine's almost spartan."

"The slideouts give it so much room. And your kitchen has an island! My apartment's kitchen doesn't have one. The cabinets, what kind of wood are they?"

"Cherry."

"A little dark for my taste but perfect for a man."

She laid her purse on the desk and picked up the framed photo of Alison. "She's lovely."

"She was indeed."

"Oh, before I forget . . ." She fished something out of her purse and held it out to him. "Ollie from SCPA gave me this to give to you."

"Thanks." He took the flash drive from her and set it next to his laptop. Armed with several incriminating still photos from it, he and Hopple would pay Van Guy a surprise visit.

"How about a quick tour before dinner?"

"Sure," he said. "Follow me." He led her down the hall, pointing out the sights. "Pantry. Washer-dryer combo. Guest bathroom. Guest stateroom."

"Very nice."

"All the way aft, the master stateroom." He presented it with an expansive gesture.

"Wow," she said. "A king-size bed and giant flat-screen TV. And the bathroom—double sinks, glass-enclosed shower, even a skylight. Dan, you live like a sultan."

"It'll do in a pinch," he said over his shoulder as he led the way back to the kitchen. He opened the wine, poured two glasses, and handed her one. "To Alison and Daryl."

"I'll drink to that," she said, and clinked her glass with his. After taking a sip, she inspected the lasagna. "This looks and smells so delicious, my stomach is growling and I'm salivating like a starving dog."

He carried the lasagna over to the table and placed it on a pad in the center, next to the salad and garlic bread. He had set the table with Alison's favorite dishes, old-fashioned ones decorated with fruit.

Kelly sat down and unfolded a linen napkin. "Everything's so lovely. You've gone to a lot of trouble."

"Not so much." In fact, he'd taken pains with every detail. He served generous portions of lasagna and filled their salad bowls and then sat down across from her.

She tasted a forkful of lasagna and smiled. "You missed your calling. Should have been a chef."

"Then you won't have any trouble choking it down?"

She laughed. "Only if I can't chew fast enough. It's fantastic. Best I've had lately."

"Thanks." He reached for a slice of garlic bread.

"So you talked to the old gyp—Roma woman again?"

"The phuri dai. Yes, I did. I had a hunch she hadn't told me everything she knew about the killings, and I was right."

Kelly took another bite of her lasagna and waited.

"She told me the killer's name is Viktor Kardos and that he's a two-hundred-year-old Romanian prince who became a vampire and later came to the United States."

She stopped chewing. "Two hundred?"

"Two hundred ten, according to her."

"And what do you think?"

"I think she believes it completely."

"But you don't buy it?"

He took a sip of wine. "I'm proceeding on the assumption that some of it is true. His name, where he's from—not his age or the vampire nonsense. But since there's no record of Viktor Kardos in any major database, it stands to reason he's using a phony name."

"So where does that leave you?"

He shrugged. "In limbo, for the time being."

"How frustrating."

"More wine?" He refilled her glass and then his. "My best bet is to find his motor home. That could be a tall order."

"And you think he's hiding in the Rogue-Siskiyou forest?"

"A needle in a haystack."

"Just like our missing ranger."

They were silent for a time, and then they both spoke at the same time: "I wonder if there's any—"

"Jinx, you owe me a Coke," she said. "One, two, three, four, five—"

"Stop."

They laughed at the juvenile nonsense.

"You first," he said.

"I was just going to say, I wonder if there's any connection between the two?"

"Right, find one and you find the other. The trick is to find the first one."

She put her fork down and sat back. "That was wonderful."

"Hope you left room for sherbet. Raspberry and peach."

"Yum. I could go for some raspberry."

"Coming right up."

While he was dishing it up she said, "The Forestry Service doesn't have a helicopter at its disposal—at least, not around here—but why don't you charter one?"

"You know, that's not a bad idea." He'd have to shell out a couple hundred bucks, probably, but it would be worth it. "Where is Brookings' airport located?"

"About a mile northeast of town. Take Parkway Drive all the way out and you'll end up at the airport."

He set the dish in front of her. "Kelly, you just earned your dinner."

"I try to pay my way."

He sat down and carved out a spoonful of sherbet. "I'll run out to the airport tomorrow after I pick up my car from the paint shop. Time is of the essence. Today's the tenth, which leaves only five days to locate that black motor coach. On the fifteenth Kardos will come out of hiding and hit the road under cover of night. So I need to get on the stick."

"My vacation starts on the fifteenth.," she said. "Two restful weeks away from the Forestry Service."

"You going anywhere special?"

She shook her head. "I'd planned to fly to Nashville and visit my boys, but their tour schedule changed and they'll be in Tokyo."

"Too bad. Well, if you're not doing anything, you want to go vampire hunting?"

She laughed. "As enticing as that sounds, I'd rather go to the beach, lie in the sun."

"Don't blame you a bit."

Despite his protests, she insisted on helping him clear the table and load the dishwasher. Then he suggested they retire to the lounge and polish off the rest of the Cabernet. He put on Chet Baker's *Daybreak* at a low volume and joined her on the sofa.

She smiled. "Jazz buff?"

He nodded. "Guilty."

"Daryl played alto sax. He was good, too. But he got tired of playing smoky bars for fifty dollars a night. Joining the force was his fallback. I still have his horn."

He took a sip of wine. "I know about the smoky bar scene. I play guitar. Gigged around Portland before I became a cop." He got up and went over to the hall closet and hauled out a thick guitar case. He set it on the coffee table in front of the sofa, unsnapped the latches, and opened the case to reveal his prized Gibson L-5, in all its sunburst glory.

"It's beautiful," she said. "I'd love to hear you play it."

"Maybe a few bars." He took it out of the case and gave it a quick tune. "Close enough." He muted the stereo and played a few bars of "Naima," Wes Montgomery style. "A bit rusty," he said and returned the instrument to the case.

"I couldn't tell. It sounded great to me. You're talented."

"You're too kind. The only talent I can lay claim to is self-deprecation. And I'm not even much good at that."

It took her a moment, and then she laughed. "Talented *and* funny."

He put the guitar back in the closet and sat down again.

"Can I ask you a question, Dan?"

"Ask away."

"Are you a germaphobe?"

It caught him by surprise. "Why do you ask?"

"You've used hand sanitizer a half-dozen times since I've been here."

He felt his face flush. "I thought I was being discreet."

"Sorry, I didn't mean to embarrass you."

"I've always had a touch of it, but it has gotten stronger since I lost Alison."

"No big deal. Everyone has idiosyncrasies. I have mine."

"Such as?"

"You think I'm going to tell you? Forget it. But there's an upside to yours." She made a sweeping gesture. "This place is absolutely spotless. You could eat off that floor. You've harnessed a harmless eccentricity for good."

"I guess that's one way to think about it."

"In fact, you can come over and clean my place any time. Maybe earn some extra cash."

"Not sure I can fit it into my busy schedule."

She took his hand and held it. "Does this cause any great anxiety?"

He shook his head. Holding her hand felt nice. Real nice.

After several minutes of comfortable silence she said, "I should get home. I've had a lovely time. Dinner was divine and the company congenial." She gave his hand a squeeze and then let go. "Want to grab a beer tomorrow?"

"Uh, sure."

"The Pine Cone, five fifteen. Be there or be square."

He escorted her to the door. "See you tomorrow."

She turned and gave him a dimpled smile.

After he closed the door behind her he stood there for a minute or two.

Then he reached in his pocket for the sanitizer.

14

Having the little red Honda Fit back made him feel like whistling a merry tune. He'd been so delighted with the flawless paint repair that he gave Saderman a fifty-dollar tip, which brought a smile to the man's normally sullen face. Van Guy would be coughing up the five hundred anyway.

On the winding road to the airport the agile little car hugged the curves as though on rails. The morning had been overcast when he set out, but by the time he reached the destination he'd needed to pull out the sunglasses.

The airport was about what he expected: a single runway almost 3,000 feet long, a scattering of hangars and other buildings, and a half-dozen light planes tied down on the tarmac. Parkway Drive snaked around the northwest end of the runway to the airport entrance. He parked next to a building with a sign over the front door that proclaimed BROOKINGS OREGON AIRPORT ELEV 462 WELCOME.

No one was inside the office. As he waited for someone to show up he perused the notices pinned to the bulletin board, thumbed though brochures extolling the virtues of learning to fly, and leafed through dog-eared copies of *Private Pilot* and *Flying* magazines. He was about to leave when he heard a toilet flush. A door in back opened and a burly man appeared, buckling his belt. Crocetti couldn't help thinking that, unless he'd flushed afterward, the man hadn't washed his hands.

He looked up and saw Crocetti. "Can I help you?"

"Perhaps," Crocetti said. "I'm looking into chartering a helicopter."

"Then you want to talk to Doug Klindt. He's got the only commercial chopper around here."

"How do I get hold of him?"

He pointed. "The hangar on the end. I believe he's down there doing some maintenance."

"Many thanks."

The last hangar in the row had a wide-open door. A faded blue and white helicopter squatted inside, and benches full of tools lined the back and side walls. No sign of Klindt, though.

"Hello?" Crocetti called.

"Hold on," came a reply from somewhere above. A man in tan coveralls climbed down from on top of the helicopter. He had a gray beard and shoulder-length gray hair.

"Are you Doug Klindt?"

"It depends," the man said. "What do you need?"

"I understand you're the guy to ask about chartering a helicopter."

"That's right. Where to?"

"Over the national forest near Brookings, low and slow."

"When?"

"Anytime between today and Monday night."

Klindt made a pained face. "That might be a problem. I have to replace the push-pull tube bearing on a rotor blade, and I'm waiting for the bearing to get here."

"Too bad. I need to go before nightfall on Monday."

"Well then, let me think . . ." Klindt pulled on his beard. "Today's Thursday. I ordered the part this morning, two-day delivery via UPS, so it should be here Saturday. Can't install it until Sunday, though. A friend of mine is getting married Saturday afternoon. It'll be cutting it close, but I can probably have you in the air bright and early Monday."

"But you'll have to work on it on Sunday."

"Wouldn't be the first time." He inclined his head toward the craft. "She's my baby."

Crocetti nodded. "Monday morning would be great." He looked at the baby's faded paint. "How old is this helicopter?"

Klindt patted the fuselage with obvious affection. "This is a nineteen seventy-two Bell JetRanger, a real workhorse and in my humble opinion the most reliable helicopter in the sky. I wouldn't be afraid to fly her to New York."

"We haven't discussed rates."

"Five hundred an hour, up to three people."

Crocetti winced. "That's a whole lot more than I thought it would be."

"What are you trying to find in the forest?"

"A motor home."

Klindt pulled on his beard. "Tell you what. Three hundred an hour. I can cover fuel costs and make a happy buck. That work for you?"

It was still more than he'd expected, but he could live with it. "You've got a deal." He gave Klindt his card. "Please let me know if you run up against a problem with that repair. Otherwise, I'll see you Monday at eight a.m."

"Here you go, partner. Hopple handed him a printout. He had run the van's plate to get the owner's name and address.

Crocetti scanned the sheet. "Leroy R. DeWitt, eh? Half-wit is more like it. He lives on Memory Lane. We're going to pay him a visit he won't forget."

"How do you want to play it?"

"Threatening to haul his ass off to jail should work. If that doesn't shake the money out of him, you can arrest him for malicious mischief and destruction of property."

"I should arrest him anyway, but we'll do it your way."

"Okay, then. Let's go see this hump."

DeWitt lived at the run-down Fairview Apartments. Unfortunately, his van wasn't there and neither was he. But no worries—they would catch up with him sooner or later.

15

Camping Emporium south of town contained an acre of RV and camping supplies, accessories, gadgets, and doodads under its warehouse-like roof. Crocetti stopped in to pick up some treatment packets for his coach's black water tank. It was Saturday morning and he had time to kill before running by the Fairview again, for the sixth time since he and Hopple had been there on Thursday, so he wandered aimlessly down the aisles filled with mostly useless stuff.

Over beers on Friday night he'd jokingly asked Kelly if she wanted to kick off her vacation with a helicopter ride, and to his astonishment she jumped at the invitation.

"I've never flown," she said. "Not in a helicopter, not even in an airplane. It's something I've always wanted to do."

"Then it's settled. I'll pick you up at seven thirty Monday morning and we'll head on out to the airport. I'll need your address."

She wrote it on a beer coaster and he slipped it into his shirt pocket.

"Who knows, you might spot the missing ranger's truck. Think the Forestry Service would give you a raise?"

She snorted. "Doubt it. I sure would love to locate that pickup, though."

She had surprised him again by agreeing to his offhand suggestion that they go out to dinner on Saturday.

He stopped at an aisle end-cap display. "Track your RV using satellite GPS with MotoTek™ next-generation vehicle tracking technology!" a placard proclaimed. He read the spiel: "Unlike most vehicle tracking units, the MotoTek™ does not depend on unreliable cellular technology, but uploads GPS location data to a satellite network for real-time vehicle-position display on a smart phone or other mobile device. Features: Rechargeable lithium-ion battery lasts over three weeks! Convenient, secure magnetic mounting! No monthly contract! Only $299.99!"

The notion pierced Crocetti's brain like a titanium bullet. If he could manage to stick one of those devices on Kardos' coach—assuming he could find it—he'd be able to track it no matter where it went. And after Kardos was safely behind bars, Crocetti could use the device to locate his own coach if it should be stolen. Either way, it was a terrific investment. He grabbed one off the shelf and made a beeline for the cashier.

As soon as he got home he unboxed his purchase and read the instructions as the device was charging. Next, he down-loaded and installed the MotoTek app on his phone. After the device was fully charged, he switched it on so it could "pair" with the app. The app then displayed a map with a flashing purple dot at the precise location of the Plush Horse. GPS coordinates were also displayed. He let out a whoop that echoed off the walls.

Later, sitting in front of the Fairview after determining DeWitt wasn't there, Crocetti checked the app to see the flashing dot. Correction: dots. Besides a red dot at the Plush Horse, the map also displayed a blue dot on Memory Lane, his current location. He'd seen a single purple dot before because he'd been right next to the tracking device. He tapped on Directions and the app provided turn-by-turn directions from blue dot to red dot. They'd thought of everything.

On the drive home he remembered something that might come in handy. After he got home he rifled through almost every drawer and cupboard in the coach before he found it.

The powerful UV flashlight had been indispensable when he was looking for a used motor home. Several possibilities were eliminated when the flashlight revealed the presence of urine, semen, and other body effluvia on carpets, upholstery, and other surfaces.

We would destroy him with a portable sun. Ultraviolet. So the old woman had said. Utilizing it on vampires aside, UV light could reveal blood residue, and that earned the flashlight a place in his arsenal. He put in a fresh set of batteries.

From the top shelf of the closet he got a black satchel large enough to hold the tracking device, the UV flashlight, extra rounds for the Colt, a spare bottle of hand sanitizer, and assorted other items.

He had an hour to kill before he was supposed to pick up Kelly for dinner at six. He smiled to himself. Despite making it crystal clear at the outset that she wanted to keep him at arm's length, that arm of hers seemed to be getting shorter every day.

After laying out slacks, knit shirt, and a pair of loafers he undressed and stepped into the shower, where he delivered a rendition of "My Way" that even Sinatra might have approved of. Anyway, the Chairman wasn't around to object.

16

On Sunday Crocetti woke with a dull headache and urgent signals from his bladder. The inside of his mouth felt like the mohair upholstery in a 1951 Packard. He crawled out of bed and limped into the bathroom and took a leak that surely set a record for volume. Then he padded out to the kitchen and washed down two aspirins with a big glass of milk. The microwave's digital clock indicated 11:19.

What a night.

After they'd gnawed their way through tough sirloins at a joint south of town misnamed Steak Heaven, he and Kelly stopped by the Pine Cone for a beer and some live music. He lost count after the fourth beer and the night became a blur. Of necessity, he took a taxi home. In a toasted haze, he had fretted and stewed about leaving the Honda behind.

And now, badly hungover, he felt the need to phone Kelly and apologize. "I hope I wasn't too much of an ass."

"Not at all," she said. "In fact, you were quite funny. I haven't laughed so hard in ages. You quipped, you sang, you even danced. Life of the party."

He groaned. "Please. I feel bad enough as it is."

"The management wants you back for a two-week engagement, if you can fit it into your schedule."

"You got a mean streak, you know that?"

She laughed. "Actually, you were fine, if a bit talkative."

"Thank God."

"Listen, I have to run some errands later. How about I swing by and pick you up, take you over to get your car?"

"If it's not too much trouble, that would be great."

"No trouble at all. See you around two."

He trudged into the bathroom and turned on the shower as hot as he could stand it. After ten minutes under the stinging spray he felt halfway human again.

By noon, figuring he should get something in his stomach, he made a ham and cheese omelette and gobbled it down with buttered wheat toast and coffee. He'd just finished washing the dishes when Hopple dropped by.

"Sorry for not calling first," he said. "I was just down the street taking a domestic violence complaint and thought you wouldn't mind. Especially since I come bearing gifts." He held out a sheaf of printouts.

Crocetti flipped through them. They were copies of police reports for the three previous murders. "Hey, thanks. I do appreciate it."

"If the brass finds out I got them for you it'll be my ass."

"They won't find out from me, Scout's honor."

"Okay." Hopple opened the door and nodded to Crocetti. "Later, partner."

Crocetti sat down on the sofa and read the reports. The first victims, in Lakeview, were a couple from Calgary. The second, Tillamook, was a man from Des Moines. The third, La Grand, were a young couple from Medford. Given the details in common and the lack of witnesses, all the reports could have been describing the same murder. But none of them mentioned a black motor home.

He reached for the phone and punched in the number for Goose Lake RV Park in Lakeview. A woman answered after two rings, sounding impatient.

"Hello, ma'am, my name is Dan Crocetti," he said in his most official voice. "I'm doing some post-investigation follow-up of the murder that took place there back on—" He glanced at the report. "June nineteenth."

She sighed. "Haven't you people bothered us enough? The Lakeview police, the state police, the sheriff, the F.B.I., and now you. We're trying to put this terrible business behind us, if you'll let us."

"I understand completely, ma'am. I just need to clear up a few details. It won't take but a minute."

"Fine, go ahead."

"Around the time of the murders was there a black motor home—all black, with dark-tinted windows—in the park?"

"Yes, it was here. Stayed two nights."

Bingo.

"What can you tell me about the coach's owner?"

"Is he a suspect in the murders?"

"Let's just say he's a person of interest."

"He was only in the office maybe five minutes."

"Can you describe him?"

"Strange," she said after a pause, "I can't remember what he looked like."

"Age, height, hair color, foreign accent—anything?"

"He was tall, but other than that I'm drawing a blank."

"Did he fill out a registration form?"

"Certainly. Give me a minute to find it." It was a long minute. "Ah, here it is. Victor Kaminski. And he came in on the fourteenth."

Two days before the murders. Crocetti's pulse quickened. "Did you get his license plate number?"

After a pause she said, "No, he left it blank. I should have caught that."

"Any information besides the name and date?"

"The time he registered. Nine thirty-seven p.m."

After dark, of course.

"He stayed two nights, you said. Did you see him again during that time?"

"No, not that I recall."

"Do you know what time he left?"

"His motor home was gone when I opened the office at eight a.m. on the sixteenth."

"When were the bodies discovered and by whom?"

"Not until later that night, around nine. The people were supposed to check out by noon. The space had been reserved. Chet—he's my husband—knocked on their door to ask them why they hadn't left. It was unlocked, so he opened it and called out to them. Then he saw the bodies. He closed the door fast and called the police."

It almost mirrored how it had gone down in Brookings. According to the police report, the medical examiner determined the time of death to be approximately 3 a.m. on the 16th. Kaminski, a.k.a Kardos, killed them and then holed up for two weeks on nearby public land.

"Sure is odd that I can't recall what he looked like," she said. "I have a good memory for faces, usually."

"If you remember anything else, I'd greatly appreciate a phone call." He gave her his number and thanked her.

After he got a cup of coffee he punched in the number for Kilchis River RV Park in Tillamook. He talked with the manager for twenty minutes, and then he called Oregon Trail RV Campground in La Grande and talked another twenty.

Their accounts differed from the Lakeview manager's only in superficial details. They both remembered the black motor coach but neither could recall what Victor Kaminski looked or sounded like. Like the Lakeview manager, they were both perplexed about not getting the license plate number.

By the time Kelly arrived to pick him up he had perused a half-dozen online articles about hypnosis. Because, although chances were nil that the killer was an honest-to-God vampire, it was beginning to look as though he did have an ability to hypnotize people, to make them forget things. A talent that could come in mighty handy in the fake-vampire biz.

He cruised by the Fairview Apartments, hoping to see DeWitt's green van. No such luck. But he noticed a fat woman sitting outside an apartment in a rusted metal lawn chair, drinking a beer and smoking a cigarette. He stopped and got out.

"Howdy," he said as he walked toward her.

The woman wore a faded floral-print muumuu with what looked like coffee stains on the front. She gave him a curt nod.

"Leroy been around today?" he asked her.

"I seen him this morning, but he took off pretty early."

"Does he have a job?"

She flicked the ash off her cigarette. "He works now and then. I think he does drywall."

"Listen, if you see him again I would appreciate it if you wouldn't mention I stopped by. I want it to be a surprise."

"No problem. I don't care to talk to that asshole anyways."

"Not one of your favorite people?"

"Leroy's a mean son of a bitch." She took a drink of her beer and then stifled a belch. "He shot up my bird feeder with a pellet gun and then swore up and down it wasn't him that done it. Worthless cuss needs a good beating."

"Well . . . you have a good day."

The woman raised her can of beer in salute.

At least he learned that DeWitt hadn't flown the coop. Now all he had to do was catch him home. Patience and persistence were a cop's stock in trade.

17

They arrived at the airport a little before eight, just as the sun peeked through the overcast Monday morning sky. The temperature was a pleasant sixty degrees, with a breeze that ruffled their hair. A small silver plane rolled down the runway and took to the air, crabbing into a crosswind.

Kelly could hardly contain her excitement, head darting around like a parrot. "I don't see a helicopter."

Crocetti grabbed the satchel and shut the door. "This way. The hangar on the end."

As they approached the last hangar, the blue and white helicopter emerged on a dolly towed by a motorized device, its operator too busy to notice them.

Crocetti and Kelly stood aside watching him position the craft on the tarmac and disconnect the towing device. He saw them and walked over. He wore a navy polo shirt with tan Dockers, aviator sunglasses, a billed cap with "Vietnam Veteran" on the front and a gray pony tail out the back.

"Doug Klindt, Kelly Buchanan," Crocetti said.

"Hi, Kelly," Klindt said. "I'd shake your hand, but mine's a bit greasy. Everybody up for a helicopter ride this morning?"

"I can't wait," Kelly said.

Crocetti grinned. "Kelly's never flown before."

"Well then," Klindt said, "you're in for a treat. Give me a second to shut the hangar door and we'll be all set."

Kelly turned to Crocetti and spoke softly. "He looks like an old hippie. Are you sure he can fly that thing?"

"Relax, I checked him out. This old dog's one of the most experienced helicopter pilots in the state."

Klindt reappeared and opened the chopper's door. "Ready to go, folks? Sit anywhere you want except the right-front seat. That's mine."

"Oh goody," Kelly said, "I get to have the back seat all to myself."

They climbed in. The craft's interior showed its age. Over four and a half decades countless butts had worn the seats in places, plastic moldings had cracks, and paint was chipped here and there. Crocetti hoped the engine and mechanicals were in better shape.

"Everyone buckled in?" Klindt noticed Kelly struggling with her seat belt. "The latch is a little stubborn. Just give it a firm push."

"Got it," she said.

Klindt held up a headset. "You each have your own set. Cabin noise can exceed a hundred decibels, making conversation impossible without shouting. Headsets will protect our ears and allow us to talk at a normal volume. Try them on."

They put on their headsets. Crocetti took out his phone and snapped a photo of a grinning, dimpled Kelly wearing hers.

Klindt's voice came through the earphones: "Can you hear me okay?"

"Ten-four," Crocetti said.

"A-okay," Kelly said, giggling.

"Then we're good to go." After a pause, they heard him say, "Brookings unicom, JetRanger seven niner whiskey for takeoff from hangar six, heading due east."

"*Roger that*," was the nasal reply.

The turbine engine came alive with a sibilant whine and the rotor blades began turning slowly overhead. The whine increased as the blades rotated faster. The chopper hovered for a moment, and then the ground fell away and they gained altitude with breathtaking suddenness.

Klindt looked over his shoulder. "Having fun yet, Kelly?"

"It's exhilarating."

"We'll maintain an altitude of about a thousand feet until we're clear of residential areas, and then we can drop down low as we want."

"Sounds good," Crocetti said. "So you flew helicopters in the service?"

"Army. Cobra gunships, mostly. I was a pilot-instructor. Retired after twenty years as a warrant officer four."

"You don't say."

"After the service I consulted at the RAND Corporation—the think tank—about helicopter design."

"Then we're certainly in good hands," Crocetti said, looking at Kelly.

Klindt had more to say. "This is the civilian version of the Kiowa, which I flew a time or two in 'Nam. When I got the chance to buy this baby I snapped it up. I named her Bella. She's a good old gal."

"Bella feels solid."

"As a rock." He pointed through the windshield. "That's the forest dead ahead. When we reach it I'll reduce speed and altitude and then you can start looking for your motor home. What color is it?"

"All black."

"Black might be tough to spot down there."

"Maybe we'll get lucky."

Two minutes later they were skimming the tree tops and experiencing a breathtaking sensation of speed, although the craft had slowed considerably. Dense in places, the forest also had streams, gullies, clearings, and rocky outcroppings.

Kelly pointed. "My god, is that a bear?"

Klindt banked the chopper to get a better look.

"It sure as hell is," Crocetti said. "A mama bear and her two cubs."

Shortly after that, Klindt called their attention to a pair of deer drinking from a small stream. The animals looked up at the strange bird flying over.

"We're interested primarily in the access roads," Crocetti said. "Roads that can easily accommodate a forty-foot motor home."

"Okay, you got it," Klindt said. "And unless my eyes are playing tricks on me there's a road that might qualify right down there."

The road he pointed out snaked through the forest below. They followed it for miles, with no sign of a motor home. As Klindt said, a black coach would be hard to spot. Impossible, perhaps. Ten minutes later they found the second road, with the same result. After the third road came up empty, Crocetti was ready to throw in the towel. It was a waste of time. They had nearly used up the hour with nothing to show for it.

Still, they were getting a memorable ride. Kelly seemed to be having the time of her life, and that alone made it worth the cost of the charter.

"C'mon, you guys, let's check out just one more," she said. "North Bank Chetco River Road winds alongside the river."

Klindt looked over at Crocetti. "Your call."

Crocetti shrugged. "Make it happen."

When they encountered the river, the helicopter banked right and followed the road next to it.

"There's a small campground up here a ways," Kelly said. "Miller Bank Campground, beside the river."

Before long a narrower road branched off to the left.

"Follow it," she said. "That's the road to the campground."

After winding around, curving back on itself, for several thousand feet, the road ended at a hundred-foot-wide sand-bar that stretched along the river for perhaps half a mile. Scattered here and there, a half-dozen RVs of various types dotted the beach. Klindt made a low-and-slow pass that brought campers out of their trailers and motor homes, craning their necks to look upward. Several waved.

Crocetti sighed. "Okay, let's head on back to the airport." As the chopper banked, he saw a flash at the tree line, like a glint of sunlight reflecting from a windshield. "Wait. Go back. I thought I saw something."

The southern end of the sandbar narrowed to a strip just wide enough accommodate a vehicle. After a hundred feet or so it widened out again, forming a smaller sandbar that at first glance appeared to be empty, but wasn't. Tucked in under the tree line, partially concealed by the shadows, a long black shape crouched.

Jackpot.

He pointed. "There it is, folks."

"Yeah, I see it," Klindt said. "Clever hiding place."

"Can you land this thing back there in the main part of the sandbar?"

"No problem."

"Wait a minute," Kelly said, "what do you have in mind?"

He took the vehicle-tracking device out of the satchel. "I thought I would knock on the door, hope Kardos invites me in for tea."

"Yeah, right. What's that you've got there?"

By the time he finished filling her in about the device, Klindt had set the helicopter down on the sandbar before an audience of curious campers. After the rotor blades stopped, Crocetti opened his door and hopped down onto the sand.

"Be careful," Kelly said.

"Don't worry." He opened his jacket to reveal the Colt in the shoulder holster. "Back in a few minutes."

Walking in loose sand with a cane proved to be a challenge. He kept to the tree line. It took him ten minutes to cover the five-hundred-yard distance. When the black coach was in sight a rush of adrenalin gave everything a sharp-edged clarity.

He ducked behind a big tree near the front of the coach. It crouched, silent and sinister, its black windows watching him. It had a Florida license plate. He wrote down the number.

He took a deep breath and crawled under the rig's front bumper. The undercarriage had plenty of places to mount the tracking device. He chose a thick metal panel that would have minimal vibration. Thanks to its powerful magnet, the device adhered to the panel as though it were bolted there. Satisfied it would stay put, he switched it on.

He clambered out from under the coach, used the cane to hoist himself to his feet, and set off in the direction he'd come from. Icy shocks coursed up and down his spine until he was out of sight of those black windows.

The helicopter was a welcome sight. He climbed in and looked at Klindt. "Let's get the hell out of here."

Two minutes later they were in the air, heading toward Brookings. As they flew over, he took a final look at the black coach. Still silent, still sinister.

Kelly tapped his shoulder. "How did it go?"

"Like clockwork." He took out his phone and started the tracking app. On the map the red dot was exactly where it should be. He showed her the screen.

Klindt leaned over and had a look as well. "I need to get one of those things for Bella, in case someone steals her."

"They're cheap insurance," Crocetti said.

"Kelly told me you were a cop. And that you got that knee injury in the line of duty."

"You heard right."

"I have a service-related disability, too. PTSD."

"Sorry to hear it, but thank you for your service. I did a three-year stint in the Marines just out of high school."

"*Semper fi.* See any combat?"

"I stood a lot of guard duty. At the American embassy in Seoul, mostly."

"I was stationed in Korea after Vietnam. Married a Korean woman. We're divorced now. One son."

Crocetti nodded. It was hard not to like Klindt. He was the amiable sort of guy it would be fun to hoist a few beers with. Kelly might be up for inviting him to join them at the Pine Cone sometime.

As they neared Brookings, Crocetti had an inspiration. "Before we head back to the airport, would you mind making a pass over a certain street?"

"Which one?"

"It's named Memory Lane. Honest to God."

Klindt laughed. "I used to live on Memory Lane."

When they passed over the Fairview Apartments, Crocetti spotted DeWitt's green van parked in front. Proving once again that patience and persistence paid off. "Okay, thanks. I wanted to see if a certain person was home before I drove over there."

Back at the airport, Crocetti asked Klindt how much he owed for the charter.

"Call it an hour," Klindt told him. "Three hundred even."

Crocetti's mouth dropped open. "We were gone longer than an hour. More like two hours. Six hundred."

"Three."

"Take at least five."

After much arguing he finally got Klindt to accept four.

"Hell of a way to run a business," Crocetti said as he doled out four hundred-dollar bills.

"Care to fill out a complaint form? I'll file it in the Shut-the-Hell-Up drawer."

"Okay, okay, you win. And thanks."

"Most fun I've had in years," Kelly said. "Thank you."

Klindt grinned. "My pleasure. Any time you want to do it again, you know where to find me."

They shook his hand and left.

After dropping Kelly off, he ignored the speed limit on the way to the Fairview, looking forward to the encounter. This was personal. He squealed the car's tires rounding the corner to Memory Lane . . . and then he swore.

The van was gone. The bastard must have E.S.P.

At least he'd found the black coach. One out of two wasn't a bad score for the day.

18

The first order of business on Tuesday morning was to call Lewis Cheng, a former colleague at the Portland Police Bureau, and ask him to run the black coach's plate. It turned out to be registered to Victor Lucian Kaminski, age 37, Fort Lauderdale address. Florida, with no state income tax and low vehicle registration fees, was a sensible choice for an RVer. But Lauderdale? Seemed like a frivolous place for a vampire impersonator to have a home base.

He'd asked Lew to run the plate instead of Hopple because so far he had not mentioned anything to the detective about Kardos or the black coach. He felt a twinge of guilt about it, but for the time being he would play it close to the vest. When he had something solid he'd brief Hopple and probably his superiors as well.

True, he'd shared every detail about the case with Kelly, rationalizing that he used to bounce puzzling cases off Alison all the time, and Kelly's intelligence and intuition made her an equally useful sounding board. It paid off. She had already been of enormous help to him.

For the dozenth time that morning he checked the tracking app, and saw that the red dot still hadn't moved a single pixel from its original position on the map. But then, it was only one day past the two-week mark. Kardos could hit the road any time.

The phone rang when his hands were slathered with sanitizer. The screen indicated it was Kelly, speak of the devil. He wiped his hands on a towel and answered it. "Yes, ma'am?"

"It's such a nice day, I'm heading over to the beach in a bit. Thought I'd ask if you want to join me."

"You're not tired of me yet?"

"Not quite yet."

"Then sure. I haven't been to the beach in years."

"Great. I'll swing by and pick you up in half an hour. I'll bring lunch."

He went back to the bedroom and pawed through the stuff on the closet shelf until he found his beach gear—shorts, sandals, and a floppy straw hat. Completing his ensemble, a tropical-print shirt he'd bought when he and Alison were in Hawaii. Add sunglasses, SPF-30 sunblock, and a paperback edition of Hemingway's *Islands In the Stream* that he'd started but never finished and he had everything he needed for a day at the beach.

Almost everything. He slipped his cell phone in the shirt's breast pocket. Priority number one was keeping close tabs on Kardos' whereabouts.

Kelly arrived wearing a broad-brimmed hat and huge sunglasses. "Look at you," she said. "Hawaii Five-O."

"Aloha, haole girl."

They climbed in Kelly's SUV. During the five-mile drive to Lone Ranch Beach north of Brookings, she thanked him again for letting her tag along on the helicopter flight. "I had a blast. I'm sure it will be the high point of my vacation."

"Glad you enjoyed it. Think we should invite Klindt to toss back a few beers with us one of these evenings?"

"Sure, absolutely. He's a character. While you were gone putting the tracker thingy on that motor home, he kept me entertained with stories about flying."

"Bet he's got a zillion of them."

The entrance to Lone Ranch Beach on Route 101 led to a parking loop that overlooked the ocean. After they got out, several seagulls swooped down to investigate.

Kelly slung an enormous bag over her shoulder and then opened the rear hatch to get the cooler. They each grabbed a handle and toted it down the steep path to the beach.

Families with squealing kids and barking dogs had staked a claim on the northern end of the beach. Crocetti and Kelly slogged through the sand to the unoccupied southern end.

Kelly spread out a blanket on the warm sand and opened the cooler. She handed him an ice-cold bottle of beer and got one for herself. They sat down side by side.

The sea was relatively calm. A mile or so out, several fishing boats plied their trade; beyond them a tanker headed south. Contrails crisscrossed the cloudless sky.

"What a perfect day for the beach," she said. "Not too hot, not too cold, a gentle breeze."

"Couldn't be better." He took out his phone and tapped on the weather app. "It's sixty-five in Brookings, but hot as hell inland. Ninety-eight in Portland, and a hundred and one in Medford. Gotta love the Oregon coast." While he had the phone in hand he checked the tracking app. Then he sighed and slipped the phone back in his shirt pocket.

Kelly opened the cooler. "I don't know about you, but I'm famished. Ready for lunch?"

Lunch was lean roast beef sandwiches two inches thick and homemade potato salad. Washed down with cold beer. As lunches went, it was as close to perfect as you could get.

Kelly's bag trilled. She dug out her phone and talked for perhaps four minutes, forehead furrowed. After she put the phone away she stared out to sea a moment and then she turned to Crocetti. "That was Dale Kennedy, one of our rangers, calling to inform me that an abandoned forest service pickup has been found. But no sign of Vern Lachlin, our missing ranger."

"Who found the truck?"

"A couple of hikers. They reported it to a ranger."

"Where'd they find it?"

"On one of the smaller access roads. We flew over that road yesterday without spotting it."

"Any sign of foul play?"

"The driver's-side window had been busted out."

It was Crocetti's turn to stare out to sea.

"So now the state police are involved," Kelly said. "They've issued a state-wide A.P.B. on Vern's disappearance."

"How far from where they found the truck is Miller Bank Campground?"

"Quite a ways. Several miles. Why?"

"Just wondering."

Perhaps there was no connection at all. Maybe the ranger just went nuts and dumped the truck. Only one thing wrong with that theory: Crocetti didn't believe in coincidence.

"Anyway," Kelly said, "it's pretty damn strange."

Crocetti nodded and then took out his phone and checked the tracking app. The red dot hadn't moved a bit. He showed it to Kelly.

"Maybe he's taken a liking to where he's at," she said.

"I guess that's as good an explan—what the holy hell?"

A gull had sneaked up behind them and flapped away with a chunk of leftover crust from his sandwich in its bill.

He shook his fist at the avian thief.

Kelly laughed. "It knows a mark when it sees one."

"Guess so."

The truth was, he didn't begrudge the bird a free meal. He would have tossed the crust to it, if not for the likelihood that every gull in sight would then have descended on them like a scene from *The Birds*.

When she leaned over to fetch a couple of fresh beers from the cooler he couldn't help admiring the way her white shorts and halter top hugged her figure. She was slender and long-waisted, a different physical type than Alison, who had tended toward the voluptuous.

She caught him looking and raised an eyebrow as she handed him the beer. He finessed the situation by pointing past her at the approach of an inquisitive dog from the pack up the beach. A shit zoo or lopsided asshole, one of those fuzzy-faced breeds.

"Beat it," he called out.

The dog skidded to a stop ten feet away and delivered a yapping lecture before scampering away.

"Mangy cur."

Kelly frowned. "Dog hater?"

"Hardly. Alison and I had a springer spaniel named Dutch. He was a great dog."

"I have a cat," she said. "My sweet Cleo."

Dogs and cats were walking germ factories, that was the reality. Down the beach a Labrador retriever stood on its hind legs with its front paws on his master's shoulders and licked his face. Crocetti's gorge rose.

After using some hand sanitizer he took out his phone, checked the app, swore, and put the phone away. It would be ironic if the coach he'd planted the device on didn't belong to Kardos and was just a random black coach. Pessimism was always whispering in his ear, trying to spoil his mood.

Kardos supposedly holed up for only two weeks between killings, according to the phuri dai, and the timing of the four killings bore it out. Why change now? Crocetti chewed his lip. Deviations from established patterns bothered him, like an itch deep in his brain's striae.

He had to figure out a way to get a look at the report after the lab crew finished going over Vern's pickup. It could confirm a connection with Kardos.

Kelly leaned over and with her index finger traced the network of surgical scars on his knee. "Is it painful?"

"Not any more. Not unless I overdo it or come down on it wrong. Marathons and deep knee bends are out."

"By the way, you made quite an impression on Rhonda, from the SCPA office. She said you remind her of George Clooney."

"Come on."

"No, I can see it. There's a physical resemblance, but it's also your voice and the way you carry yourself."

"Blame the limp for that last one."

"Anyway, that's what Rhonda told me."

He took a swig of beer. "You and Rhonda need your eyes checked."

"Change of subject. You're retired, you have time on your hands and money enough to enjoy it. Instead, you're trying to catch a killer. Why not leave it to the police?"

He took another long pull on his beer to give himself time to think about it. Finally he said, "In the four years since Alison died, I've felt like I was in a fog, like I was just going through the motions. I told myself that, given time, I'd snap out of it. But the feeling it was a permanent condition kept tapping me on the shoulder.

"Then I stumbled on the double murder. It was like those black and white movies that suddenly change to technicolor. I felt alive again. Kelly, I was a damn good homicide cop, with a knack for solving murders. I haven't lost that.

"If I can bring Viktor Kardos to justice then I'll have done something that makes a difference, something that counts." He looked in her eyes. "Does that answer your question?"

She leaned over and kissed him on the cheek. "Yes."

They sat silently under the sun-washed sky and watched the seagulls wheel and dive in an aerial ballet above the surf. After a time Kelly slipped her hand in his.

19

It was 7:33 a.m. when he pulled up in front of the Fairview Apartments, hoping to catch DeWitt there at an early hour.

No van.

"Just missed him," a man in a tattered bathrobe said as he tossed a bag of garbage into a dumpster. "He's working today, won't be back until later."

"Any idea what time?"

"Depends. Could be early as four or late as six. That's if he don't stop someplace for a beer."

Crocetti nodded thanks and got back in the car. Over eight hours to kill. Kelly had gone down to Crescent City for the day to visit a friend. He didn't feel like going back to the Plush Horse, so he started the car and drove to Denny's. After putting away a cheese omelette, a half-dozen link sausages, and two cups of coffee he was ready to face the day.

He drove around for a while and then went back to the Plush Horse after all, for a midmorning nap in his recliner. Where he dreamed.

In the dream Kardos was ten yards behind him in the darkness, keeping pace as he slogged through the sand along the tree line of the Miller Bank Campground sandbar. His knee was on the verge of giving out, but he didn't dare slow down until he reached the safety of a cluster of RVs ahead. The nonchalance of Kardos' pursuit heightened his dread.

Somewhere along the tree line the Colt had fallen out of the holster, so he was utterly vulnerable. Kardos would no doubt soon tire of playing with him like a cat with a mouse and then pounce on him. Then he remembered the UV flashlight in his jacket pocket. He drew it as though it were a pistol, whirled around, and switched it on.

Kardos halted and held up his cape as protection against the ultraviolet, but not before the skin on his face began to bubble and sizzle like bacon on a grill.

"You will regret that," Kardos said from behind the cape, in an accented voice that was half growl, half hiss.

Crocetti backed away, keeping the light pointed at Kardos, who made no attempt to follow him. A jolt of adrenalin gave him strength and anesthetized his knee, allowing him to move faster than usual. He made it to within a hundred yards of an Airstream parked near the river when a dark shape descended on him from above, engulfing him in a powerful embrace.

He screamed.

He was still screaming when he woke up and found himself in his coach's salon, embraced by his recliner, his heart playing an up-tempo calypso in his chest.

"Jesus Christ," he said aloud. He didn't often have nightmares, but when he did they were lulus.

He walked back to the bathroom and splashed cold water on his face. After toweling off he opened a beer and drained half of it in one pull.

Dream or not, he would make damn sure he had the UV flashlight with him if he should encounter Kardos.

He arrived at the Fairview a few minutes after four and was delighted to see the faded green van parked in front. What's more, his timing was even better than he'd first thought: DeWitt was just getting out of the van. Crocetti pulled into the diagonal space next to him.

"Howdy, Leroy," Crocetti said after he got out of the car.

DeWitt's work clothes and shoes were covered with white drywall dust. He didn't return Crocetti's greeting but only stared at him, a sullen look on his face. "Do I know you?"

"We haven't been formally introduced, Leroy, but I think you know my car." Crocetti handed him the stills he'd made from the video. "A few shots of you making a modification to the door. The video's even more compelling."

Understanding dawned on DeWitt's face as he looked at the photos. "You're the asshole that cut me off."

"First come, first serve, Leroy. That's the way it works."

DeWitt looked him up and down and sneered. "Buzz off, Grandpa."

"Tsk, tsk, tsk. That's all you have to say? No apology for defacing my brand-new car?"

"Shit happens when you steal a man's parking space."

Crocetti sighed. "I guess we'll have to do this the hard way." He took out his wallet and flashed his shield and I.D.—but not long enough for DeWitt to see the *Retired* designation. "Malicious mischief and destruction of property carry a fine or jail time or both."

Blood drained from DeWitt's face until it blended with the white dust on his shirt. "Am I under arrest?"

"That depends on you, Leroy."

"What's that supposed to mean?"

"It cost five hundred bucks to get my door fixed. Cough it up, along with an apology, and we'll call it square. Otherwise we can take a ride downtown." No need to mention he'd have to call Hopple to come make the arrest.

DeWitt shoulders slumped. "Wait here." He went over and unlocked his apartment and disappeared inside. Four minutes later he reappeared and held out five greasy hundreds. "Here you go. I'm sorry."

Crocetti put the money in his pocket. "How sorry?"

"Sorry enough to never key a car again."

Crocetti nodded and opened his car's unblemished door. "See you later, Leroy. Stay out of trouble."

And that was how it's done.

20

Hopple phoned him Thursday midday, just as he finished cleaning up after emptying the coach's black water tank, a task that always made him wish he could wear a hazmat suit instead of only disposable latex gloves.

"I got a message for you," Hopple said. "Popejoy wants to talk to you."

"Yeah? Who the hell is Popejoy?"

"My boss."

"What does he want to talk to me about?"

"Damned if I know. Maybe he wants to give you a job."

"Why did he pick you to relay the message?"

"You and I had lunch at the Flying Gull a couple weeks ago. Popejoy was also there. I didn't see him, but he saw us."

"Did he say when he expects me to come see him?"

"Right away, if not sooner."

"Sounds more like a command than a request."

"That's Popejoy's style."

"Hell, I'm not busy. I'll drive over now."

"Partner, I'm sure I don't need to point out that Popejoy would go ballistic if he found out I gave you copies of those police reports."

"What police reports? I didn't see any police reports."

"Good man. Now listen, Popejoy can be intimidating, so be ready for it. Let me know how it goes."

Crocetti drove over to the Brookings Police Department's station house on Elk Drive, next to the Elk's Lodge. He had no idea what Popejoy wanted, but when the chief of police summons you, you damn well go.

"Popejoy sent word he wants to see me," he told the desk sergeant.

"Name?"

"Dan Crocetti."

The sergeant led him back to an office with NORMAN H. POPEJOY, CHIEF OF POLICE on the door. He knocked and then opened it. "A Dan Crocetti here to see you, Chief."

"Send him in," came the answer.

Popejoy had a face like a doubled-up fist. He had another distinguishing physical characteristic: hairlessness. He wasn't just bald, but completely hairless—no eyebrows or eyelashes, no beard, no body hair. *Alopecia areata universalis* it was called, a rare condition caused by an immune system malfunction. Crocetti had taken several criminology classes at Portland State, and one of his professors had the condition. Ironically, his name had been Harriman.

"Sit down, Crocetti." So much for formal introductions.

Crocetti dropped into a chair facing the desk and waited.

"I'll come right to the point. Just what the hell do you think you're doing?"

"Excuse me?"

Popejoy's pale gray eyes bored into him. "My sister said you told her you were working with the Brookings police on an investigation."

"Your sister? Sorry, but I don't remem—"

"She said you questioned her about removing blood from a body."

Crocetti made the connection. The woman he'd talked to at Meecham's Funeral Home was Popejoy's damn sister. "Yes, I guess I did at that."

Popejoy leaned back, arms folded. "Today I gave the Portland Police Bureau a call and had a chat with your former boss. Seems before you retired you were a homicide hot shot."

Crocetti shrugged. "I cleared a case or two."

"You've been busy since you came to Brookings."

"What do you mean?"

Popejoy ticked off points on his fingers. "One, you arrived in Brookings the night the Ostrows were murdered. Two, you set up camp at the scene of the crime. Three, the next day you inquired about methods of removing blood from a body. Four, you've been hanging around town for more than two weeks, digging around." He smiled, "gotcha" variety. "You're freelancing, conducting your own private investigation of the Ostrows' murders. Tell me I'm wrong."

No point in denying it. "I've been poking around a bit, just for the hell of it."

Popejoy leaned forward and the fluorescent lights overhead reflected off his shiny pate. "Listen here, Crocetti, and listen good. I don't give a shit if you were the Second Coming in Portland, here you're just in the way. Brookings is a small town, but we have a crack homicide team of our own. Either back off or I will arrest you for interfering with an official police investigation and toss your ass in jail. You're retired. Stay retired. Got that?"

Crocetti clenched a fist, fantasizing about the satisfaction he'd get from smacking Popejoy's hairless pink face. Instead, he said, "Got it."

Crocetti drove home nursing his wounds. Apparently, collegial courtesy was a foreign concept to PopeJoy. That was bad enough, but the dumb son of a bitch didn't even want to know what Crocetti's efforts had turned up, things his "crack homicide team" didn't have the slightest clue about. Popejoy could kiss his ass.

Reclining in his La-Z-Boy at home with his second beer in hand and Stanley Turrentine's *Cherry* album playing softly in the background, Crocetti's blood pressure had returned to a semblance of normal. He was dozing off when he heard a soft scratching sound. He killed the music and listened.

Nothing, only a muted hum from the refrigerator.

When he heard the noise again it seemed to come from under the floor. Probably a squirrel. The surrounding trees were crawling with them. The coach's undercarriage had no exposed wiring or other vulnerabilities, so a squirrel couldn't do any damage. His eyelids refused to stay open.

The scratching, more insistent this time, woke him from a dream about Alison. She'd been about to tell him something important. Swearing, he grabbed his cane and got to his feet.

Outside, he looked for something to throw at the intruder and found a stick. He bent down and peered under the coach, but he couldn't see a squirrel or any other critter. Whatever it was, he likely frightened it away when he stepped outside.

And then the scratching began again, so close he jumped away from the coach. It had come from behind the door to the "basement" storage compartment. Something was inside. He unlocked the door and eased it open, wishing he'd had the foresight to get protective gloves first.

Inside the compartment was a small dog. Fuzzy faced and mostly white with brown patches covering one eye and the opposite ear, it looked at him with head tilted, as if to say, Who the hell are you?

"How did you get in there, pally?" Crocetti said. Then he remembered he'd had the compartment open that morning to store some things from the coach. It was open for perhaps ten minutes. The pup must have hopped in then. It had been trapped in there for hours.

The dog growled and bared its teeth when Crocetti reached in and tried to pick it up.

"Come on, pally," he said. "I'm not going to hurt you. Wait here, I'll be right back."

He closed the compartment and went inside to the fridge and cut a big hunk from the chicken breast he'd been planning to use in a sandwich. As he was trying to coax the dog out with the chicken, a man and woman wearing matching lime green jump suits came walking by. They stopped to watch.

"Hello," the man called out, "What you got in there?"

"A stowaway," Crocetti said.

They came over and leaned down to have a look.

"Honey," the woman said to her companion, "ain't that the little dog we saw on the road?"

"Sure looks like the same one," the man said. He turned to Crocetti. "We come in Monday, from Newport. Ten miles out or so we come upon that dog, sittin' by the side of the road, and figured somebody dumped it there and took off."

"Some folks is so cruel," the woman said.

"Anyways, we stopped and called to it, thinking we'd take it to the animal shelter when we got to Brookings, but it run off. Hope you got better luck."

They nodded to him and continued on.

If they'd seen it on Monday, that meant it took the dog three days to cover the ten miles to Brookings. It probably hadn't eaten in a good long time.

The animal's eyes were riveted on the chicken, its nose twitching. Hunger finally overcame fear; it crept forward and snatched the chicken and gulped it down. Then it allowed him to pick it up.

Holding it, he learned three things: First, beneath its silky coat, the kind that didn't shed, the dog was terribly thin. Second, it had no collar. Third, it was male.

"Poor little guy. How long you been on the bum, pally?"

Crocetti carried him into the coach and set him down in the guest bathroom. It had a tile floor, impervious to everything short of explosives. Then he filled a bowl with water and took it to him. The dog lapped up all of it.

"Thirsty, eh?" Crocetti refilled the bowl at the basin.

As he watched the little dog walk around the bathroom sniffing this and that, Crocetti learned something else about him: He had a limp. His right hind leg didn't work properly, although he didn't act like it was painful to use.

"You, too? Well, at least you don't have to use a cane."

He found an old flannel blanket in the linen closet and took it to his visitor, who immediately curled up on it.

"Too bad you can't tell me your name. I need to call you something, so I guess it'll be Pally. Any objection?" The dog closed his eyes, so apparently not.

After washing his hands thoroughly, followed by a dollop of sanitizer for good measure, Crocetti got in the car and drove to Fred Meyer, where he bought Pally a nylon collar and leash—brown, to match his markings—and six cans of dog food and a bag of kibbles. Not that he had any intention of keeping him. That was out of the question, for any number of reasons. But it appeared he was stuck with the dog until he could make other arrangements.

When he got back he filled a dish with dog food and set it down next to the water bowl. Pally looked up at him and wagged his tail. The dog had manners. He ate every scrap and licked the bowl clean.

Crocetti put the collar on him and attached the leash. "C'mon, time for a bathroom break."

They limped together to a wooded area next to the park, where Pally did his business. He seemed perfectly happy to go back to the guest bathroom and flop down on the blanket.

After washing his hands again, Crocetti opened a beer and tried to figure out what he was going to do with his guest. No way was he going he drop him off at some shelter. A dog with a bum leg wouldn't have much chance of being adopted, even one as cute and well behaved as Pally. He had to find a home for him. Maybe Kelly would have some ideas about that.

In the meantime the germ problem loomed large. One of the rundown buildings downtown was a pet grooming parlor. He'd take the dog there tomorrow, get him shampooed. Even though his stay was temporary, while Pally was his guest he *would* be clean. And face licking was of course forbidden.

One good thing about finding the dog—he hadn't had time to stew about his run-in with Popejoy. *You're only in the way. You're retired. Stay retired*, the hairless son of a bitch said. He could feel his blood pressure rise just remembering it.

He checked on Pally and then opened another beer.

21

Pally wagged his tail when Crocetti arrived to pick him up. His coat was whiter and fluffier. He had a blue satin ribbon with a bow around his neck (which would remain only until they got to the car).

"Such a handsome boy," the large woman who owned the grooming parlor said. "He got the deluxe treatment—flea shampoo, blow dry, brushing, nail clipping, ear cleaning, and coat trimming. He loved the attention."

"Good job," Crocetti said. "How much do I owe you?"

"Thirty-five. By the way, I noticed he doesn't have a tag on his collar. I got a machine that engraves tags. I can make one for him in just a few minutes. Five dollars."

"Make it happen." In for a penny, in for a pound. He gave her his card. "Engrave 'Pally' and my cell phone number on it, please."

"You got it."

After she was done, he handed her a fifty and told her to keep the change. On the way to the car, Pally walked with a spring in his step, despite his limp. Crocetti held the door open for him; he hopped up and sat on the passenger seat.

Back at the coach, Crocetti got a fresh blanket and put it in the corner of the lounge and then set the bowls next to it. Pally wagged his tail and curled up on the blanket, as though he wanted to be as little trouble as possible.

Kelly arrived shortly after two. "Where is he?" she asked as she walked in.

"Pally, come meet a friend," he said, pointing to Kelly.

The dog left his blanket and went over to her. He sniffed her and showed his approval by wagging his tail.

"He's adorable," she said. She bent down and stroked his fur and then picked him up. He nuzzled her neck. "And he's so sweet. How could someone be so heartless as to dump him by the side of the road?"

"Maybe it was his bum leg."

"Poor baby. It's not his fault." She nuzzled him back. "I'd take him, but Cleo cat would never forgive me."

"Klindt said he'd join us at the Pine Cone later. Maybe he would like a dog."

"And maybe you'll decide to keep him."

"Not likely."

"Too bad." She hugged the dog and gently set him down. "I think he'd be good for you. And you for him."

Pally stood at attention and faced the door. Then he made a soft *woof* sound. Ten seconds later someone knocked.

"Good boy, Pally," Kelly said. "You're Dan's early warning system."

It turned out to be Hopple at the door. Crocetti introduced him to Kelly and then to Pally.

"Kelly and Pally," Hopple said. "Sounds like a tumbling act."

Kelly shook his hand. "Nice to meet you. Sorry to rush off just as you get here, but I have an appointment at four thirty to get my hair done."

"See you later on," Crocetti said.

"Very nice," Hopple said after she left. "Very nice indeed. I had assumed Pally was her dog."

So Crocetti filled him in about the Pally situation. "You and Meg wouldn't by any chance want a dog?"

Hopple shook his head. "Sorry, not a fan of little dogs. If we get a dog it'll be big and intimidating. A mastiff or a Rottweiler."

"Just thought I'd ask."

"Speaking of intimidation, let's hear about your meeting with Popejoy. What did he want?"

"He found out I was snooping around after the Ostrow murders and told me to back off."

"He didn't find out from me. I didn't say squat to him."

"It was his sister. I dropped by the funeral home she works at and asked her some questions about removing blood from a body. My mistake was telling her I was working with the Brookings police in an advisory capacity. She mentioned it to her brother."

"Tough break. So he told you to knock it off?"

"In no uncertain terms. Threatened to toss my ass in jail if I didn't stand down."

"You can't say I didn't warn you about him, partner."

"To hell with Popejoy. I finally caught DeWitt at his apartment. Shook five hundred out of him."

"Glad to hear it. He give you any trouble?"

"Not really. I had him by the short hairs and he knew it."

"Perfect timing. Medford has a warrant on him. Failure to appear. We're going to pick him up today."

"Care for a beer?"

"You talked me into it. We'll drink to your new dog."

Crocetti sighed. "Go ahead, break my balls. I don't mind.

A Friday night crowd had filled the Pine Cone even before he and Kelly got there at eight sharp. As they sipped beer they watched a group of shaggy musicians set up equipment on the bandstand. A mustachioed individual setting up drums wore a cowboy hat so dilapidated it looked like it had been stomped by a flamenco dancer on coke.

"Klindt just walked in," Kelly said and waved him over.

As he made his way over to them he was intercepted four times by people who shook his hand and slapped him on the back. He waved at several others, who shouted their greetings across the room.

"Mr. Popularity," Kelly said.

He nodded to them and pulled out a chair. "Hi, folks."

"Evening," Crocetti said. "How goes the helicopter biz?"

"It has its ups and downs."

Crocetti and Kelly groaned in unison.

Klindt called a waitress over and ordered another round for them and an IPA for himself. He watched her walk away and then turned to them. "So what's new?"

"Well," Crocetti said, "I found a dog in need of a home. I thought of you."

"Thanks, but I have a dog, a Belgian Malinois named Grace. War dog, sniffed out bad guys in Iraq. She's a sweetheart."

"I'll find somebody who'll want him." Crocetti drained the last of his beer and set the empty glass down. "I hope."

"Or maybe you'll decide to keep him," Kelly said.

Crocetti shot her a look.

"Oh, by the way," Klindt said, "I ran over to Camping Emporium and bought one of those tracking devices for Bella." He took out his phone and showed them a flashing red dot at the airport on the map. "How's yours working out?"

Crocetti checked his app. "Fine, except the goddamn coach hasn't moved an inch."

"Want me to fly you out there again so you can knock on the door, ask him why?"

"Thanks, I'll stick with the app."

Crocetti excused himself to go to the restroom. While washing his hands he inspected himself in the mirror. His assessment: not bad for sixty-three. At least he'd kept all his hair. Steely gray now, it would eventually turn white like his dad's, but that beat being bald all to hell. He turned to the side and sucked in his gut, what remained of it. The crunches he'd added to his morning routine were paying off. Come to think of it, he did kind of resemble George Clooney. A little. After George aged a decade or two.

As usual, a sheaf of paper towels prevented direct contact with the door handle. On the way back to the table he heard Klindt's distinctive falsetto laugh above the tavern's background din.

A small crowd had congregated around their table, most of them with some mileage on their odometers. Klindt seemed to be holding court. Standing on the fringe, Crocetti caught Kelly's eye and she shrugged.

"... so there we were," Klindt was saying, gesturing with his hands, "at three thousand, engine out, autorotating. I'm looking for a clearing in the jungle below to set down in, and my copilot, young and green, says, 'Does this mean we're going be late getting back?' I said, 'No, dickhead, it means we're going to die.' Which I immediately regretted saying, because he threw up."

They all laughed. "So what happened next?" one asked.

"All the way down I kept trying to restart the engine and finally, just as we were about to kiss the top of the jungle, it caught. I had to smell his barf all the way back to Da Nang."

It drew howls of laughter and then the impromptu audience drifted back to their tables.

Crocetti pulled out his chair and sat down. "Your fan club?"

"Fellow Vietnam vets," Klindt said. "Insisted on hearing an anecdote, as usual. And I got anecdotes up the wazoo."

The band started playing at nine sharp, kicking off the first set with "All My Ex's Live In Texas." The singer, who also played a Fender Telecaster, sounded a lot like George Strait. The steel player added some tasty fills. Obviously, they had spent some time on the arrangement. All in all, a cut above the usual bar band. The dance floor filled up fast.

Kelly leaned over to him. "You're a jazz buff. How do you feel about country music?"

He smiled. "I like it, if it's played well. These guys are good players."

Klindt sang along with the chorus, so drastically off pitch it was in a key unknown in western cultures, but he delivered it with enthusiasm.

During the next number a fortyish blonde walked up and asked Klindt if he wanted to dance. "Hell, yes," he said and escorted her to the dance floor. His dancing turned out to be, like his singing, eccentric and exuberant.

Crocetti and Kelly looked at each other and laughed.

"Such a character," she said. "Do you dance, Dan?"

"Only if it's a slow song."

They didn't have long to wait. At the first few bars of "The Chair," another George Strait song, he took her hand and led her to the dance floor, leaving the cane behind.

He had almost forgotten what it felt like to hold a woman in his arms. It evoked memories of dancing with Alison, even though proportions, textures, and scents were all very different. The physical closeness felt good.

"Dan." She tapped him on the shoulder. "The song's over."

"Oh." On the way back to the table he held her hand, reluctant to break contact.

"By the way," she said, "after my hair appointment I went to Pet World and bought Pally a couple of presents."

"Yeah? What did you get him?"

"A soft, fluffy bed and a stuffed toy. They're in my truck."

"That was nice of you. I'm sure he'll appreciate it."

The steel player picked up a fiddle and the band launched into a blistering rendition of "The Devil Went Down to Georgia." The dance floor became a sea of laughing, whooping, writhing humanity. He and Kelly watched with fascination.

Klindt dropped into his chair, out of breath after dancing with a tall brunette. He finished the last half of his beer and then signaled the waitress for another. "I need to pick up a can of lady repellent," he said. "They won't leave me alone."

"We all have burdens to bear," Crocetti said.

Klindt took out his phone. "I can't resist the urge to check this damn tracking app every five minutes." He held it up for them to see. "Looks like nobody's stolen Bella yet."

Crocetti fished his phone out of his pocket. "I haven't checked mine since you got here. I've almost given up expecting to see any—holy mother of Jesus!" The red dot was now on North Bank Chetco River Road, a few miles south of Miller Bar Campground.

Kardos was on the move.

22

Crocetti looked over at his copilot. Kelly had her glasses on, studying a fold-out map of Oregon. They were about seven miles north of Brookings on U.S. Route 101. According to the tracking app, Kardos was almost to Port Orford, roughly forty miles ahead of them. Crocetti had not hesitated even a microsecond before giving chase, Popejoy's warning be damned.

He'd tried to discourage her, concerned about her safety, but Kelly had insisted on coming with him. "I can help drive," she said. It was a persuasive argument. A relief driver would be invaluable, and he felt certain he could keep her out of the way if things broke bad.

After leaving Klindt at the Pine Cone, they'd rushed over to Kelly's place to drop off her truck and give her a chance to throw some things into a suitcase. They arrived at the Plush Horse twenty-five minutes after leaving the tavern. Another twenty minutes to unhook the power and water connections, retract the slides, and hitch up the car behind the coach, and then they were ready to hit the road. The space was paid up through Sunday, not that losing a couple days' rent mattered a diddly damn.

"He has no choice but to stay on the coast highway," Kelly said. "At least until Reedsport, and then he could head east on Route 38."

"What's the next eastbound highway after Reedsport?"

"Let's see . . . Oregon Route 126, from Florence. Then U.S. 20, out of Newport. After that, there's half a dozen places he could cut over."

But then, Kardos might stay on Route 101 all the way up the coast to Astoria. Whatever he did, they'd be hot on his trail, thanks to the tracking device.

High-pitched squeaks from the rear of the coach made them turn around. Pally was in his new bed, biting his new toy. It was a cartoonlike stuffed vampire, complete with fangs and cape, that squeaked when squeezed.

"Very funny," he'd said when Kelly showed it to him.

"I couldn't resist," she'd said. "It was too perfect."

Pally wouldn't let it out of his sight. He acted like it was the first toy he'd ever been given.

Kelly swiveled her seat around to face Crocetti. "Think we'll overtake Kardos?"

"We're forty minutes behind him, so I doubt it, unless he slows down or stops somewhere."

"So what do you hope to accomplish by following him?"

"For now I'm just keeping tabs on him."

As yet, he had no evidence that Kardos murdered anyone, only supposition based on circumstance and an old gypsy woman's fantastic tale. But he had a plan: find the machine Kardos used to drain victims' blood or the draculin and anesthetic he injected into their bodies, items that would qualify as incriminating evidence. So he needed to get inside that black coach somehow.

By the time they reached Port Orford, the flashing red dot was halfway between Bandon and Coos Bay on the app's map, about where he expected.

"We haven't gained on him at all," Kelly said. "In fact, he might be even farther ahead."

"Doesn't matter, as long as we know where he is."

She looked at her watch and yawned. "Almost midnight."

"Why don't you go back and lie down, get a couple hours shuteye? Then you'll be fresh when it's your turn to drive."

"In a while."

"There's a rest area up ahead. I'm going to stop for a few minutes so Pally can do his business."

"Good thinking."

As they pulled into the rest area, a semi loaded with lumber exited at the other end. Crocetti parked in a pull-through and shut off the engine. They got out and stretched. A westerly breeze carried a whiff of salt air. Pally saluted every bush, light pole, and sign post in sight.

"Want to drive?" he asked Kelly.

"Sure," she said. "It'll give me a chance to get the feel of this thing."

Two minutes later they were underway, Kelly behind the wheel. To his surprise, she handled the rig confidently, as though she'd driven big coaches all her life.

"My folks had a Winnebago," she said. "Dad taught me to drive it. It was a bit smaller than this one, but I don't notice much difference. This is really nice, all the power assists. It almost drives itself."

It was only one of the reasons he was glad he'd brought her along. Hopefully, she didn't regret coming. He looked over at her. "Not quite the vacation you'd imagined, huh?"

She laughed. "It's more exciting. I'm having a terrific time."

"I'm glad to hear that. I've been feeling a little guilty"

He sat back and made some quick calculations. Sunrise would be at 6:17 a.m. He'd looked it up. Kardos was a night traveler. It was 12:37 a.m., so he had six hours and twenty minutes driving time remaining. Assuming a 50-mph average, that would take him 300 miles from his current position. Crocetti checked the app. The red dot was nearing Lakeside, ten miles south of Reedsport. So would Kardos take Route 38 when he got to Reedsport? With a 300-mile range he could make it to almost anywhere in Oregon before sunrise.

"I just realized," Kelly said, "if you stress the first syllable of Crocetti instead of the second, it sounds like 'crotchety.' Are you crotchety, Crocetti? You seem pretty congenial to me."

"Until someone gets on my bad side. But I don't think you have anything to worry about."

She laughed. "When it comes to bad sides you're a piker. You haven't seen me before I've had my morning coffee."

"Fortunately, we've got plenty of coffee on hand."

She pointed through the windshield. "Looks like there's an accident ahead."

Flashing lights from an ambulance and several state police units lit up the night. Traffic slowed to a crawl. As they passed they didn't see any wrecked vehicles, but emergency medical technicians were loading a body on a stretcher into the ambulance. Crocetti asked Kelly to pull over and stop.

"Just leave the engine running," he told her. "I'm going to find out what's going on."

He walked back and approached a young state trooper, who eyed him suspiciously until Crocetti showed him the retired police shield and I.D. "What happened here, officer?" he asked.

"A state trooper was killed."

"How?"

"Someone broke his neck. The body was on the other side of the guard rail, tossed there like a rag doll. His gun was beside him, three rounds fired. It was me that found him. I rolled up on his unit and stopped to investigate." The words had come out in a torrent, his voice wavering. One of the other troopers motioned him over. "Excuse me," he said over his shoulder.

Crocetti returned to the coach and climbed aboard. Kelly was sitting in the passenger seat. Apparently, she'd driven enough. She didn't say anything, merely raised an eyebrow. He recounted the trooper's story.

"Strange," she said.

"Yeah, it's strange all right." He slid behind the wheel and eased the coach into traffic. He drove on silently, trying to work it out.

"Think it was Kardos?"

"Seems likely. Wonder why he did it."

He has the strength of ten men, strength enough to lift a car with one hand. No man can stand against him.

Or so the old woman had said. Assuming it was true, just hypothetically, it would mean he was strong enough to snap a man's neck like a twig.

Okay, but why would Kardos kill a state trooper? It didn't make sense. Unless ... what if the trooper had stopped the black coach for some reason?

The scenario unfolded like a movie in Crocetti's mind.

The black coach slowed and stopped at the side of the road. The state police cruiser pulled up behind, lights flashing. The trooper walked up the right side of the coach to the open door and peered into the darkness within. He called out, "Hello?" No answer. He called out again, but again there was no response. He drew his .357 and carefully entered the coach. A dark shape moved toward him. He fired at it, three shots. It kept coming. He screamed ...

But even if it did happen that way, it didn't necessarily mean there weren't logical explanations. Kardos might have worn body armor that blocked the bullets. And although it would take enormous strength to break a man's neck, maybe he had pharmaceutical help. From, say, PCP.

"When you were talking to that state trooper," Kelly said, "how come you didn't mention Kardos?"

"What would I have told him—a wackjob who drives an RV and impersonates a vampire might have killed your trooper? He would've patted me on the head and told me to run along. Or maybe taken me into custody for psychiatric evaluation."

"I guess you're right."

"When I get some hard evidence, that's when I talk to law enforcement about Kardos."

"By the way, where is he now?"

He checked the app. "Almost to Reedsport."

"One dollar says he continues on north instead of turning east at Reedsport."

"You're on."

Ten minutes later he handed her a dollar bill.

"Thank you, sir." She yawned and stretched.

"The sofa's quite comfortable," he said. "I've taken many a nap there. Or there's the guest room."

"Talked me into it. I'll give the sofa a try." She got up and went aft.

Crocetti yawned. He considered pulling over long enough to make some coffee. Instead, he opened one of the bottles of 5-hour Energy he kept handy. It contained enough caffeine to vanquish any drowsiness. He emptied the little bottle in two gulps.

They had left in such a hurry he hadn't had time to phone Hopple and let him know he was taking off. First thing tomorrow he'd give him a call, although he probably wouldn't tell him why he'd left. Not just yet.

Twenty minutes later Kelly returned. "I can't sleep in a moving vehicle," she said. "Never could. I start to drop off, but then I wake up with a start."

"Too bad. I can sleep most anywhere." He checked the app. "Kardos is approaching Florence. How about another bet?"

"Sure. I say he goes straight through."

Five minutes later Kardos turned east on 126. Crocetti held out his hand. "Pay up."

She returned his original dollar. "Even-Steven."

As they drove through Florence forty-five minutes later, Kelly got up and walloped him in the shoulder with her fist, hard enough to smart.

"Slug bug red. No hit backs." She pointed to an older red Volkswagon beetle ahead of them.

He rubbed his arm. "What are you, twelve?"

"Thirteen."

He flinched when something cold touched his right forearm. It turned out to be Pally's nose. First slug bug and then a dog's wet, slimy nose. It must be break-Crocetti's-balls time. Fortunately, a bottle of sanitizer was within reach. And so he patted the animal, very glad he'd taken him to the salon. "How's it going, fella?" Pally gave his hand a lick.

"He's been sacked out in his new bed for several hours," Kelly said. "Such a good boy."

"There's chicken in the fridge. Bet he'd like to have a few bites."

She leaned down. "How about some chicken, Pally? C'mon with me, your Aunt Kelly will hook you up."

Crocetti reached for the sanitizer before they'd gone two steps.

A few minutes later she returned to her seat. "Pally loved the chicken. He gulped down three big chunks. Now he's back in his bed."

"That's a very good place for him." And for his billions of germs.

The winding road passed through Mapleton and Vida. In Veneta, ten miles west of Eugene, he realized he'd forgotten to check the app for almost forty-five minutes. When he saw the screen he almost dropped the phone.

The red dot wasn't moving.

Kardos had stopped a half-mile east of Coburg, next to the I-5 interchange. A quick calculation revealed he'd been stationary at least twenty minutes. As though waiting for them to catch up.

Route 126 bordered the south end of Fern Ridge Lake, and before long they reached the outskirts of Eugene. He turned left on Beltline Road and took it to I-5. Then he drove north for three miles, to the Coburg exit.

Kardos was near, and Crocetti had a good idea where.

He took an immediate left into Truck 'n Travel, a truck stop that offered fuel, food, merchandise, service, lodging, entertainment, and recreational facilities for travelers. Kardos must have stopped for fuel, although Crocetti didn't see the black coach. But it had to be there somewhere; the tracking app attested to that.

His own fuel gauge registered just a quarter of a tank, so he got in line behind a Peterbilt loaded with plywood. When it was his turn he pulled up next to a diesel pump and shut off the engine. He stepped down from the coach and nodded to the attendant. "Evening," he said and handed him the key to unlock the fuel filler hatch. "Top 'er off, please."

After the fuel began flowing he asked the attendant, a skinny guy with a pony tail, if an all-black coach with dark-tinted windows had come through.

"When?"

"Thirty, forty minutes ago."

"I been here just twenty minutes." He turned around and shouted to another attendant across the bay. "Tyler . . . you seen a black motor home in the past half-hour or so?"

Tyler nodded and pointed to yet another attendant in the next bay. "Jimmy took care of him."

Crocetti walked over there. "I understand you had a black coach in here a little while ago."

Jimmy scratched his three-day beard. "What about it?"

"Might not be the right one. What can you tell me about the man driving it?"

"Tall . . . paid in cash. That's all I can remember. Weird."

"What's weird?"

"I talked to him for several minutes. I should remember more about him."

"What did you talk to him about?"

"He wanted me to replace his taillight bulb. I told him we couldn't get the part until tomorrow. He gave me fifty bucks in advance, told me to keep the change. It's a ten-dollar job. You'd think I'd remember someone who tips like that."

"So his coach is still here?"

"Yeah. He said he'd leave it here and I could just go ahead and replace the bulb tomorrow."

No doubt Kardos would hide inside the coach during the day and hit the road after nightfall.

"Where's it parked?"

"Back there somewhere." He pointed toward several dozen semis and a handful of RVs parked in formation in back.

He thanked Jimmy and paid the bill. After he started the engine he eased the coach forward and steered it toward the parking area.

"Well," Kelly said, "did you find out anything? Where's Kardos?"

"He's here. Parked in the back, hidden among all those big trucks." Crocetti filled her in. "They can't replace his taillight bulb until tomorrow, so he's staying over. But now we know why the state trooper stopped him."

"The trooper pulled him over because he had a taillight out, and Kardos killed him. Is that your theory?"

"I'd bet money on it. He couldn't take a chance on getting stopped again, so he's having it fixed."

"Shouldn't you report all this to the police?"

"Not without evidence. For now, I want to find out where he's parked."

The parking area in back was jam-packed with trucks, so locating it wasn't easy. Then Kelly spotted it in the back row, tucked in between two big trucks. He found a back-in space in the next row, facing the black coach. He couldn't have asked for a better vantage point.

"Lordy," Kelly said, "I didn't expect it to look so . . ."

"Sinister?"

"That's the word for it."

"It's deliberate. Listen, I'm going take Pally out so he can do his business. You're welcome to tag along."

"Do you think it's safe?"

"Kardos won't dare do anything here. Too many truckers coming and going. I'll take a gun along, just to be sure."

"A gun? But that state trooper's bullets didn't any effect on him."

"Bullet-proof vest, probably. I'll aim for his head."

They took Pally to a grassy strip along the side of the parking area. Mercury vapor lights cast long shadows. The rumble of idling diesel engines filled the night. The air itself had a preternatural stillness.

"New moon tonight," Kelly said.

"That's good. We don't have to worry about werewolves."

She laughed. "Only vampires."

An odd thing happened on the walk back. Pally stopped facing the black coach as though frozen. It took a determined pull on his leash to make him continue.

"So what now?" she said after they were back inside the coach.

He looked at the clock. "It's three fifteen. Sunrise will be at six seventeen. We'll take turns keeping an eye on that coach for the next three hours. I'll take the first watch, until four forty-five."

"Aye, aye, Captain. Roust me if I don't wake up by then." Yawning, Kelly stumbled back to the guest stateroom.

Around four o'clock the 5-hour Energy wore off, and he had trouble keeping his eyes open. He fought it but finally succumbed.

Pally's growling woke him. The dog was standing stock-still in the middle of the lounge, staring at the ceiling.

Crocetti stood. "What is it, Pally?"

Pally answered with a low growl.

Crocetti got a flashlight and the Colt and slipped out into the night. He checked all around the coach but saw nothing. Then he shined the flashlight on the roof. Again, nothing. He went back inside.

Pally met him at the door, tail wagging. Whatever had spooked him was no longer a concern, apparently. Probably heard a trucker walking by.

He put the gun away. Between Pally's false alarm and the night air, his drowsiness had vanished completely.

But it had returned by the time Kelly put a hand on his shoulder and said, her voice groggy, "My turn to stand watch, Captain. You see anything?"

"Not a thing," he said. "Wake me up when it's daylight." He shuffled back to his bedroom and collapsed onto the soft bed, practically snoring before his head hit the pillow.

Fitful dreams invaded his sleep, including one in which he heard footsteps on the roof. That one woke him. He lay there listening but heard only idling trucks. He said to hell with it and went back to sleep.

23

Sunlight streaming in through the window above the bed woke him. The bedside clock indicated 10:41, almost four and a half hours past daybreak. He'd slept six hours, much longer than he'd intended. He was still in yesterday's clothes.

He used the bathroom and then splashed cold water on his face, deferring his customary morning shower. The door to the guest room was closed, so he assumed Kelly was still asleep. But he found her sitting on the sofa in the lounge reading a newspaper, Pally curled up on her lap.

"Good morning," she said. "You look rested."

"Yeah? I feel rocky. Had some bad dreams. I didn't intend to sleep so damn long. I thought you were going to wake me when the sun came up?"

"I decided to let you sleep a while longer. You were running on fumes. Just got up a half-hour ago myself. I fed Pally and took him for a walk already. And got a newspaper."

"That guy show up to replace his tail light?" He inclined his head toward the black coach.

"Not yet."

"Kardos won't come out during the day, so we don't need to keep an eye on his coach. Want to go have breakfast in the restaurant?"

"Now you're talking. I'm starving." She set Pally on the floor and he trotted over to his bed and hopped in.

The restaurant was packed with hungry truckers, but they found an empty booth next to the window. Bacon and eggs, hash browns, toast, and coffee seemed to be the morning specialty, so they ordered it.

"Wish there was a way to lure Kardos out of his coach," Crocetti said. "I'd sure like to have a look inside."

Kelly shuddered. "Not me, not for any amount of money. That black thing creeps me out."

"I've got a feeling all the answers are in there."

The waitress brought their coffee.

"When I was sitting there after you went to bed I thought I heard footsteps on the roof," Kelly said, adding cream to her coffee. "Pally and I stared at the ceiling for several minutes, until I realized I was hearing things. Then I felt silly."

Crocetti nearly choked on his coffee. He had forgotten about the dream that woke him up. It could be a coincidence. "It's understandable that you'd be a little jumpy. Hope you're not sorry you came along."

"Lord, no. As I said before, I'm having a terrific time. I haven't had this much excitement in years."

The waitress set their breakfast in front of them. They attacked the food with single-minded determination, hardly talking. As she mopped up the last bit of egg yolk with a slice of toast, Kelly's face was a picture of contentment. Then she sat back and sighed.

He grinned at her. "You're not going to lick the plate?"

"I'm tempted to."

He picked up the check. And she let him.

After they got back he sat down in the recliner and pointed through the windshield. "A guy with a toolbox just walked behind the black coach to replace that taillight bulb."

"Know what I wonder? If Kardos is behind one of those windows, looking out. They're so dark we'd never know if he was or not."

"I've wondered that myself."

His phone rang. It was Hopple. "Hey, partner," Crocetti said, "what's going on?"

"I called to ask you the same question. I dropped by the Plush Horse, learned you'd taken a powder."

"I'd planned to give you a call today. It's Kelly's vacation and we're taking a little trip."

"You dog."

"Right now we're camped just outside of Eugene."

"You *dog*."

"Yeah, well . . ." Hopple could think what he wanted.

"Want to hear something funny? Popejoy has a theory. The killer used some sort of machine to drain the victims' blood."

"Yeah? Wonder where he got that idea."

"He thinks the perp might've worked at a funeral home."

"Logical." But wrong.

"So we're contacting funeral homes to ask them if they had any ex-employees who were nutjobs. Know how many funeral homes there are in Oregon?"

"A bunch?"

"A shitload. But we don't have anything else to go on."

"Well, let me know if you turn up anything."

"You got it, partner. In the meantime I'm sure you and Kelly will have loads of fun. Later."

After hanging up, Crocetti sighed heavily. He felt guilty as hell for leaving Hopple in the dark. All the more reason to get a look inside that black coach and find some solid evidence.

Pally hopped up on Kelly's lap. She stroked his silken fur. "Poor baby. He's starved for affection."

"Yeah," Crocetti said. "He needs a good home. Hope I can find him one."

"He seems to love it here."

"I know what you're trying to do, and it won't work."

"Okay, Crotchety Crocetti."

Then it was her turn to get a phone call. She covered the mouthpiece and whispered, "It's one of my coworkers at the office." She spoke for five minutes and then hung up, her forehead furrowed.

Crocetti reclined all the way. "Problem?"

"He called to tell me they found Vern Lachlin's body."

"Where?"

"About a thousand yards from his truck, hidden in brush. Backpacker found it. And this ought to interest you—his body had been drained of blood."

"Any holes in his neck?"

"Impossible to tell. Animals had chowed down on his face and neck. They identified him by his uniform."

"Five'll get you ten the medical examiner will find draculin and anticoagulant present in the body."

"Dan . . . don't you think it's time you tell the authorities what you know?

"Tell them what, exactly? I have a hunch a deranged RVer is playing vampire, killing people and draining their blood? They'd demand to see my proof. Evidence, I need evidence. Something concrete I can present to them."

"How are you going to get it?"

"I don't know yet. Sooner or later I'll find a way."

"I hope it's soon. Kardos scares me."

"He *wants* to scare people. That's the whole point. He's a psychotic serial killer. The shrinks are going to have a field day with him."

"As the one who catches him, maybe you'll be famous."

"Like I give a diddly damn about that. Besides getting a killer off the street, the only thing that interests me is the challenge, pitting my skill and intellect against his."

"I'll stick with crossword puzzles."

Crocetti looked out the window. "The guy with the tool-box is headed back after fixing the taillight."

"With all his blood intact."

"It's a safe bet Kardos will hit the road again at nightfall, which will be . . . shortly after eight. It's almost two, so we have about six hours of daylight left."

"How do you suggest we spend that time?"

"We're liable to be up all night again, so we should prob-ably grab some shuteye."

"Good idea. Would it be possible to take a shower first?"

"Yes, but you'll need to take a Navy shower."

"What's that?"

"It's how we conserve water when the coach isn't hooked up to an outside faucet. You get wet, then turn off the water, lather up, and rinse. Like sailors do on ships and submarines."

"Okay, I can do that." She headed for the guest bathroom, with its smaller but perfectly adequate shower.

While she was occupied, there was something he needed to check. He went outside, walked around to the back of the coach, and climbed the aluminum ladder. When he reached the top he blinked, sure he was seeing things. But in the thin layer of road dust on the smooth rubberized material coating the roof, there they were, clear as could be.

Footprints.

24

They had given Kardos a ten-minute head start so that it wouldn't be obvious they were following him. He had led them east on Route 126, through Springfield and one-horse towns with names like Walterville, Leaburg, Vida, Nimrod, Finn Rock, and Rainbow. Now Kardos was approaching the junction with Route 20, where he'd have the option of turning west to Sweet Home or Lebanon or continuing east over the mountainous pass to Sisters or Bend.

In the passenger seat, Kelly sat with Pally asleep on her lap. "I was thinking," she said, "maybe you should have some cards printed that say 'Daniel Crocetti, Vampire Hunter.'"

He looked over at her. "Funny."

"It's a niche market. You could have it all to yourself."

"Thanks for the tip. In case you're interested, Kardos just turned east on Route 20."

After a few minutes she said, "I haven't been to Sisters in years, not since Daryl and I skied at Hoodoo after we were first married. Next, we skied at Mount Bachelor, near Bend. We spent more time in our chalet than we did on the slopes." She sighed. "Anyway, it's beautiful country."

"I'm guessing sightseeing is the last thing on Mr. Kardos' mind."

"It's only five after eleven. Any guesses as to where he'll light?"

"Hard to say. He's on the hunt, and RV parks are his hunting grounds. There are several hundred of them within range. One thing you can count on—wherever he chooses will be close to public land, where he can hide out for a couple weeks."

"There's plenty of public land within a two-hundred-mile radius, so he'll have his pick."

"Fuel range isn't the only thing that determines how far he'll travel to find a victim. A more important factor might be his thirst for blood."

"So you're admitting that Kardos is a real vampire that requires blood?"

"That was an unfortunate choice of words. I'm just saying serial killers tend to escalate, to become more blood-thirsty, figuratively speaking, as time goes on."

"I have a question. Unless you catch Kardos red-handed, in the act of murdering someone, won't any evidence you find just be circumstantial?"

"Probably, but that's not a bad thing. There's a misconception that circumstantial evidence is less valid than direct evidence. Not true. Criminal prosecutions often rely entirely on circumstantial evidence such as fingerprints, DNA, and ballistics tests. Circumstantial evidence can be incriminating as hell. Just ask Ted Kaczynski."

"But don't you need a warrant to search for evidence?"

"No. That's one advantage to being a civilian investigator. I can snoop with impunity. If I come up with something solid I'll call in law enforcement and they can get a warrant."

"Then please promise me you'll be careful. Ever since we learned about that state trooper with a broken neck I've been worried about you."

"I'll be careful, I promise."

Her concern was touching. It made him feel guilty that he still hadn't told her about the footprints on the roof. He'd put it off, stalling until the right time. And now wasn't it.

Kelly was quiet for a time and then said, "You want to see inside Kardos' coach. How are you going to pull that off?"

He'd been giving the problem some thought. "Obviously, I can't have a look while he's in the coach, so I'll need to get him out of there somehow. I'm going to play it by ear and hope for an opportunity. I was a Marine. I will improvise, adapt, and overcome." He saluted smartly. "Oorah."

"Semper fi," she said. "Daryl was in the Corps, too. I didn't want to butt in when you told Doug you were in the Marines."

A half-hour later he checked the app and did a double take. The red dot was motionless. Kardos had stopped again, this time near the town of Sisters. He handed Kelly the phone.

She looked at the screen. "Think he's had more trouble?"

"We'll find out in about fifteen minutes."

Remarkably, the highway into Sisters did not suffer from strip mall blight, offering only a lone gas station and general store combo. Downtown Sisters consisted of eight blocks of galleries, antique stores, and artsy-fartsy gift shops, save for the occasional charming little cafe. The buildings had facades with styles ranging from rustic to Tyrolean village. Despite its eagerness to attract tourists, the town seemed like it would be a pleasant place to live. That is, if you didn't mind winters with snow drifts tall enough to bury a car.

"I expected it to look a lot different," Kelly said. "But it hasn't changed all that much. More upscale, maybe."

On the other side of Sisters the road branched: McKenzie Highway went to Redmond, Route 20 continued on to Bend. Kelly pointed to a sign: THREE SISTERS RV PARK. Crocetti turned into the entrance and stopped to check the app.

The red and blue dots had almost merged into a single purple dot. They had found Kardos.

Crocetti made a slow circuit of the park, which was laid out with three rows, each able to accommodate twelve rigs. And in a pull-through space in the middle row, the black coach crouched, looking as sinister as ever.

The only spot available was a back-in space on one of the side rows. But it would give them a decent view of the black coach's front and back doors through a side window. He backed in with an expert's confidence.

"I don't get it," Kelly said. "After hours, people can come in unannounced and just park wherever they please?"

"Pretty much, with the expectation they'll register in the morning, although some RV parks provide registration cards you can fill out and drop in a box when you get there. I didn't see any when we drove past the office, though."

"Pally needs to go out. Will you come with us?"

"Just a sec." He opened the desk drawer and reached for the shoulder rig but instead shoved the Colt into his belt, grip concealed by his jacket. "C'mon, Pally."

They stepped out into an eerie silence. No night sounds of frogs and crickets and dogs barking in the distance. The trees had the look of still photographs. Pally did his duty and then seemed anxious to go back inside. They were glad to accommodate him. Crocetti returned the gun to the drawer.

Sitting on the sofa in the dark, they watched the black coach, only fifty feet away but poorly illuminated by the parking area's feeble lighting. Visibility was good enough, just barely, to see anyone entering or exiting.

"Like I told you back at the truck stop," Kelly said, "I can't help wondering if Kardos is watching us from behind those black windows."

"Not unless he has night-vision goggles."

"Maybe vampires don't need them. Maybe they have natural night vision."

Crocetti answered with a grunt. She was doing her best to get a rise out of him. Damned if he'd give her the satisfaction. "Tell you what, I would like to own a pair of night-vision goggles myself."

"Are they expensive?"

"Several thousand for a decent pair. I'm beginning to think it might be a good investment."

"Only if you plan to continue being a freelance detective."

It was a distinct possibility. Everyone had something they were good at. Some people's talent was solving crossword puzzles. His was solving murders. And truth be told, he was no slouch at crossword puzzles.

Kelly put her hand on his arm. "Did you see that?"

"See what?"

"I think . . . I thought I saw something, a dark shape next to the back door. But I wouldn't swear to it."

"I didn't see anything. Maybe your eyesight's better than mine."

Light streaming in through the windshield wasn't helping. He got up and closed the curtain across the front.

"That's better," Kelly said. "I might've been seeing things."

He put on a jacket and grabbed the Colt and flashlight. "I'm going to have a look around anyway."

"For God's sake, be careful."

He stepped down onto the asphalt pad and stood there a moment, listening. In the strange silence the rush of blood in his ears was all he could hear. He took a deep breath and set off around the loop encircling the middle row of RVs. As he passed by the black coach, the hair on the back of his neck rose. It pissed him off. Kardos was probably observing him, but so what? They'd be eating Eskimo Pies in hell before he'd let some loony perp spook him. A sidelong glance confirmed that Kardos hadn't hooked up his water and electrical connections. Easier to make a quick exit after his grisly work was finished, if indeed he was on the hunt.

Continuing around the loop, Crocetti saw no activity at all, as might be expected at two thirty a.m. As he walked up to his coach from the other direction he shined the flashlight on the roof—just in case the unhinged son of a bitch was up to his old tricks.

"It's me," he called as he opened the door, so he wouldn't startle Kelly.

"See anything?"

"Not a damn thing." He sat down beside her. "You?"

"Ditto."

"This might be a long and boring night. Tell you what—I'll take the watch while you doze, and then we'll trade off."

"Sounds like a plan." She adjusted a throw pillow behind her head and settled back into the sofa.

Sitting there in the dark, listening to her regular breathing, Crocetti couldn't help thinking about the hundreds of times he'd been on a stakeout—watching a door, waiting for someone to arrive or depart. He'd usually had backup, though. Here, he was on his own. But he had no doubt that he could take Kardos, if it came to that.

With a soft *woof*, Pally left his bed and stood rigidly alert, facing the front of the coach. Crocetti listened, not taking his eyes off the black coach, but he didn't hear a thing. A few minutes later Pally returned to his bed.

As he was considering tossing back some 5-hour Energy he heard an engine start and soon afterward the black coach began moving. The rush of adrenalin made caffeine unnecessary. He nudged Kelly awake and pointed out the side window at the departing coach. "Kardos is hitting the trail."

She yawned. "What time is it?"

"A bit before three. Time for us to go." He got to his feet, went forward, and threw back the curtain that closed off the cockpit. Then he recoiled as though from a viper.

Scrawled across the windshield in reddish-brown letters, a message:

STOP FOLLOWING ME

Ignoring Kelly's cry of alarm, he grabbed the gun and flashlight and hurried outside.

The message was on the outside of the windshield, written in reverse so it would be readable from inside. His guess was that it had been written with blood. He got a sample with a swab and dropped it in a small plastic bag and then took flash photos of the windshield. Fuming, he scrubbed off the blood with the long-handled pad he used to remove bugs.

"Dan, I'm scared," Kelly said in a small voice.

He put his arms around her. "He wants to scare us, honey. Let's not give him the satisfaction."

The tracking app indicated that Kardos was heading southeast on Route 20, toward Bend.

Crocetti started the coach's engine.

25

The distance to Bend from Sisters was twenty-three miles. Halfway there Kelly broke the silence. "You haven't said a word since we hit the road. You're glowering, and the corners of your jaw are bulging. That warning message really upset you. Want to talk about it?"

Crocetti looked over at her. "It's just that the guy's getting nervy, trying so—what's the word—overtly to scare us off. And what really chaps my ass, he smeared blood on my prized coach. I consider that a very personal insult."

"Okay, but I hope you're not so wound up about it that you do something rash and get yourself hurt . . . or worse."

"I appreciate your concern, but I'm not a rookie. Kelly, I've put over two hundred killers behind bars. This bogus vampire, defacer of windshields, will be one more."

"Fine. But you promised me you'd be careful, dammit, and I'm going to hold you to it."

"Yes, dear," he said in the voice of a browbeaten spouse.

After several seconds of shocked silence, she laughed. "Okay, no more nagging."

The clock in the dash indicated 3:45. Two and a half hours until sunrise. That gave Kardos plenty of time to find another place to hole up until nightfall. Now that he knew Crocetti was on his tail, would he alter his plans? Perhaps under pressure he'd screw up. If so, Crocetti would be there.

"I've been sitting here wondering," Kelly said. "How do we know that Kardos didn't kill anyone back in Sisters? I mean, we didn't see him slip out of his motor home to write on our windshield, so who knows what else he did?"

Crocetti thought about it for a minute. "How do we know he didn't? Just a hunch. I think our presence spooked him."

"How did he know we weren't just another coach?"

So he told her about finding the footprints on the roof back in Coburg. "Somehow he knew then that we were tailing him."

"How could he?"

"I'll be sure to ask him after he's in cuffs."

A half-mile ahead traffic had come to a standstill, a necklace of motionless taillights adorning the night.

"What now?" Crocetti said, slowing the coach.

They stopped behind a pickup with huge off-road tires and a suspension that elevated the cab to almost the same height as Crocetti's coach. And yet the truck looked like it had never left the pavement even once. The driver was wearing a Seattle Mariners baseball cap backwards.

Thirteen places ahead of the pickup a dark shape loomed. The black coach.

A man wearing a hard hat and an orange vest came walking down the line, stopping at each vehicle to say something. Crocetti lowered his side window.

"Rock slide," the man said. "You'll have a twenty-minute wait while the crew clears the road."

An idea coalesced. Crocetti got up and walked back to the desk. In a drawer that contained odds and ends he found the items he was looking for and pocketed them. He hesitated before reaching for the Colt but decided to take it.

He grabbed his cane and turned to Kelly. "I need a distraction. I want you—better yet, you and Pally—to walk up to the front of Kardos' coach, on the driver's side, and just loiter there a few minutes and watch the workmen clear the road. Then come back here. Think you can do that?"

"Okay, but it'll be creepy, knowing Kardos will be looking at me. Where will you be in the meantime?"

"Close by," he said, "I'll fill you in after we get back."

They walked next to the guard rail, and because the road curved slightly, they were mostly out of sight of Kardos' side mirrors. One vehicle length behind the black coach they split up. Kelly and Pally crossed to the left side of the coach and he stepped over the guard rail so he could approach from the right without being seen in the side mirror.

He kneeled by the coach's big front tire and fished from his pocket two stout four-inch nails. One he wedged in front of the tire, between the asphalt and tread, and the other he wedged in back, in case the coach rolled backwards. Either way, the tire was sure to pick up a nasty puncture.

First to arrive back at his coach, Crocetti had just washed his hands when the door opened and Pally hopped in, followed by Kelly. "How'd it go?" he asked her.

"Fine, except for having a bad case of the heebie-jeebies. I swear, I could feel his eyes boring into my back." She stood with her hands on her hips. "Well? Talk to me."

He smiled at her. "I'm feeling prescient. I predict Kardos' right-front tire will develop a slow leak due to a nail puncture. When he realizes it's going flat he'll have to stop and get it fixed. And then I'll play it by ear."

"Adapt, improvise, and overcome?"

"Oorah."

"We'd better get ready to go. Looks like the workmen are about finished clearing the road."

Several minutes later traffic started to move, and before long they were up to speed. He crossed his fingers that the leak would be slow enough to let Kardos make it to Bend, only about seven miles further, where there was a good chance he'd leave the coach unattended for several minutes while he made arrangements to get the tire fixed. At least, that was Crocetti's hope.

"By the way," Kelly said, "I practically had to drag Pally up to the front of Kardos' motor home. The poor pup didn't want any part of it. He trembled the whole time. Can't say I blame him."

"Kardos' scent is probably all around his coach. Dogs are intuitive. Pally must've sensed he's a bad guy. Anyway, you both did good. I couldn't have pulled it off without your help."

Less than a mile out of Bend, traffic began slowing again.

Kelly groaned. "Another rock slide?"

But the obstruction turned out to be the black coach, poking along and causing frustrated drivers to take foolish chances to get around it.

Crocetti looked over at Kelly. "Gotta love it when an idea pans out."

Up ahead, the black coach signaled a right turn and hobbled into a large, brightly-lit truck stop. Crocetti followed, lagging back a bit, staying out of sight.

Kardos drove through to the back and stopped in front of a large steel building with a sign proclaiming, "24-Hour Service Center." Crocetti pulled up next to a propane tank the size of a school bus and switched off the engine.

"Keep an eye on him," he told Kelly. He pocketed a flashlight and got two small walkie-talkies from the desk. After making sure they were both charged and set to the same channel, he slipped into the shoulder rig, holstered the gun, and put on a jacket. "Any movement over there?" he called out to Kelly.

"Kardos just went into the building, wearing either a cape or a long black coat, I couldn't tell which. He looked scary as hell."

"I don't have much time." He handed her a walkie-talkie. "Let's make sure these work."

They worked just fine, other than an earsplitting screech of feedback resulting from their proximity.

Crocetti grabbed his cane and headed for the door.

"I hope you know what you're doing," she said.

He traversed the distance across the asphalt as quickly as his knee allowed. At the black coach he tried the door. It was unlocked, just as he'd hoped. He spoke into the walkie-talkie: "I'm going in. Warn me if Kardos reappears."

"*Please be careful*," came the reply.

Crocetti stepped inside and switched on his flashlight. The interior was like a Victorian parlor, not exactly typical decor for a modern motor coach. Wine-red velvet curtains blocked the light from the heavily tinted windows, giving the place a funereal pall. Edgar Allen Poe would have felt right at home, had it not been for the smell, the unmistakable stench of decay, like rotting meat—the same unholy smell that had been present in the Ostrow's coach.

The flashlight's beam swept across a grouping of ornately framed photographs on the wall. One in particular caught his eye. It featured a man, a woman, and a dark-eyed girl about five posing stiffly, their faces somber. The three subjects' clothes were old-fashioned and formal; the man wore a cut-away coat, the woman and girl long dresses. Looming over them in the misty background, a medieval castle. He didn't want to take the time to examine the other photos. The flash in his phone's camera was set to automatic, so he stood off to the side to minimize reflection and snapped a close-up of each photograph for further study, and then he took a wide shot of the eccentric room.

All very well, but he was there to ferret out evidence, specifically the machine Kardos used to drain his victims' blood and his stash of draculin. Crocetti checked the cabinets and closets in the lounge and the kitchen cupboards. Empty.

The refrigerator most definitely wasn't empty. It contained several dozen bags full of blood, all types. One would think even a fake vampire would be more particular. Crocetti's eyes widened when he opened the freezer. It was packed with stacks of banded currency, seemingly all hundreds, giving a literal meaning to "cold cash." Based on his experience with drug seizures before joining the homicide squad, he estimated it to be several hundred grand. He photographed the stacks of money and bags of blood.

Highly suspicious findings, but they wouldn't incriminate Kardos in any of the murders. Crocetti moved down the hall toward the rear of the coach. Hopefully, the machine and draculin were back there somewhere.

He checked the guest bathroom and found that it had no soap, towels, or even toilet paper. Nothing in the medicine cabinet. The guest stateroom was also totally empty except for a bed without bedding, its closet bare as could be. Apparently, Kardos didn't often have company stay over.

One room left.

He opened the door to the master stateroom and shined the flashlight into the darkness within. "Holy mother of Jesus," he said aloud. The beam illuminated a large object in the center of the room.

A coffin. Of course. For verisimilitude.

Made of ebony and decorated with elaborate carvings, its lid was open. It was lined with soil.

So it wasn't merely an act, some kind of performance art. Kardos actually believed he was a vampire. The crazy bastard belonged in an institution for the criminally insane.

After photographing the coffin he shined the light in the master bathroom. Same story as the other bathroom, totally bare. One thing was sure: Kardos saved a fortune on soap and toilet paper. And no one could call him a clothes horse. The closet contained a row of dark clothes on hangars and a half-dozen pairs of unfashionable black shoes, nothing else.

On his way back to the lounge, the walkie-talkie crackled. "Dan, he just left the building and he's headed your way. For God's sake, get out of there!"

Just then—at the worst conceivable time, of course—the flashlight slipped out of his hand and blinked out when it hit the floor, dead as roadkill.

His only hope was to slip out the rear door in the master stateroom, assuming he could find his way back there in the almost total darkness. But before he'd gone three steps the front door opened and the coach rocked slightly.

Crocetti froze, not daring to even breathe.

Faint light from the windshield silhouetted a tall figure. The figure stood silently, sniffing the air like some type of animal.

Then it came toward Crocetti.

Crocetti reached for the gun, but before he could get his hand on the grip, Kardos was there. He wrapped an icy hand around Crocetti's throat and lifted him off his feet and held him suspended against the wall, a prodigious feat of strength.

"You should have heeded my warning," Kardos said in a thickly accented baritone, his cold, wet breath fetid as the sewer drain in a slaughterhouse killing floor.

With great difficulty, Crocetti said, "A word of advice . . . you should think about . . . using breath mints."

Kardos hauled him out of the hallway by his neck and tossed him as though he were a sack of styrofoam packing peanuts. He landed hard, ending up on his back against a divan. A mixture of fear and adrenaline blunted the pain as he scrambled to his feet. In the salon's dim light, Kardos was a shadowy shape coming for him.

As Crocetti reached for his gun, a young guy appeared in the open doorway. "Hello? Mr. Kaminski? If you could go ahead and pull your rig into the shop I'll get you fixed up."

While Kardos hesitated, Crocetti bolted for the door, bum knee forgotten. "Excuse me," he said to the young man as he brushed by him.

As his feet touched the asphalt outside, the walkie-talkie in his jacket pocket crackled. *"Dan? Are you okay?"*

He answered her while limping toward the sanctuary of his coach. "I'm fine, more or less. See you in a few."

When he got there she helped him up the steps. "Where's your cane?"

"Left it behind. I've got a spare."

Her eyes searched his face and then dropped lower. "What happened to your neck? It's all red! And that looks like a— damn, it is. It's a handprint."

"I guess things got a little out of control."

"Sit down. I want to hear every detail."

He dropped into a chair and told her what had happened, start to finish. "And if that kid hadn't shown up when he did, no telling how it would have ended up."

"Sounds to me like you would have ended up dead."

"Not if I shot him in the head first."

"What were you thinking, taunting him about his breath? You must be a crazy person."

"Old cop tactic. Get them mad so they'll make mistakes. I got away, didn't I?"

"You were lucky."

Hard to argue with that.

"So what are you going to do now?"

The shaking started in his hands and spread throughout his body, as though he'd stuck a fork in an electrical outlet. He crossed his arms to conceal it. "I think I'll go lie down for a bit," he said.

"Are you all right, Dan?" A vertical furrow had appeared between her brows.

"I'm fine. I just need to . . . collect my thoughts."

By the time he made it to his bedroom the shaking had become uncontrollable. And he was cold. Teeth chattering, he threw back the covers on the king-size bed and kicked his shoes off, not bothering to untie them, and got between the sheets and pulled the covers up over his head. He was five again, hiding from the monster in the closet. Except this time the monster lurked inside a motor coach across the way.

Even with the gun, he'd been badly outmatched. Going up against Kardos was like Pally challenging a Rottweiler. The worst part was that he had nothing to show for the risk he'd taken, only photos of bags of blood, stacks of money, a coffin.

Kelly knocked lightly and opened the door. "Dan?"

He poked his head out from under the covers. "Yes?"

She came in and sat on the side of the bed. "Please hear me out. I know you love the excitement of the chase and the challenge of pitting your intellect against Kardos. But I'm scared. For you. For . . . us. If chasing after Kardos gets you killed—well, the thought makes me crazy. The truth is, you don't need to do it. You could turn it over to the state police or FBI anytime." She got up to leave but paused at the door. "Please promise me you'll at least think about it."

"Okay."

He thought about it. He was sixty-three with a bum knee and bad prostate. His ego and mulishness had nearly gotten him killed. Next time he might not be so lucky. The smart move would be to step aside and let someone else take over. Someone who had not stared into that maw of pure evil and been totally, utterly terrified.

After the chills and shaking subsided, he tossed back the covers and swung his legs over the edge of the bed and stood. He found Kelly sitting in the lounge, flipping though a *Downbeat*. She looked up, eyebrows raised.

"We'll head back to Brookings in the morning," he said.

"Thank God." She got up and hugged him. "I'm relieved."

In the master suite's bathroom he splashed cold water on his face, toweled it dry, and stared at himself in the mirror. His face looked haggard, the skin slack, as though too big for the supporting structures underneath. Was it his imagination or were more veins than usual visible in the whites of his eyes? And he'd never noticed before that one eye was larger than the other. Or was it a trick of the lighting?

So he'd hightail it back to Brookings. Retreat. It was a wise decision under the circumstances . . . right?

Not so fast, partner.

The price was too high—his self respect. He would despise himself for the rest of his days. What he should do—what he *needed* to do—was clear. And Kelly was not going to like it.

"Sorry, but I can't leave," he told her. "I can't run back to Brookings with my tail between my legs. I wouldn't be worth a diddly damn if I did."

Kelly stared at him. "Fastest change of heart on record."

"I've never been a quitter. I'm not about to start now."

"That's admirable, but—"

He held up his hand. "So I think you'd better take the bus back to Brookings."

"No way," she said, "I'm staying. Someone has to call the ambulance. Or hearse."

He opened his mouth to say something and then closed it. What could he say to that?

26

It was almost daybreak when the black coach emerged from the shop and parked in a back corner of the paved area, where it was almost certain to remain until nightfall.

A couple hours later Crocetti unhitched the car as Kelly looked on. The car would be much more convenient for running errands in town while their coach remained parked next to the huge propane tank, an excellent vantage point for keeping tabs on Kardos.

They drove to Applebee's and had pancakes for breakfast. Between bites Kelly said, "I don't understand something. How has Kardos managed to avoid being caught for so long? You'd think they would've gotten him long before now. Are they a bunch of bozos or what?"

He took a sip of coffee. "I can only speculate. City, county, state, and federal agencies are conducting ongoing investigations. Bureaucracies are cumbersome. They sometimes move at a snail's pace. So I have an advantage."

"I don't imagine they'll be pleased if you show them up."

"Probably not, but the important thing is to get that psycho off the street."

"Another question. The old Roma woman told you he kills every two weeks, regular as clockwork, because he needs the blood to survive, and then hides again. Today's the twenty-first, so he's six days late. How do you explain that?"

"That's been bothering me, too. By now he knows we're following him, so maybe we fouled up his schedule. And it's not as though he actually needs blood to survive. He's only a make-believe vampire, remember."

She pushed her plate aside. "Kardos is tall, but not particularly muscular. How was he able to lift you by the throat and toss you across the room with one hand? How was he able to withstand that state trooper's bullets and break his neck?" She sat back and crossed her arms. "I think Kardos is a genuine vampire. It would explain everything."

He sighed and shook his head. "Sorry, I can't accept it. If I did, I'd have to accept the existence of werewolves, zombies, wizards, goblins, elves, the Easter Bunny, and Santa Claus."

"Wait a minute. Are you saying there's no Santa Claus?"

"Kardos is not a supernatural creature. He's rich, cunning, and physically powerful. He's unhinged, a textbook psychopath, and possibly on PCP. But he's as human as you and me."

"Crocetti, you're the most stubborn man I've ever met."

"You're not the first to tell me that. Ready to go?"

Their next stop was Walmart, where Kelly went looking for a lightweight jacket and some facial cleanser while he browsed in the sporting goods department. Their firearms section was well stocked. He grabbed a box of .38 cartridges for the Colt and then stopped to look at an assortment of pepper spray canisters.

A salesclerk sidled up and pointed to a canister with red flames licking up the sides. "See that one there? It'll make a grizzly bear turn tail and run."

"That so?" But how effective would it be against Kardos, that was the question. It might be worth a try. "I'll take one. Got any tasers?"

"Nope, sorry. Gun World, they got some wicked tasers. But they're not open Sundays."

Damn. Chances were, they would be long gone by Monday.

He found Kelly near the front, thumbing through *People* magazine. They got in line behind a skinny girl with enough piercings to make a metal detector go nuts.

On the way to the car, Kelly walloped him in the shoulder with her fist. "Slug bug blue. No hit backs." She pointed to a beat-up Volkswagon beetle.

"Sweet Jesus, I'm babysitting here," he said, rubbing his shoulder.

"Oh, don't be so crotchety, Crocetti."

Their last stop was Albertson's, to stock up on groceries. No telling when they'd get another chance. They filled a cart until it was heaping with food, including wine and several types of cheese, one a smoked cheddar, his favorite.

Back at the coach after they put away the groceries, he said, "I'm going to sack out for a few hours. Kardos will be hitting the road after dark and we might have a long night ahead of us."

She yawned. "I could use some sleep myself."

As he shuffled back to the master stateroom he couldn't erase a mental image of the coffin, its black-garbed occupant waiting to emerge after dark.

The light through the stateroom window had grown dim by the time he woke up. Stretching made his joints crackle and pop. He stumbled into the bathroom and splashed cold water on his face. He could use a shave, but it would have to wait.

He met Kelly as she was just coming out of her stateroom. "I could have slept three or four more hours, easy," she said.

It was fully dark outside by the time he'd made coffee and poured two cups. They sat and talked in the dark lounge while they kept an eye on the black coach, expecting it to leave at any moment. But it remained where it was for nearly an hour after the sun had set.

Kelly sipped her coffee. "Think Kardos plans to stay here another night?"

"No," he said. "I've got a feeling he's going to leave pretty soon."

And twenty minutes later the black coach began to move. They gave it ten-minute head start and then followed.

Or tried to.

Something was wrong. The coach acted as though it were mired to the axles in tar. He put it in park and went out to see what the trouble was.

"Come out and have a look at this," he called to Kelly. When she joined him he pointed to the very flat front tire. "See there? The sidewall's been slashed. Same story with the other front tire. Both destroyed."

"What are we going to do now?"

"No way around it, I'll have to buy two new tires."

"How much will that cost?"

"Maybe a grand apiece."

She shook her head slowly. "My god."

"I haven't priced tires lately. They might cost more."

"Looks like Kardos got you back for the nail in his tire."

"Listen, I'm going to walk over to the shop and get the ball rolling. Want to tag along?"

"I'll stay here, maybe fix us some sandwiches."

After he walked into the shop he spotted the young fellow whose splendid timing in appearing at the door of the black coach had allowed him to get away from Kardos. The guy stopped stacking tires when he saw Crocetti. "Did you need some help, sir?" Then recognition dawned. "Hey, we ran into each other last night."

"It's more like I ran into you. Sorry about that. I was in kind of a hurry."

"What can I do for you?"

"My coach is in dire need of two new front tires. Got time to walk over and take a look?"

"Sure, lead the way."

While they walked, the guy asked him if the owner of the black coach was a friend of his.

"No," Crocetti said, "we were just comparing notes about our coaches."

"Did you notice his breath could gag a maggot?"

"Why do you think I was in such a hurry to get out of there?"

The guy grinned. "I kept my distance, believe me. He gave me a fifty-dollar tip, though."

"Nice little score."

"Funny thing, though—other than being tall and having bad breath I don't remember much about him. Hope I don't have early-onset Alzheimer's, like my grandma."

"Some people just aren't very memorable." Crocetti said. Especially if they have Kardos' skill at hypnosis.

The guy let out a whistle when he saw the slashed tires. "Any idea who did it?"

"Some teenagers were hanging around out here. They did it, probably. My insurance covers vandalism, but it's still a pain in the ass."

"We don't have the tires you need in stock," the guy said, "but I can have a pair here tomorrow. You'll be on the road by the end of the day."

"The price?"

"I can let you have a set of Michelins for eleven-fifty apiece. They retail for fifteen."

"Okay, make it happen."

Kelly had food ready when he got back to the coach, chicken sandwiches and fruit salad. He delivered the good news first: She would have a chance to catch up on her sleep. And then the bad: They would be stuck there for another day.

She shrugged. "Sit down and eat."

27

Gun World appeared to be doing a brisk business for a Monday, its aisles filled with steely eyed hunter types. Stuffed and mounted animals were on display everywhere: bobcats, wolves, bear, deer, elk, and a huge moose, its long face wearing an expression that seemed to say, "What a revoltin' development this is."

Behind a counter, a rack full of AR-15s and other military-style rifles generated intense interest. Prospective buyers handled them with the reverence usually accorded to sacred artifacts.

"I'm the only female in the whole damn store," Kelly said.

"Not so," Crocetti said and pointed to a camo-clad woman with a bulldog jaw and unibrow looking at a Glock. "Probably stopped in on the way to Victoria's Secret."

He finally located an assortment of tasers under a glass counter and beckoned to a salesclerk, a plump young man trying, with limited success, to grow a mustache.

"Interested in a taser, sir?"

"Possibly. Show me the one you recommend."

The salesclerk unlocked the case, removed a device, and laid it on top of the counter. "This is the JoltMaster 3000. Not the most expensive, but it has everything the spendier units have. But don't tell my boss I said that."

Crocetti picked it up. "It's just as powerful?"

"All tasers use the same current, voltage, and waveform. They are all equally effective at stopping an attacker in his tracks."

Kelly asked if she could hold it. "How does it work?"

The salesclerk launched into a spiel he'd obviously reeled off many times: "Tasers fire two pronged darts propelled by compressed nitrogen. The darts are connected to insulated copper wire which conduct the electricity from the taser into the attacker's body. When both darts strike the target, it completes an electrical circuit. Electricity flows through the attacker's muscles causing loss of voluntary muscle control."

"What if it's a big guy?" Crocetti asked.

"Size doesn't matter. A taser will be just as effective on a three-hundred-pound man as it will on a hundred-pound woman. A taser will even take down a full-grown bull."

"Do you have to hit an area with exposed skin?"

"No. The darts will penetrate several layers of clothing."

"What if the attacker is high on PCP or other drug?"

"Doesn't matter. Neuromuscular incapacitation will immobilize any attacker, regardless of their mental state."

"One last question. What's the range?"

"The length of the wires, fifteen feet."

"Okay, I'll take one. And three spare cartridges."

Back at the coach he unbagged his purchase. The taser came with a belt-clip holster. Holstered, the pistol-shaped taser looked and carried like a gun.

He grinned at Kelly. "Next time—assuming there is a next time—Kardos is going to get a big surprise. A shocking one, I predict."

"Like a kid with a new toy. But explain this to me—from the questions you asked the sales clerk it was obvious you'd had no experience with tasers. How can that be the case? You're a thirty-year veteran policeman."

"Us old timers dint have no truck with them newfangled gadgets. Besides, they were issued only to uniformed officers."

After he stashed the taser in the drawer with the gun, he loaded some photographic-quality paper in the printer and, via bluetooth, sent it the photos he'd taken in Kardos' coach. Then he spread them out on the dinette table, eight in all, and he and Kelly examined them.

"These five have an old, silvery look," she said.

"I did a little research online this morning before you got up. I think they're daguerreotypes."

"Any idea how old they are?"

"According to Wikipedia, daguerreotypes became widespread in eighteen thirty-nine. In that year Kardos, the original one, would've been thirty-two." He pointed to one of the photos. "That's about how old I'd guess this man is."

Kelly scrutinized the print. "You think that's Kardos?"

"The original one. The killer's ancestor."

"He has an overbite. That must be his wife and little girl."

"I would assume so."

She pointed to another photo. "Here he is alone, and he looks about ten years older."

"According to the phuri dai, he became a vampire when he was thirty-seven. Supposedly."

"So this photo was taken after he became a vampire."

"I said supposedly."

"Twice, you've said it. Anyway, he seems sad."

Crocetti agreed. Sorrow haunted the man's dark eyes. "Perhaps he lost his wife and child." Or his humanity, he almost said, but she would have pounced on it.

"Look at this one," Kelly said. "A bunch of young girls at some sort of party in a garden." She pointed to one of the girls. "There's Kardos' daughter. She seems to be having a terrific time."

In another photo an imperious-looking man with a gray beard sat stiffly, a German shepherd at his feet. The man had a regal air. It had to be the elder Kardos, the prince. Even with the beard the family resemblance was unmistakable. Crocetti made a mental note to Google Romanian royalty the first chance he got.

He pointed to a daguerreotype of a huge medieval castle, its turrets shrouded in mist, an elegant black coach drawn by two white horses standing in front. "This must be the family homestead."

"Looks cozy," she said.

"The last three photos are contemporary."

She was fascinated by the Victorian parlor and refrigerator full of bags of blood and stacks of cash, but the photo of the coffin took her breath away.

"My god, look at the indentation in the dirt," she said. "Kardos actually sleeps in it. No doubt about it."

"Which further confirms he's a wackjob."

"Or a vampire."

He got up and stretched. "Anyway, there you have it."

Pally left his bed and stood on his hind legs to get the leash dangling over the edge of the desk. He came over to Crocetti with it in his mouth, his eyes pleading.

"Okay, okay," Crocetti said. "Let's go for a walk. C'mon, Kelly, go with us."

"Sure. I could use the exercise. But that's one intelligent dog, to bring you his leash when he wants to go out."

"Pretty smart, I have to admit."

Fifteen minutes into their walk the young guy from the shop hailed them from across the parking lot. After he caught up with them he said, "Thought you'd want to know. Your tires will be here this afternoon."

"Great," Crocetti said. "Are you going to need to get my rig into your shop? That could be a challenge with front tires completely flat."

"No need. I can make the switch where it sits. I have a portable power wrench and a monster jack."

"Sounds like you've got everything under control."

Pally pulled on the leash. Crocetti nodded to the guy and they continued on their way. Pally strained at the leash, leading them over to the area where the black coach had been parked, and then he began sniffing the ground.

"He's looking for something, but what?" Kelly said.

With Crocetti in tow, Pally crisscrossed the area a half-dozen times, until he homed in on a section of scrub grass at the edge of the pavement. He barked once and looked up at them.

Crocetti leaned down to see. "What is it, boy? What'd you come up with?"

It was a bag that had once held blood and now held only blood residue. Crocetti found a twig, inserted it through the hole at the top, provided for hanging the bag when delivering its contents, and picked it up.

Kelly made a face. "What do you plan to do with that?"

"Preserve it. It's evidence. Might have Kardos' saliva and prints on it."

"Why would he discard it out here?"

"Who knows? Maybe he had an outdoor picnic and left his trash behind."

"You'd think he'd be more careful."

Crocetti leaned over and patted Pally's head. "Good boy. I owe you a steak."

"And it's well deserved."

On the walk back to the coach Crocetti made a snap decision. "Pally," he said to the dog, "how would you like to be my permanent partner?"

Pally looked up at him and wagged his tail. But then, he'd probably react that way no matter what was said to him.

"Hear that, Pally? You've got a forever home." She leaned over and kissed Crocetti's cheek. "I knew you were a big softie. I predict this will be a legendary detective partnership."

"I'm as surprised as you are, you want to know the truth. I hope to hell I won't regret it."

Usually he avoided making snap decisions. Impulsiveness wasn't one of his personality traits. He preferred thorough, careful deliberation. But he'd jettisoned his customary caution and made a serious commitment, one that would affect his life for the next decade, possibly longer. Why? He looked down at the animal limping along on his bum hind leg and had his answer: Gimps had to stick together.

Back inside the coach Crocetti dropped into a chair and Pally hopped in his lap, to Kelly's amusement. He stroked the soft fur as the dog dozed, totally relaxed. He managed to make it a full ten minutes before the urge to wash his hands became too urgent to ignore.

28

The sun was setting by the time they reached Prineville, on their way to the the eastern Oregon town of John Day. Kardos had been in John Day all day, according to the app. Now that night had fallen he would most likely be on the move again.

It might have been his imagination, but it seemed to Crocetti the new front tires had improved the coach's ride and handling. And after shelling out two-and-a-half grand by the time all was said and done, he wanted to think so.

When they came upon a Dairy Queen on the west end of town, with—wonder of wonders—three long, empty parking spaces on the street in front, he pulled over.

"Dan, you're a genius," Kelly said.

"My dear mother would have agreed with you. Let's get some ice cream."

At the counter inside he ordered a chocolate-dipped cone while Kelly deliberated. Finally she said, "Damn it, I'm going to splurge and have a hot fudge sundae. I haven't had one in ages." They decided to sit at a table inside.

"Ummm," she said, savoring the first bite. "Hits the spot."

"You feel like you're caught up on your sleep yet?"

"Pretty much. You?"

"I took a long nap. Then I got up and did some research on Romanian royalty, courtesy of Google."

"Find out anything interesting?"

"I learned that Prince Nicolas Kardos the Third, born in seventeen seventy-two and died in eighteen forty-one, had two sons, Viktor and Vladimir. Vlad died at nineteen when his horse threw him during a fox hunt, broke his neck. There's nothing about Viktor."

"Well? Isn't that consistent with what the old Roma woman told you?"

"I suppose, but it doesn't mean the weirdo we're chasing is the same Viktor Kardos. He could be a relative, or perhaps he's no relation and simply appropriated the name."

She sighed. "What would it take to convince you that Kardos is a real vampire, a look at his fangs?"

"Nope. They could be prosthetics."

She pushed the half-eaten hot fudge sundae away. "I can't finish it. Want it?"

He shook his head. "The only thing that will convince me is witnessing Kardos do something that can't be explained by scientific means."

"You, sir, are one stubborn man."

"So you've said."

A beat-up brown car with a headlight out pulled into the parking lot. Two young guys, a redhead and a brunette, got out and came in. Both were skinny, both had sallow skin that looked almost green under the fluorescent lights. The redhead was a mouth breather, exposing very bad teeth. After looking Kelly up and down they slouched over to the order counter.

Crocetti inclined his head in their direction. "I'd say Archie and Jughead have been hitting the meth pretty hard."

After buying soft ice cream cones, the pair sat down several tables away and talked in low tones, punctuated with a laugh from time to time, and sneaked looks at Kelly. The meth-addled punks would be lucky to see thirty, the way they were going. One would think a relatively remote place like Prineville would be free of the scourge of methamphetamine. And one would be dead wrong. The drug was everywhere these days.

On the way out, Crocetti ordered a child-size soft vanilla cone. "For Pally," he said. "To celebrate our new partnership."

When Crocetti bent down and held it out to him, the dog sniffed it, took an exploratory lick, and then looked up at him, confusion on his fuzzy face.

"That's right, it's for you," Crocetti said. "Go ahead."

Tail wagging, Pally devoured the ice cream, a dreamy look in his eyes. Then he licked his chops for several minutes.

Ten miles past Prineville, Crocetti realized that they had forgotten to give Pally a bathroom break before they took off again, so he pulled into a rest area.

He and Kelly were watching Pally explore a patch of grass when a car with one headlight entered the rest area. It pulled up behind the coach and two men got out.

Archie and Jughead.

Archie took a pistol from a jacket pocket and pointed it at them. It was only a .22 but still plenty lethal. He ordered them into the coach. They complied, not wanting to argue with a methhead with a gun. He made them sit together on the sofa.

Jughead opened the freezer compartment of the refrigerator and rifled through the contents. "It's not here," he said.

"Check the rest of the fridge," Archie said. "All the shelves and drawers."

"Just food," Jughead said after he finished looking.

Archie turned to them. "Okay, where is it?"

"Where's what?" Crocetti said.

"The fifty-freakin' grand."

Crocetti glanced at Kelly. She looked as confused as he felt. "Fifty thousand? That's nuts. I never keep much cash on hand, no more than fifty, sixty bucks."

Archie said to Jughead, "Check all the drawers, cupboards and closets. It's here somewhere."

"I don't understand," Crocetti said. "Where did you get the idea there's money hidden in here?"

Archie smirked. "Don't bullshit us, pops. We have it on good authority."

"Yeah? Who would that be?"

"A guy we met last night, he told us. Said you'd be coming through."

Then the pieces fell into place. "This guy—what did he look like?"

Archie's brow furrowed. "Just a guy. Tall, I think. A righteous dude.

"How did you happen to run into him?"

The furrows deepened and then he shrugged. "We were pretty high at the time."

"I'll check the bedrooms," Jughead said over his shoulder.

Archie had made a careless mistake. He'd allowed Crocetti to keep his cane. At a perfectly timed squeak from Pally's stuffed vampire, Archie turned his head to look, and Crocetti saw his chance. In a move worthy of a ninja he cracked the cane across Archie's wrist, making him drop the gun. He roared and grabbed his wrist. Crocetti scooped up the pistol before Jughead came running, a Bowie knife in his hand.

"Never bring a knife to a gunfight, son," Crocetti said. Surely you've heard that before? Now drop it."

He did. Kelly picked it up.

"I think you broke my freakin' wrist," Archie said.

"And I feel terrible about it. I want you two nitwits to lay on the floor on your bellies with your wrists crossed behind you. Do it, unless you want another orifice or two."

They did as he said.

Crocetti didn't trust the .22, so he got the Colt from the desk. For a moment he considered giving the taser a real-world test but decided against it. Maybe if there had been only one he'd have been tempted.

"Kelly, you'll find some zip ties in the top drawer over there. Get a couple of large ones and tie their wrists behind them. It'll keep them nice and docile while I figure out what to do with them."

After they were securely bound he helped them sit up with their backs against the wall. Then he took out his wallet and showed them his badge and I.D. It got the expected oh-shit reaction.

"That's right, boys. You're a pair of brain-dead, tweaked-out screwups."

"Are we under arrest?"

"I'll ask the questions. You said this righteous dude told you I had fifty large hidden in this coach. And you believed him? Are you that gullible?"

"He was pretty convincing," Archie said.

No doubt. Up against Kardos' hypnosis skill, weak-minded Archie and Jughead had about as much chance as popsicles on a Las Vegas casino roof at high noon in July.

As for what he was going to do with them, he could file a complaint against them with the sheriff or state police, but then he would have to stick around and give a statement. It would take up the rest of the night.

"Tell you what," he said to them, "I'm going to cut you a break, because I'm feeling magnanimous. That means generous. Anyway, I will keep the knife and gun and send you on your merry way."

They looked at each other and then at him, astonishment on their faces. "No shit?" Jughead said.

Crocetti motioned for them to stand up. Kelly clipped the zip ties and he gestured to the door with the gun. "After you, gentlemen. I use the term loosely."

They stepped out and took off in a dead run toward their car, no doubt worried he'd change his mind.

From the open doorway he called some parting advice to them. "Better mind your mamas' warnings about talking to strange righteous dudes."

They jumped in the car and squealed the tires getting out of there.

He closed the door and turned to Kelly. "How about that Kardos, siccing those tweakers on us? And they had weapons. Bet he told that pair to use them on us if we didn't come across with the fifty thou. Lucky for us they turned out to be a couple of clowns."

"It's hard to ignore the escalation, though."

"What do you mean?"

"First, Kardos writes a message in blood on your windshield. Next, he slashes your tires. Then he brainwashes those two idiots into trying to rob you, and perhaps even kill you. Kill both of us. He's escalating, getting progressively more vindictive."

"You're dead right about that."

"It's almost as though he's trying to discourage you."

He smiled at her dry humor. "We need to stay on our toes. I've got a sneaking feeling this attempt won't be the last."

Before they motored off into the night, he checked the app and was surprised to see that Kardos was still in John Day. The big question was why?

29

The distance between Prineville and John Day was 115 miles, average driving time two hours fifty-two minutes. It took them a bit over five hours, not counting the time they'd spent dealing with Archie and Jughead. An overloaded log truck had jackknifed on U.S. Route 26, just past the town of Mitchell, flinging logs as though they were tinker toys. The highway department had to bring in special equipment to clear the road, which took several hours. So once again Crocetti and Kelly arrived at their destination at daybreak.

The app directed them to the northeast part of town, to Grant County RV Park, sandwiched between the fairgrounds and John Day River. Twenty-five spaces with full hookups, only half of them occupied. The black coach was on an adjoining grassy area that had been set aside for dry camping, parked between an older red Dodge pickup with a camper and an Airstream trailer with severely corroded aluminum skin, towed by a Jeep Cherokee. Compared to them, the gleaming black coach looked out of place.

There was no on-site manager, but the park had a website with a phone number for reservations and credit or debit card payments. Crocetti had to wait forty-five minutes, until seven o'clock, when the online office opened for business. He paid thirty dollars for a space with full hookups and a decent view of the black coach.

Given the park's vacancy rate it wouldn't be a problem if they needed to stay longer than one night. That depended on what Kardos did.

Setting up the coach—leveling, hooking up, and deploying the slideouts—took fifteen minutes, much of it requiring only the touch of a button. A tree provided shade for the starboard side, so extending the awning wasn't necessary.

He got the binoculars and trained them on the black coach. It crouched there, sinister as ever, its obsidian windows glaring malevolently at unsuspecting passersby.

A hundred feet from the black coach, an older woman in a blue work shirt and shorts emerged from the Airstream and removed a laundry basket from the Cherokee and toted it back to the trailer.

A few minutes later a guy in a tank top stepped out of the Dodge pickup camper, his muscular arms and neck covered in tattoos, his head shaved. He lifted the pickup's hood and uncapped a brightly colored container—oil or transmission fluid, presumably—and leaned into the engine compartment to pour it. After closing the hood he swaggered over to a trash barrel at the corner of the grassy area and tossed the empty container in. The muscles, tattoos, and swagger were telltale signs: He'd done time in the joint.

Kelly touched his arm. "See anything interesting?"

He lowered the binoculars. "Nothing much. No activity at the black coach, not that I expected any."

"I made fresh coffee."

"Good. I could use some."

Kelly poured two cups and brought one to him. "What do you think Kardos is up to?"

He shrugged. "He's been here since yesterday, God only knows why. I'm pretty sure he hasn't preyed on anyone around here. He wouldn't stick around afterward."

"Have you considered the possibility that he stayed because he wanted to lure you here? So he can get rid of you once and for all?"

"He can try. This time I'm prepared for him."

"You didn't find the evidence you were looking for when you searched his motor home, so why are you still hounding him? What's the point?"

Before he answered he went to the desk and got a small black leather case from the top drawer. "I didn't get to search the locked storage compartments underneath that coach." He unzipped the case, revealing oddly shaped metal tools. "This is a set of picks, used to pick locks. It's been a while since I've used them, but I'm pretty sure I've still got the knack."

"When are you going to try?"

"Kardos is nocturnal. I'll need to do it during the day."

"Aren't you worried that someone will see you?"

"The way that coach is angled, only the hump with the pickup camper would be able to see me. And he doesn't look like the type to get involved."

"You're going to have me biting my nails."

A glance across the way told him he couldn't attempt it right away. Tattoo Guy was lounging on the hood of the pickup, his back against the windshield, catching some rays. No sense making certain the guy saw him picking the locks. Maybe the sun would go behind the clouds and the bastard would go back inside his camper.

He got up and refilled their cups. It was early as yet, not even nine, and it would not be dark until after eight p.m. At some point during those eleven hours he'd surely get a chance to slip over there and have a look in the compartments. In the meantime he'd relax, have a beer, maybe take a nap. And mentally prepare for the excursion.

But Kelly had other ideas. She seemed to go out of her way to make him very aware of her presence. When they passed in the hall, she contrived to bump a round hip against him. While handing him coffee, she managed a lingering contact. She hung on his every word, giving him smoky looks through long lashes. When leaning over to show him something in a magazine, she pressed a warm breast against his arm. In contrast, her small-talk was totally innocent.

It created in him an acute awareness of her undeniable femaleness. And with the awareness, bewilderment. What had happened to the woman who went to such great lengths to make sure he understood she wanted no entanglements?

Finally she managed to trip and have him catch her just so, a silken weight, eyes half-closed, breath humid, lips soft and available.

He took hold of her upper arms and stood her up straight. "Kelly, what the heck is going on?"

Her face lost all trace of sensuality. "I—I'm sorry, I just thought—never mind. Bad idea."

"No, honey," he said, "good idea. Great idea. Bad timing."

She wasn't listening. "How could I be such a damn fool? I could just die."

He tried to hold her, but she wasn't having it. She yawped and reared and bucked until she broke free, protesting that the special moment had passed, to hell with it, etcetera.

"Stop that." He caught her and made her look at him. "Kelly, you are an extremely desirable woman. Under normal circumstances I would've carried you back to my bed before you could catch your breath."

She sighed. "So you're practicing some kind of self-denial, huh?"

"I guess you could call it that. And don't think, even for a second, that it didn't cost me. Isn't costing me."

"Because the time isn't right."

"Unfortunately. But after this is over, after Kardos is safely behind bars, wild horses won't keep me away."

"Well . . . if it won't violate your vow of chastity, will you at least kiss me, as a consolation prize?"

She didn't have to talk him into it. He took her in his arms and kissed her, softly at first, then with more urgency than he'd planned. It burgeoned, becoming an unspoken promise. She shivered against him. After they parted, a curious mixture of longing, sadness, and guilt washed over him.

"I'm feeling kind of strange," he said. "Alison was the last woman I kissed."

She nodded. "I'm a little confused myself. I felt like I was betraying Daryl. That's crazy I know."

He hugged her. "We'll take it slow. No expectations, no pressure. Deal?"

"Deal."

His lips still tingled from the kiss. He picked up a *Jazz Times* magazine and dropped into a chair. After he read the same paragraph three times he tossed it aside and picked up the binoculars. Tattoo Guy had apparently retired to his camper. No activity around the black coach or Airstream.

Kelly tapped him on the shoulder. "We passed a bookstore on Main Street. I need something to read. Want to take me?"

"Tell you what, I'll unhitch the car for you and then you can take yourself. I'm going to stay here and take a nap."

After he saw her off, he went back inside. His eye fell on the case of lock picks. The black coach and its secrets awaited. He could sneak over there, check the compartments, and be back—with photos of the evidence, hopefully—before Kelly returned, a fait accompli. He slipped the picks in a front pants pocket and grabbed his cane.

He made his way across the grassy area to the black coach and glanced around. Nobody seemed to be looking, so he made his move, sticking close to the coach's starboard side, and kneeled next to the basement compartment. After several minutes of fumbling with the picks in the lock, he heard a satisfying click. He put the picks away and reached to open the compartment door.

He sensed movement behind him, but before he could turn around to see what it was, a granite fist slammed into the side of his head, blurring his vision and sending him reeling. As he lay there, dazed and helpless, the unseen attacker began punching and kicking him with a savage fury. He tried to ward off the blows but couldn't see them coming. He curled up in a fetal position and shielded his head with his arms. Not much protection, but better than nothing. For the coup de grâce, his attacker delivered a kick to his side so agonizing he began to black out.

As he slid toward the event horizon he wondered if this was the end of the line for him, and he beseeched the Infinite, *Please, not yet.*

"Nothing personal, Pops. It was only business." Male voice. It sounded almost jovial.

Crocetti heard retreating footsteps and then the blackness swallowed him.

30

Kelly woke him with soft, sweet kisses that covered his face and neck. Her sensuous tongue bathed his closed eyelids and darted into his ears, mouth, and nostrils. Of their own accord, his loins began to respond—

"Mister? Can you hear me? Say something, mister." A woman's voice—but not Kelly's.

With supreme effort he hoisted one eyelid and saw a dumpy woman with hair like steel wool and a lined face full of concern. The woman with the Airstream. Clutching a small white poodle struggling to get free.

He took a deep breath and regretted it at once, wincing at a sharp pain in his left side. "Would you . . . help me sit up, please?"

The pain stabbed him again, more intensely, before their combined efforts managed to get him into a sitting position on the ground.

The woman shook her head. "You're a sight, mister. Who done that to you?"

Although he hadn't seen him clearly, undoubtedly it was Tattoo Guy. Crocetti pointed at the empty area the pickup camper had occupied. "Do you know when that man left?"

"I seen him take off about a half-hour ago. He's the one who beat the crap out of you?"

Crocetti nodded. "He blindsided me."

"I'm not surprised. He looked meaner'n a rattlesnake."

"Probably took off right afterward." Which meant he'd been out cold thirty minutes.

"It was Popsie that found you. I forgot to hook the screen door and she slipped out and made a beeline over here."

Popsie gave him a baleful look. She had a deformed lower jaw and protruding tongue, giving her a demented expression.

The cane was on the ground about two feet to his right, but reaching for it made him cry out. That final kick to his side must have broken something.

"Do you think ... do you think you could help me to my feet? I need to go back to my coach."

She handed him the cane. "Are you sure you don't want me to call an ambulance to take you to the hospital?"

"I'll be all right. Just lend me a hand, if you would."

She transferred Popsie to her other arm and offered her hand.

He took hold of it and braced himself, holding his breath, which escaped through clenched teeth when the excruciating pain hit. The process of getting to his feet took almost a minute, and at the end of it he was drenched in sweat. But he made it.

"I'll walk you over," the woman said.

"I appreciate it."

Between the support she provided and his cane he managed to hobble the thousand miles to his coach, and then he had to sit down on the bottom step to gather his strength for the attempt to scale the remaining steps.

Kelly drove up and jumped out, looking alarmed. "My god, Dan! What happened?"

He managed a grin. "You oughta see the other guy."

She looked at the woman, eyebrows raised.

"Kelly, this is—I'm sorry, I didn't get your name."

"Lurlene," she said. "Lurlene Fetty."

"Mrs. Fetty was kind enough to help me walk over here."

"Call me Lurlene. And this is Popsie."

"Lurlene, I am in Popsie's and your debt."

Lurlene turned to Kelly. "I wanted to call an ambulance to take him to the hospital, but he wouldn't hear of it. Maybe you can talk some sense into him."

Kelly put her hands on her hips. "Don't be a fool, Dan. You need medical attention. You look like death warmed over. I'm serious."

"Okay, okay. If you'll help me into the car I'll let you take me to the emergency room, and on the way I'll tell you the whole sordid saga."

The emergency room intake staff took one look at him and put him on a gurney, despite his objections. A young doctor examined him and sent him off to have his ribs x-rayed. After that, he had a cranial MRI. Then he got a room of his own. Kelly sat by the bed and held his hand.

A while later the doctor came in, smiling. "You're in luck, Mr. Crocetti. The MRI scan showed no evidence of subdural hematoma—that's intracranial bleeding—or bone splinters from the trauma. You must have a hard head."

"That's what I've been telling him," Kelly said.

"You do, however, have three cracked ribs. We taped them up, which is about all that can be done. Other than those two non-life-threatening injuries, you have more contusions than a hockey player."

"Sounds like I'm going to live," Crocetti said.

"All the same, we're going to keep you twenty-four hours, just to be sure you're in the clear. Standard procedure when a patient's been knocked unconscious."

Crocetti sighed. "Doc, I'd rather not stay here overnight. Can't I just come back tomorrow?"

The doctor shook his head. "Twenty-four hours. Doctor's orders."

After he left, Crocetti looked at Kelly. "Well, this is a hell of a note. Know the worst part? I didn't get to see what's in those storage compartments."

"I can't believe that thug jumped you in broad daylight."

"Kardos paid him to. 'Nothing personal, only business,' the bastard said after he was finished. I'll tell you something, a beating feels very, very personal. I'm taking it personally. After I get on my feet it'll be payback time. The son of a bitch is going to wish he'd killed me when he had the chance." Tough talk, even though at the moment he felt like he was constructed of paper-mâché held together with Scotch tape.

Kelly leaned over and gave him a peck on the cheek. "You are certifiable, Dan Crocetti, but I admire you anyway."

"That so?"

"I guess I've got a thing for knights in slightly tarnished armor."

He laughed, which resulted in a stab of pain in his ribs. "It's tarnished, all right. Not to mention, dented and corroded and rusted."

"When I made a pass at you earlier today I'd been thinking about how masterfully you handled those two meth freaks. It turned me on."

"Honey, my chest would be puffing out if it weren't for these cracked ribs." Her flattery aside, the way he'd handled Tattoo Guy was anything but masterful.

"It's four o'clock," she said. "Pally's been there alone for hours. I should take him for a walk and then I'll come back."

"I had completely forgotten about Pally in all the uproar. Glad you're on it."

She kissed him and gave him a little wave before she went out the door.

He reached—very carefully—for his phone and punched in the number of the Grant County RV Park. After identifying himself to the woman who answered, he asked her for information about the man driving the pickup camper. "I think he might've accidentally taken off with something that belongs to me," he told her.

"So sorry to hear that," she said. "Let's see, he registered as Delbert Pruitt, Idaho license plate one W two N nine six five. No phone number, no email."

"Thank you, ma'am. You've been most helpful."

He looked up the number of the John Day police department and punched it in. He reached a woman with a flat, nasal tone and asked to speak to someone about filing a criminal complaint. She passed him to a bored-sounding detective who identified himself as Grantham.

"Detective, my name is Dan Crocetti. Detective sergeant, retired. I was on the job in Portland."

"What can I do for you, Crocetti?" His tone of voice was considerably friendlier.

"I'm calling from the hospital. I'd like to file a complaint for felony assault and battery."

"Tell you what. I'll drive over and talk to you in person. What's your room number?"

Thirty minutes later a stocky blond guy wearing a purple polo shirt and khakis walked in the room. He was five-two, tops. "Crocetti?"

"The same."

They shook hands.

"Jesus, look at you. Hope you gave as good as you got."

"Wish I could say I had, but the skell came up behind me and sucker-punched me. Then he went to work on me with his fists and boots. I couldn't see worth a damn, so I was at his mercy. Afterward I was out cold for about thirty minutes, no sign of the punk after I came to."

"Where did this take place?"

"Grant County RV Park. A lady friend and I got there this morning in my motor coach. The incident occurred at about eleven. I was just having a look around the park. Kelly—that's my lady friend—had gone into town."

"Any witnesses?"

"None that came forward. Another camper found me. Or rather, her toy poodle found me."

"Any idea who did it?"

Crocetti handed him the information he'd gotten from the park manager and added: "Male Caucasian, thirties, six foot tall, one ninety, shaved head, ink covering his arms and neck and probably his chest, and he'd pumped a lot of iron."

"Sounds to me like he's done a stretch or two in the joint."

"We're on the same wavelength there."

"One thing—you said you couldn't see well. Are you sure it was Pruitt?"

"The first blow to my head blurred my vision, but I could see well enough to I.D. him. Plus, the cowardly bastard got in his camper and took off afterward."

"I'll run Pruitt through CODIS, see if he has any wants or warrants. And of course run the plate and send out a bulletin on his vehicle."

"Shouldn't be too hard to spot. It's an older Dodge pickup, red in color, with a ratty slide-in camper."

"Okay, I think I've got enough. I'll be back to have you sign your statement after I transcribe it, with the help of this here handy little gadget." Grantham produced a tiny digital recorder with a blinking green light.

"I wondered why you weren't taking notes. See you later."

Kelly returned at a quarter to six and handed him a *Guitar Player* magazine. "I swung by the bookstore again. I thought you might want something to read."

"Thanks, hon. Listen, I've been thinking. I want you to go throw some stuff in an overnight bag and then take Pally and check into a motel tonight. It's not safe for you to stay in the coach alone after sundown with Kardos a only few hundred feet away."

"That didn't even cross my mind, but you're right."

"Let me know when you're all checked in."

"Sure, but we still have a couple hours of daylight left. I want to stay with you a little while longer."

"That's fine. I'm grateful for your company. I definitely don't feel like reading or watching TV."

She sat in the chair beside the bed. "Are you in a lot of pain, hon?"

He shook his head, smiling. "I've got enough oxycodone in my system to lay out a Clydesdale, so I'm doing fine. You missed Detective Grantham from the John Day Police Department. I'm filing an official complaint against Delbert Pruitt."

"That's the guy who attacked you?"

"The RV park office gave me his name and license plate number, and I passed it on to Grantham."

"I'd like to get my hands on Delbert Pruitt." She had said it quietly, the feral look on her face lending credence to the mythos that the worst thing that could happen to captured prisoners was to be given to the enemy's women.

"Anyway, they're looking for him. He's probably in Idaho by now, though."

"Did you say anything to the detective about Kardos, since he paid Pruitt to beat you?"

"No. It would just muddy the waters."

"Think Kardos will move on tonight?"

"My guess is he will. Now that he thinks I'm out of commission he doesn't have much reason to stick around."

"*Thinks* you're out of commission? You mean you're not?"

"Only temporarily."

"And after you get back on your feet you plan to don your tarnished armor, mount your spavined steed, then galumph after Kardos to do battle once more?"

"Something like that."

She threw up her hands and sighed. "I guess I'd better get going. I saw a Best Western on the main drag, so I'll get Pally and check in there." She leaned over and kissed him softly. "Bye, hon."

Forty-five minutes later she phoned to tell him they were settled in and she'd visit him tomorrow after breakfast. After the call, his eyelids became too heavy to keep open, and he slid down into a dreamless, opioid-induced sleep.

31

Crocetti was eating a light breakfast—bran cereal, stewed prunes, wheat toast, Jello, orange juice—when Grantham appeared in the open doorway and knocked lightly.

Crocetti motioned for him to come in. "I didn't expect you back so soon."

"You were on the job so you get priority." He gave Crocetti a printout. "Have a look at that."

Delbert Pruitt's rap sheet was six pages long. No stranger to assault and battery—the sheet listed three arrests and two convictions for it—other highlights were menacing, breaking and entering, robbery, auto theft, and even a kidnapping and extortion attempt. He'd been a guest of the state penitentiary in Salem on several occasions, the last a three-year stretch for accessory to an armed robbery of a 7-Eleven. He'd driven the getaway car.

"He's versatile," Crocetti said.

Grantham nodded. "Jack-of-all-trades, illegal variety." He handed Crocetti a typed document and a pen.

Crocetti looked over the statement, signed it, and handed it back.

"We'll slap Pruitt with second-degree assault, a class B felony, maximum penalty ten years. He'll probably get five, since a deadly weapon wasn't involved."

Crocetti grinned. "Five would be just dandy."

"How are you feeling?"

"Not too bad, considering. The cracked ribs are the worst. If I move wrong they get my attention."

"When are they going to cut you loose?"

"Later this afternoon."

"After my shift ends today, Margie and I are heading over to the coast for a few days. I'm taking some vacation days. It's either that or lose them."

"Have a good time, Grantham. Thanks for all the help."

"We'll find Pruitt, count on it." He stuck out his hand. "Nice to meet you, Crocetti. Take it easy."

Kelly arrived shortly after eleven with another magazine, *Downbeat*. She leaned down and kissed him warmly. "How are you doing?"

"Good. Slept like a baby. My ribs are sore as hell, but that's to be expected. How was the Best Western?"

"Worked out well. I brought my swim suit, hoping they had a pool, and they did. Best of all, it wasn't packed with kids. I had it all to myself."

"Grantham was here earlier with Pruitt's rap sheet. He's been in and out of jail his whole life. When they find him he'll face an assault-two charge, a felony. So he'll be out of circulation for a few years."

"Hope they find him soon."

"What did you do last night besides swim?"

"Read, mostly. Pally looked for you all evening. He knows he's your dog."

"Looks like I'm stuck with him, all right."

She stayed another two hours and then said, "Think I'll go back to the coach, do some laundry. I'm running out of clean clothes. What time should I come back to pick you up?"

"Probably late afternoon. How about I give you a call when they're getting ready to discharge me?"

"And then I shall come on the run." She kissed him. At the door she turned around. "Open or closed?"

"Leave it open six or eight inches, please."

"'Bye, hon."

Listening to her fading footsteps he again marveled at the astonishing evolution of her attitude toward him, from arm's length to affectionate, bordering on proprietary. He didn't mind a bit, and that surprised him as well.

He yawned. Perhaps a mid-day nap was in order. On the verge of dropping off, in that surreal state between wakefulness and sleep, he saw a man peering in at him through the partially open doorway. The man had a shaved head and wore blue scrubs. An orderly? But orderlies didn't act furtive. And not many orderlies had hypermuscular arms, necks covered with ink, or teardrops tattooed below the outer corner of one of their eyes.

Delbert Pruitt.

And it was a safe bet he wasn't there to drop off a get-well card.

Adrenaline chased away the drowsiness. Pretending to be asleep, he snaked his hand toward the call button. It turned out not to be necessary.

"Excuse me," a blond nurse said. Pruitt moved aside to let her pass and then disappeared. The nurse entered the room, checked Crocetti's vitals, and left again, leaving the door open eight inches.

He had to work fast. He swung his legs over the side of the bed and stood swaying, ten feet tall. Hastily arranging extra pillows under the bedding, he managed to create the impression, if you didn't look too close, that the bed had an occupant. Then he grabbed the cane hooked over the bed rail and walked over to stand behind the door. And waited.

He didn't have long to wait. The door slowly opened and Pruitt appeared, moving stealthily, his attention riveted on the bed.

Gripping the cane near the bottom like a baseball bat, Crocetti swung with all the strength he could muster, aiming at a spot just below the occipital bump at the back of Pruitt's head and hit it dead center. Pruitt pitched forward and crumpled to the tiled floor. Then, to Crocetti's astonishment, he started to get up. The man had a thick skull.

So Crocetti gave him another good whack with the cane. Double tap.

Pruitt went down and began snoring softly.

Crocetti closed the door. Then he called the police and asked to speak to Grantham. When the detective came on the line, Crocetti said, "Busy? This is Crocetti."

"Not too busy. What do you need?"

"I've got something to show you. I think you'll find it very interesting."

After a pause, Grantham said, "Okay, see you in ten."

Crocetti opened the door partway and beckoned to the blond nurse. She hurried over, eyebrows raised with concern. "Mr. Crocetti, why are you out of bed? You should have used the call button."

"Thought I'd stretch my legs. The doctor said it was okay. Listen, I need something. Do you happen to have a large zip tie I can have?"

Eyebrows knitted, she returned to the nurses' station and rummaged in a drawer. She came back holding a large black zip tie. "You're in luck. That's the only one we had. What do you need it for?"

As he was casting about for a plausible explanation, a call buzzer sounded and the nurse excused herself.

With Pruitt's wrists fastened behind him, Crocetti could relax a bit. He was stretched out on the bed when Grantham knocked and entered the room. With a sweeping gesture, like a magician presenting an astounding trick, Crocetti motioned to the still-unconscious Pruitt on the floor. Ta-da!

Openmouthed, Grantham looked at Pruitt and then back to Crocetti. He did this once more and then said, "I'll be damned."

"Pruitt sneaked into the hospital, filched some scrubs, and slipped into my room with the intention of finishing the job," Crocetti said. "I discouraged him with this." He held up the cane.

Grantham shook his head slowly. "You are one tough old bird, Crocetti."

On the floor, Pruitt groaned.

Crocetti couldn't help smiling. "He's going to have one hell of a headache, might have a concussion. I can't say I feel sorry for the bastard."

Grantham took out his phone. "I'll get a couple uniforms over here to take him into custody."

Pruitt turned his head to look at them.

"Payback's a bitch," Crocetti said. "Right, Delbert?"

"Kiss my ass." Pruitt spat the words.

"Tsk, tsk. Such language." Crocetti lowered his voice so Grantham wouldn't hear. "Tell me, how much did the tall man in the black coach pay you?"

"Five bills for the first round, another five for the second. Shoulda skipped out after the first."

"Instead, you'll be going away on a long vacation in Salem. You've been there before, Delbert. You will get to see all your friends again."

"Wish I'd taken care of you the first time."

"Wish in one hand and . . . well, you know the rest."

Grantham ended the call. "They're on the way."

The door opened and the nurse walked in. She saw Pruitt on the floor, his wrists bound behind him, and let out a cry of alarm. "My god," she said, bending down to examine him, "what have you done to this orderly?"

"He's only dressed like an orderly," Crocetti said. "And this is Detective Grantham of the John Day Police Department."

A few minutes later two uniformed police officers entered the room. "Stand him up," Grantham told them. When Pruitt was on his feet, Grantham said, "Delbert Pruitt, you're under arrest for assault in the second degree." After Mirandizing him, Grantham told the officers to accompany him while a doctor examined his head injury. They left the room with their prisoner, the nurse in the lead.

Grantham turned to Crocetti. "Well, my hat's off to you, partner. Wait until I tell the guys back at the House. You're going to be a celebrity. And when you come back to testify against Pruitt the beers are on me."

"Looking forward to it." Not quite true. Given his choice, he'd rather not come back to John Day this century.

After Grantham left, Crocetti yawned and glanced at the wall clock. A bit after four. He might have enough time to squeeze in a nap before they discharged him. God knows, he could use one. He used the bathroom and then climbed back into bed. As he slid down into sleep, he marveled at how the adrenaline had anesthetized all his pain. Too bad the relief had only been temporary.

Kelly's call woke him up at five after five. "I take it they haven't discharged you yet."

"No, but I expect them to come get me any time now." He yawned. "I was taking a nap. Think I'll try to get back to sleep. I'll phone you after they show up."

When he opened his eyes again the clock was indicating 6:49. He swore and pressed the call button to summon a nurse. Ten minutes later he pressed it again.

It was seven thirty by the time a nurse answered his call.

"I was supposed to be discharged this afternoon," he said. "Did you forget about me?"

"Very sorry for the delay, Mr. Crocetti, but there was a four-vehicle accident on the highway, and we've been very busy. We appreciate your patience."

He phoned Kelly and told her about the delay. "So I don't know when they'll get around to me."

"I might as well come on over there," she said. "See you in a few."

He picked up the *Downbeat* and flipped through it while he waited, keeping an eye on the clock . . . and on the gathering dusk outside the window. At eight there was no sign of either a discharge or Kelly. He punched in her number.

No answer. Maybe she was on the way and didn't want to answer her phone while she was driving, illegal in Oregon. That was probably it.

He tried again twenty minutes later, with the same result. By then it was dark outside. A hunch told him something was wrong. Badly wrong.

He threw back the covers and got out of bed. His clothes were in the closet. After dressing, he phoned for a taxi and told the dispatcher he would be waiting out in front of the hospital.

One nurse was at the nurse's station, a young brunette who had overplucked her eyebrows into thin lines. They gave her a surprised expression that didn't change when he walked up to the counter.

"I'm out of here," he said. "A cab will be picking me up in ten minutes."

"Mr. Crocetti," she said, "you haven't been discharged."

"Let's correct that state of affairs. You have ten minutes to get some discharge papers for me to sign."

She pressed her lips together as she left and returned five minutes later with the discharge form. He signed it and folded his copy, nodded to her, and headed for the lobby to wait for the taxi by the entrance.

It pulled up in front at 8:50, twenty minutes late. A dispatch mix-up, the driver said. Crocetti grunted. Of course it had to happen now.

32

When the taxi pulled up in front of his coach Crocetti noticed three things right off: First, the car was still there. Second, his coach was totally dark inside. Third, the black coach was nowhere to be seen. He paid the driver and walked toward his coach, his mouth dry as parchment.

A gut feeling told him the door would be unlocked, and it was. The stench of decay hit him before he could switch on the interior lights.

"Kelly?" No answer, so he called again, louder.

He went to the desk, got his gun, and checked the entire coach, fore to aft.

Not a soul to be found.

Then he froze, gripped by an icy terror. Kelly's purse lay on the kitchen counter next to the toaster, where she always kept it.

A whimper came from behind the sofa. Pally was cowering behind it. It took Crocetti a full minute to coax him out. He picked him up and sat down on the sofa and held him. The dog wouldn't stop trembling. "What happened here, Pally?"

But Crocetti knew the answer.

He felt like tearing his hair out, beating his head against a wall, screaming, weeping. Instead, he opened windows to get rid of the nauseating smell. Then he took out his phone and activated the tracking app.

The red dot wasn't quite halfway between John Day and Burns on U.S. Route 395 south. If he left in pursuit in ten minutes, Kardos would have roughly a thirty-mile head start.

He heard a knock at the door. His heart beat faster with the hope that Kelly would be standing there when he opened it. But it was Lulene Fetty, holding Popsie in her arms.

"I seen you get out of the cab," she said, "and I thought I'd come over and find out how you're doing."

"Come on inside."

She stepped through the door and sniffed. "Jumpin' Jesus, you need an air freshener or two in here. Man, if you ain't a sight. Hope they catch that asshole, excuse my French."

"They arrested him this afternoon."

"Glad to hear it. Would you mind if I set Popsie down to say howdy to your dog?"

"No, go ahead."

After the requisite butt sniffing and tentative tail wagging, they seemed to hit it off and began playing, one chasing the other and then switching off. In spite of his bum leg, Pally managed to keep up with Popsie.

"Lurlene, did you happen to see Kelly leave?"

She hesitated. "Fact of the matter, I did. She took off at dusk and then she come back about a few minutes later. Then I seen the tall man from that black thing walk over here. Five minutes later the both of 'em come out and walk over to his motor home."

"Did she go willingly?"

"It didn't look to me like he forced her none. She was beside him, relaxed as you please."

"And she went inside his coach?"

"Yup. And then he comes out and goes into the park for a bit. Then he comes back, and several minutes later that black motor home drives away. Never did see your wife come back here, so I figgered she left with him."

Crocetti worked it out. Kelly left at dusk to pick him up, but returned for some reason. By then it was dark. Kardos swooped down and, no doubt using hypnosis, captured her.

"Look at them dogs. They's havin' a ball."

"Lurlene, thank you for the information, but you'll have to excuse me. I need to get going."

"C'mon, Popsie, we got to go now." She picked up the dog and started toward the door. "Good luck finding your wife."

"Thanks."

With oxycodone mercifully blunting the pain in his ribs, he went outside and hitched the car to the coach and disconnected the power, water, and sewer hookups. A cross breeze had cleared out the stench, so he closed the windows. Last, he retracted the slides. After he took Pally outside to do his business they were ready to hit the road.

Just as he sat down in the cockpit there was another knock at the door. Lurlene probably thought of something else.

Standing there was a balding man, fortyish, wearing a rumpled seersucker suit and an opaque stare. "Dan Crocetti?"

"That's right."

"Detective Einhorn, John Day police. May I come in?"

"Sure." Crocetti stood aside. "What can I do for you?"

"Can you account for your whereabouts earlier tonight?"

"I was in the hospital. Admitted on Wednesday afternoon, discharged this evening at eight thirty." He handed Einhorn the copy of the discharge. "Caught a cab in front at eight fifty."

Einhorn punched in a number on his phone, spoke in low tones, and then put it away. "Okay, the hospital confirmed it."

"What's this all about?"

"Do you know a man named Howard Blunt?"

"No. And I'm not answering another damn question until you tell me what's going on."

"It's like this, Crocetti. Blunt was stabbed to death tonight in this campground. Between eight and eight thirty, according to the medical examiner."

"So I'm a suspect?" Crocetti took out his wallet. "Have a look at this."

Einhorn examined the shield and I.D. and then looked up at Crocetti. "How long you been retired?"

"Three years. Portland Police Bureau."

"Then I'll come right to the point. How come a cane with your name engraved on it was found in the victim's RV?"

Crocetti gave a grunt of surprise. "No idea. As I said, I didn't know Blunt."

"I called the RV park office and got the names of all the campers here. Lo and behold, you were among them."

"It so happens I lost a cane in Bend. Been using a spare."

"How did you come to lose it?"

"Left it in another RVer's coach." Which was absolutely true. He'd left it behind getting away from Kardos.

"Do you have the name of that RVer?"

Crocetti shook his head. "I was at a truck stop in Bend and noticed a coach similar to mine. I had a brief conversation with the guy who owned it and forgot my cane." Almost true, assuming a loose interpretation of "conversation."

Einhorn questioned him about the other coach and its owner. Just a middle-aged traveler getting fuel, Crocetti told him, driving a coach like thousands of others on the road.

"Anyway, it wasn't Blunt," Einhorn said. "He had a trailer."

"Obviously, the cane was planted there."

Einhorn took out his phone, excused himself, and stepped outside for fifteen long minutes, during which time Crocetti ground his teeth. He needed to get on the road as soon as possible. Tick-tock. Each passing minute meant Kardos was farther away.

With Kelly, who must be petrified with terror.

When Einhorn came back in he looked hard at Crocetti. "The lab matched your prints on file at AFIS with the prints found on the murder weapon."

Crocetti opened his mouth and closed it again. Then he said, "The murder weapon, what was it?"

"A Bowie knife."

"Just a minute." Crocetti went over to the desk. He hadn't noticed that the drawer was partly open. The Colt, taser, and Archie's .22 pistol were in there, but Jughead's Bowie knife was missing.

The situation was turning sour. He'd been set up and now he was on the wrong end of a homicide investigation. He needed to nip this in the bud, fast.

"I took that knife and this pistol off a pair of tweakers who tried to rob me when I pulled into a rest area near Prineville. I tossed both weapons in this drawer."

"Did you file a police report for the attempted robbery?"

Crocetti shook his head. "I didn't want to take the time. Besides, they were so hyped up on crystal meth they couldn't see straight. I took their weapons without much trouble and sent them on their way."

Einhorn ran his hand through his thinning hair. "Sure do wish you'd called the police, then there would be a record. Any idea who stole the knife from you?"

"No. The door was unlocked when I got here. As to who came in here and took it while I was in the hospital, your guess is as good as mine. For all I know, those two meth heads followed me."

"First, you get the shit beat out of you, then you're being looked at for murder. You seem to be having a run of bad luck, Crocetti."

"Tell me about it."

"Hang loose a minute while I call the cab company and check out your alibi." He talked into the phone for several minutes and then turned to Crocetti. "They confirmed your story. Here's the timeline: We got an anonymous call at eight twenty-nine tipping us to the murder. The caller phoned from this campground, using a burner. At the time of the call you weren't discharged yet. Taxi picked you up at eight fifty and dropped you off around nine. That means you couldn't have done it."

"I'm relieved to hear you say that."

So before leaving with Kelly, Kardos had killed Blunt with Jughead's knife and planted the cane. And then he used a disposable cell phone to call the police and tip them off about the murder. A semi-clever frame. Probably would've worked if he hadn't had a rock-solid alibi.

"Even if you had whacked the guy, I can't imagine you'd be so careless as to leave your monogrammed cane and a knife with your prints behind at the scene. So they were planted there to implicate you. Someone have it in for you?"

"Besides the couple hundred creeps I busted, you mean? I can't think of anyone specifically." Other than Kardos.

"Can you give me a description of the two tweakers?"

Crocetti described Archie and Jughead.

"Stand by while I make one more call," Einhorn said.

Crocetti nodded, hoping he would make it short.

After talking on the phone a few minutes, Einhorn hung up. "The Prineville police know the pair well. They're going to pick them up for questioning."

"Maybe they'll catch them holding."

Einhorn closed his notepad. "That'll do it for now, Crocetti. I'll get hold of the truck stop in Bend, see if the driver of that coach paid with a credit card. Hope you don't have any plans to go anywhere. I'm sure I'll have more questions."

"Whatever I can do to help, Detective."

After Einhorn left, Crocetti hustled around as fast as his bum knee and cracked ribs allowed, packing a few essentials —extra clothes, toiletries, gun, taser, flashlight, various odds and ends. He almost forgot to toss in the UV light.

Pally followed him around, and when he picked up the suitcase the dog danced on his hind legs, his liquid eyes pleading. Crocetti found a big paper bag. Into it went Pally's food and water bowls and enough dog food for several days, plus a half-gallon container of water.

Figuring he could make better time in the car, he unhitched it from the coach. After everything, including Pally, had been loaded into the car, he locked the coach, leaving a couple of lights on inside. He didn't want to take the time to reconnect the shore power. The coach's bank of batteries would supply power to the refrigerator and lights for a week, easy.

It was twenty after ten when they took off. Crocetti felt a stab of guilt. His sudden departure was sure to make Einhorn very unhappy. Too bad.

33

When things start breaking bad, they sometimes turn into an avalanche of miserable luck. Shortly after midnight just outside of Burns a "Check Engine" light came on. He pounded the steering wheel and swore, alarming Pally. He couldn't blame this one on Kardos, and that made it worse somehow.

But how in hell could the engine go haywire? The Honda's odometer had less than two grand on it. He'd bought the car brand new so he wouldn't have to deal with any mechanical issues. The big question: How was he going to get it fixed out here in the sticks?

He'd been gaining on Kardos, in spite of the black coach's two-hour head start. The car could make better time than the ponderous coach, and he'd been pushing it, exceeding the speed limit by five to ten miles per hour. But surely that wouldn't cause the engine trouble.

Praying it wouldn't conk out on him, he eased the car into town, looking for a good place to stop. He spotted a brightly lit area up ahead and a big sign with "Chalkie's" in red letters ten feet high. It turned out to be a combination gas station, grocery, U-Haul, and—hello!—an Excelsior Rent-a-Ride. He pulled up next to the rental cars and opened his door. Pally hopped into the front seat and wagged his tail.

"Let's go take a leak, boy. You get to go first." He attached the leash. Getting out of the car was a painful experience.

They limped behind some buildings and found an area of scrub grass littered with rusty car parts. Pally's relief was evident. A sympathetic pang from Crocetti's bladder had him biting his lip. By the time he made it to the gas station's restroom the Kegel muscles that constricted his urethra were spasming.

Then he put Pally back in the car and walked around to the front of the gas station, looking for someone he could ask about renting a car. Only one attendant was on duty, a tall, sallow-faced kid with an excess of nose and deficiency of chin. He finished with a customer and came walking toward Crocetti.

"Help you?"

Crocetti nodded. "I'd like to rent a car."

The kid winced. "I'm kind of new here. I don't know squat about the rentals. The guy that knows about it called in late, said he can't make it until two. I'm here alone and I'm not thrilled about it, I can tell you that."

"But he'll be here at two?"

"I told him I'd kick his ass if he wasn't."

Crocetti sighed. He'd hoped to rent a car and be back on the road with minimal loss of time. Now he was looking at an additional delay of almost two hours. "Okay, I'll kill some time until then."

"The Pastime's down a couple blocks. It's a tavern, but they got pretty good food—chicken tenders and jojos, that kind of stuff."

Crocetti's mouth watered. He hadn't eaten anything since noon. "Thanks. I think I'll mosey on down there."

"Were you in an accident, mister?"

"Something like that."

He checked on Pally, who was curled up in his bed, and then locked the car and set off on foot in the direction the kid had pointed.

The Pastime turned out to be a neighborhood tavern with character. The Saturday night crowd had thinned out, and that was fine with him. He slid onto a stool at the end of the bar.

"I oughta see the other guy?" the bartender said. Round and bald with a well-trimmed red beard, he wore a big grin.

Crocetti laughed. "Damn right. A beer, please."

"Coming right up." The bartender poured a draft and set it down in front of Crocetti with a flourish.

Crocetti picked it up and signaled that he was moving to a table. He sat down and reached for an appetizer menu. Deep fried food seemed to be the Pastime's specialty: mushrooms, clams, scallops, cheese, and of course chicken tenders and jojos, thick potato fries. A thin-lipped woman with tightly curled graying hair came round to take his order. He decided he couldn't go too far wrong with the tenders and jojos.

While he waited for his order he sipped his beer and tried to ignore the wall-mounted TV, which was tuned to Fox News —not a surprise, considering where he was. Fortunately, the volume was barely audible. His food appeared, sizzling hot.

He checked the app. Kardos was rolling west on Route 20, about five miles from Bend. But why back to Bend, instead of heading south, as Crocetti had assumed he would?

A familiar face on the TV screen caught his attention. He stopped chewing. He had seen that face in the mirror all his adult life. He strained to hear the voice-over.

"... *person of interest in the murder of Howard J. Blunt of Des Moines, Iowa in an RV park in John Day. Anyone spotting Crocetti should call the following number ...*"

Crocetti glanced around. Not a soul was paying attention to the TV. He forced himself to relax and breathe normally. The chances of someone recognizing his swollen and bruised face as the one shown on the screen were slim.

Einhorn was playing hardball. The state police would no doubt be looking for the Honda. All the more reason to rent another car.

He paid in cash, adding a generous tip. Then he wrapped a chicken tender in a napkin for Pally and stood, resisting the urge to hide his face. With a nod to the bartender, he pushed the brass bar that opened the door. Outside, he used some hand sanitizer and started back to the car.

The tender was a big hit with Pally. After it was gone he licked his chops and wagged his tail whenever Crocetti looked at him.

It was one a.m. Still an hour to kill. Crocetti examined his insurance card. His policy had 24-hour emergency roadside assistance. He'd never had occasion to use it. He called the number. The man who answered identified himself as Steve.

Crocetti explained the situation to Steve, concluding with, "It's my understanding that my policy covers towing to a shop to perform repairs. The nearest dealer is Bond Honda in Bend, a hundred thirty miles from here."

"You can't have it repaired in Burns?"

"Not without voiding my warranty. It needs to be an authorized Honda service center."

They went back and forth for a few minutes, but Crocetti stuck to his guns and the guy folded. "Very well," he said, "we'll make arrangements to have your car picked up Monday at . . . Chalkie's in Burns and hauled on a flatbed truck to Bond Honda in Bend. You'll have to arrange for the repair."

"Of course. And you'll reimburse the cost of my rental?"

"Yes, yes. Just turn in the receipts."

"Been a pleasure, Steve. You have yourself a good night."

A perfect solution. State police wouldn't be looking for his car on a flatbed truck. Things seemed to be breaking in his favor for a change.

He checked the app again. The red dot was motionless in Bend, near the Deschutes River, which passed through the city. He zoomed in so he could pinpoint Kardos' location. A label appeared above the dot: American Red Cross. He damn sure wasn't there to donate blood.

Crocetti yawned. Forty-five minutes to go, enough time to squeeze in a nap. He reclined the seat and closed his eyes. On the floor of his mind lay Kelly, her sightless blue eyes staring at the Infinite, her bloodless face awash with ecstasy. He bolted upright, blinking.

Pally jumped into the front, his bushy eyebrows steepled with concern.

Crocetti swore. Up until then he had managed to stave off nightmarish scenarios and focus on the mission ahead. If he couldn't keep a level head, the odds of finding Kelly would be slim to none. On the job the operative phrase was "Work the problem." Giving emotions free rein only interfered with the process. True, he had a personal stake in the outcome, but that made discipline even more important.

A car drove up and parked. A young guy with curly dark hair stepped out and went into the office. Crocetti got out and followed after him.

After he walked in, the kid with the big nose and no chin said, "Mario, this gentleman wants to rent a car."

"Sure thing," Mario said. "What kind of car did you have in mind?"

"Nothing fancy," Crocetti said. "The blue-gray Ford Fusion will do just fine." It was nondescript, exactly what he wanted.

"We just got that in. Thirty-five a day."

"Make it happen, Mario."

"Okay, you'll need to fill out this form."

Crocetti handed it back after he was done. "I've arranged for a towing company to pick up that red Honda out there. I'd appreciate it if you would keep an eye on it until they come and get it. I have a car cover for it."

"No problem. And I'm ready for your credit card."

Paperwork completed, Mario accompanied Crocetti out for the walkaround, to inspect the Fusion for any damage. Crocetti spotted a small ding on the passenger door that wasn't noted on the inspection sheet. Otherwise, the car looked like it had come from the showroom.

He transferred Pally and their belongings to the Fusion. Then he opened the Honda's rear hatch and got out the cover he'd bought but never used. Mario helped him cover the car.

After a final bathroom break for himself and Pally, he got behind the Fusion's sculpted faux-leather wheel and set off for Bend.

Traveling west on Route 20, he paid close attention to the speed limit. No sense pushing his luck.

Still, he made good time. It was 4:50 a.m. when he rolled into Bend. The red dot was motionless in Chemult, sixty-five miles south on US-97. It should be much farther south.

He looked up the address for the American Red Cross and entered it in the dash-mounted GPS. A contralto female voice with a British accent began issuing directions in an imperious manner. Do it or else.

When the limey lass announced he'd reached his destination, he turned in. The American Red Cross shared a complex with an urgent-care clinic, a realtor, several physicians, and an insurance company. Four police units were in the parking lot, cherry tops flashing. He parked away from them.

The Red Cross was swarming with cops and medical types. Crocetti got out of the car and walked over, pretending to be an urgent-care patient who was curious about all the activity. An officer standing in front watched him with a gimlet eye.

Crocetti nodded to him. "Good morning, officer. What's all the excitement?"

"The Red Cross had a break-in earlier. You'll hear all about it on the news. Excuse me." He turned and went inside.

A large Hispanic man in white was leaning against a column smoking a cigarette. Crocetti walked over to him. "The punks who broke in, what were they after, drugs?"

The man flicked an ash off his cigarette. "Blood."

"Blood? They only took blood?"

"One man, alone. He cleaned us out. Three of us couldn't stop him. I'm six-four, two-fifty and he tossed me aside like I was made of straw."

"Weird."

"Here's something even more weird. On the surveillance video you can see us fine but not him, only a big blank spot where he's supposed to be. The police said the cameras must have malfunctioned. Sure. All four of them."

"Did you get a good look at the guy?"

He hesitated. "I been standing here trying to remember. I got a good eye for details, but for the life of me I couldn't tell the cops what he looked like. It was a little embarrassing."

"I heard traumatic events can cause temporary amnesia." Giving the guy an out seemed like the decent thing to do.

"Maybe that's it. Well, guess I should get back inside." He gave a parting nod.

Crocetti walked back to the car lost in thought. Perhaps Kardos had switched from killing people to knocking over blood banks. He'd certainly made a sizable withdrawal from this one. Only one thing wrong with that theory: For serial killers there was no substitute for killing. It was a need, like breathing. If Kardos was stealing blood from blood banks it had to be for show, part of his vampire masquerade. Crocetti prayed, a rare thing for him, that the distraction would buy Kelly some time.

It took every ounce of self-control he could summon not to jump in the car and charge down the highway with the speedometer needle buried. That would be a huge mistake. In light of Einhorn's APB, he couldn't risk getting pulled over for speeding. Instead, he must scrupulously obey traffic laws. To have any hope of finding Kardos' coach and getting Kelly away from him before the twisted bastard killed her, it was essential that he keep his head on straight.

Focus. Work the problem.

He took Pally for a walk and let him visit every shrub in the parking lot's planting area. Then he checked the app. The red dot was still sitting on Chemult. Sunrise was less than an hour off, so Kardos wasn't going anywhere. Another welcome break.

He started the car and slammed it into gear.

34

While passing through La Pine, he spotted a police cruiser parked at NAPA Auto & Truck Parts, a radar gun aimed out the window. He hit the brake pedal and glanced at the speedometer. He'd been doing over 40, perhaps even 45. The posted speed limit was 35. So much for scrupulously obeying traffic laws. He hoped the cop would give him a little leeway, seeing as how it was almost six a.m. with no other traffic.

No such luck. The cruiser rolled out after him, lights flashing. Crocetti pulled over, opened his window, and waited. If the cop had seen Einhorn's APB, they would haul Crocetti's ass back to John Day before lunchtime.

The uniformed officer walked up to the window, his hand on his gun. Crocetti couldn't blame him for being cautious. Traffic stops could be dangerous as hell.

"Morning, officer," Crocetti said in his most affable manner, both hands on the steering wheel.

"Good morning, sir. Could I see your driver's license, registration, and proof of insurance, please?" The officer was young and square jawed.

Crocetti handed him the license, insurance card, and the registration from the glove box. "It's a rental."

The young cop examined them carefully.

Crocetti flipped open the wallet with his shield and I.D. "Portland Police Bureau," he said. "Thirty years."

The officer handed him back the documents and closed his ticket book. "My wife and I are moving to Portland. She landed a teaching position at Reed College, and I plan to apply to the Bureau."

"That so? I'd be glad to put in a good word for you."

"That would be mighty kind of you. Name's Jim Wright."

Crocetti wrote it down. "Consider it done."

"Gosh, thanks so much. I'll let you be on your way. Have a good day."

"Same to you, Jim."

Before pulling away from the curb, Crocetti watched the cruiser make a U-turn and roar off. Professional courtesy, the Brotherhood of the Badge—which included retired badges—had gotten him off the hook. Sure, he'd put in a good word for Jim. Why not? Whether he made the grade or not depended entirely on his qualifications.

He set the cruise control to 55 on the nose, and as the car floated silently down the road he wished he had remembered to bring along some 5-hour Energy.

The next town on US-97 south was Crescent, posted speed limit 40. He maintained a conservative 35 until he had passed through it. Only a total idiot would risk another traffic stop. Chemult, his destination, was down the road another seventeen miles, according to the sign. And each mile he covered strengthened his resolve.

Talk about an unlikely hero—bum leg, cracked ribs, swollen and bruised from head to toe—yet he couldn't wait to get there. He would laugh, if it didn't hurt so damn much. Kelly had called him a knight in tarnished armor. It was a generous assessment. Creaky, rusty, dented armor was more like it. But you made do with what you had.

Not for the first time, he wondered why someone would pretend to be a vampire to the degree that Kardos had. Not that any serial killer was a paragon of sanity. They all had a screw loose. But to adopt every aspect of a classic vampire, to the point of sleeping in a coffin and actually drinking blood—it was a delusion on steroids, a horror movie come to life.

Crocetti had never been a fan of horror movies, not even when he was a kid hanging out on lazy Saturday afternoons in the balcony of the Avalon Theater on Belmont. He would have taken *Forbidden Planet* over *Dracula* any day.

A mile or so south of the Route 58 junction, he pulled over and stopped at a wide place on the shoulder to give Pally and himself a much-needed bathroom break. They walked into the woods far enough to be out of sight of the highway. Pally waited until Crocetti did his business and then added his contribution to the same spot. Having thus marked their territory in traditional male fashion, they got back in the car and continued on toward their destination.

The morning sun had cleared the horizon by the time they reached Chemult. The town was little more than a wide spot on the highway, a hodgepodge of stores, cafes, gas stations, and a seedy motel. ("Vacancy," the sign announced. No kidding.) Many former businesses were boarded up. A mobile home, its yard strewn with junk of every description, squatted near the highway.

But it also had a sizable truck stop, Pilot Travel Center. He turned in and made a circuit of the lot and counted a dozen 18-wheelers. No black coach. The app indicated he was almost on top of it. He parked and got out. After stretching, wincing from the pain, he walked around. A glance at the app showed the blue and red dots had merged into a single purple dot. He made a 360-degree visual sweep. His eye fell on a green dumpster behind a building. He walked over to it, threw back the lid, and peered in.

Completely empty, except for a dozen empty Miller High Life cans. He looked down at the app's screen. Unless there was an equipment malfunction, the tracking device had to be around there somewhere. He circled the dumpster and then checked underneath.

And there it was.

He pulled it free and switched it off. As though on cue, the sun ducked behind the clouds and a curtain of gloom descended over the area.

Kardos had wanted him to find it. The sadistic son of a bitch planted the device and took off down the road. With Kelly, who by this time must be catatonic with terror—assuming she was still alive.

He sat down heavily on the cement curb. Tears of frustration filled his eyes and streamed down his cheeks. He took out his handkerchief and blew his nose.

Some detective.

Collaring Kardos was to be his crowning achievement, an incandescent blaze of glory. But then he had underestimated his quarry at every turn, certain he was no match for super cop Daniel Crocetti—who had more balls than sense, thinking he could go up against someone like Kardos without backup. Even a disastrous face-to-face encounter hadn't tempered his overconfidence. What an arrogant buffoon he was. But self-flagellation wasn't going to get Kelly back.

When he'd checked the app in Bend at 4:50 a.m., the red dot had been stationary in Chemult. Sunrise was at 6:21, giving Kardos an hour and a half to plant the device and find a place to hole up for the day. It could be anywhere inside a sixty-mile radius, an area of over eleven thousand square miles. If he'd continued south on US-97 he could have made it as far as Chiloquin. But perhaps he had chosen Crater Lake National Park instead. Or Klamath Marsh National Wildlife Refuge. Or Winema National Forest. Bottom line, jumping in the car and roaring off in search of the black coach would be like looking for a needle in a haystack the size of a coliseum.

He could bring law enforcement into it, state police or FBI, with their vast resources. But it would take a while, perhaps even days, to get the ball rolling, due to bureaucratic inertia. By that time Kelly might have a couple extra orifices in her neck and a severe shortage of blood.

A better idea hit him. He took out his phone and tapped an entry in his contact list. While it rang he chewed on his bottom lip. He counted five rings.

"Klindt."

"Dan Crocetti, Doug."

"Well, well, well. I was just thinking about you. How goes the chase?"

"Not so good. We're in big trouble. Kelly's been kidnapped by Kardos. He found the tracking device and he dumped it in Chemult. That's where I'm calling from."

"You say Kelly was kidnapped?"

"Yes, in John Day. I followed Kardos to Chemult. No telling where he went from here, but I've got to find him and get her away from him."

"I'll top off Bella's fuel tanks and take off right away. Give me an hour and a half to get there."

"Doug, I can't express how grateful—"

"Save it. Let's focus on getting Kelly back. Is there someplace I can land near where you are?"

"I'm at the Pilot Travel Center on the south end of town. There's a clearing next to the parking lot in back. You can set Bella down there."

"Copy that. See you by oh nine hundred."

The sun broke through the clouds just then and the gloom dissipated. Likewise, the phone call had brightened Crocetti's outlook considerably. A ray of hope could do wonders for one's mood.

He needed coffee. The sandwich shop beside the Travel Center building was open, although business was slow at 7:30 a.m. He ordered a large coffee. His stomach signaled that it would also appreciate something solid, so he ordered a footlong turkey sub to go and grabbed a bag of Doritos.

He went to the Travel Center office next door and asked a guy with a linebacker's shoulders and a mouthful of capped teeth the size and whiteness of Chiclets if he could park his car there for the rest of the day and possibly overnight. Not a problem, the guy said, as long as he parked on the south side of the building.

Before he unwrapped the sub he filled Pally's food and water bowls and then they had breakfast together. Bellies thus filled, they went for a walk. A man and his dog, limping along in unison.

He phoned Grant County RV Park in John Day, paid for another night, and asked them to charge his card every day at checkout time until he told them different.

After moving the car, he inventoried the satchel's contents —gun and holster, extra .38 rounds, taser, flashlight, pepper spray, UV flashlight, lock picks, folding multitool, and phone charger.

Last on the to-do list, but definitely not the least important: a visit to the restroom. After draining his bladder he splashed cold water on his bruised and swollen face. It didn't help much with the throbbing pain.

At 9:07 he heard an approaching *thwop thwop thwop* and looked at Pally. "Guess what, gimpy dog—we're going for a helicopter ride."

35

The helicopter's blades stirred up a whirlwind of dust and sand as it landed. A group of curious onlookers, mostly truckers, had gathered to watch. Crocetti waited until the blades stopped spinning before he approached the cockpit with the satchel in one hand, Pally's leash and his cane in the other.

"Chrissake," Klindt said. "What happened to you?"

"Long story." Crocetti tossed the satchel in the back seat's footwell and deposited Pally on the back seat.

"Grab the blanket behind the seat," Klindt said. "He can lay on that."

With Pally curled up on the blanket, Crocetti buckled his seat belt and put on his headset. "I'm ready."

"Which direction do you want to try first?"

"Might as well head south."

The engine came to life with a whine that drew an anxious bark from Pally. Then the chopper lifted off and banked south to follow US-97.

"What's the maximum distance he could be from here?"

"A bit over an hour's travel, I estimate, so no more than fifty, sixty miles. But I have a hunch he didn't go that far."

"Let's hope not. Now . . . are you going to tell me why your mug looks like you ran face-first into a brick wall?"

"And why I have three cracked ribs?"

"No joke? Jesus."

Crocetti told him the story, beginning with the sucker punch and concluding with coldcocking Pruitt with his cane in the hospital.

"I would've done a number on his face and ribs to even the score," Klindt said. "So when was Kelly kidnapped?"

"Kardos snatched her while I was in the hospital. One of the other campers saw him take her."

"Gutsy bastard."

"That's not all. Before he left with her, he stabbed a man to death at the RV park and planted my monogrammed cane and a knife with my fingerprints on it at the scene."

"I'm surprised you're not in police custody."

"I had an airtight alibi. I was in the hospital at the time of the murder. Even so, a John Day police detective told me to stick around. He wasn't too happy when I took off. He put out a state-wide all-points bulletin on me as a person of interest and plastered my face on TV, sans bruises."

"I'm guessing you figured you could find Kelly faster than the police could."

"Exactly right."

"This Kardos is hardcore—paying someone to beat the crap out of you, trying to frame you for a murder, and then kidnapping Kelly."

"Doug, you don't know the half of it. Kardos is an unhinged serial killer with at least eight victims in Oregon so far. I need to make sure Kelly's not his ninth."

"How come he hasn't been caught?"

"He's careful and cunning. But he has an Achilles heel—he travels only at night and lays low during the day. That's when he's most vulnerable."

"Then let's find the son of a bitch before it gets dark."

"That's the plan."

Klindt pointed at an airstrip below. "Beaver Marsh State Airport. I landed there for fuel one time. Might need to again, depending on how things go. We've got over half a tank, so we're okay for now."

Three miles down the road, Klindt said, "We're coming up on a junction with OR 138, otherwise known as the Volcanic Scenic Legacy Byway, which branches off to the west. It passes by Diamond Lake and Crater Lake and eventually ends at Roseburg ninety miles or so away. Several little towns are in between—Clearwater, Glide, and Dixonville. It's a heavily forested mountain pass."

Crocetti grunted. "Plenty of places for Kardos to hide. What say we check it out before continuing on south?"

"Works for me." Klindt banked the chopper to the right.

Crocetti looked back at Pally. He was alert but not scared. "Well, what do you think, Pally? Got the hang of this flying business yet?" The dog ignored that and busied himself with licking his privates.

Klindt looked over his shoulder. "Wish I could do that."

"Give it a try," Crocetti said. "He'd probably let you."

Klindt laughed. "Maybe after we land."

An hour and a half later they circumnavigated Crater Lake, after investigating the area around Diamond Lake and the Umpqua National Forest as far in as Clearwater.

"Last time I flew over Crater Lake," Klindt said, "I had a wicked impulse to set down on Wizard Island, just for the hell of it. The National Park Service would have taken a dim view of that."

"No doubt," Crocetti said. "Year before last, I camped at Crater Lake for almost a week. Nice area." But the nice area had a shortage of black coaches. As in zero.

"We can continue on south if you want, but we're running a bit low on fuel. We might have enough to make it to Chiloquin State Airport to refuel, but it would be cutting it close. So we're heading back to Beaver Marsh."

"Good. It will give us a chance to stretch our legs and visit the can. Right, Pally?"

The dog opened one eye and closed it again.

Fifteen minutes later they touched down at the north end of the strip, near a fuel truck. On shutdown, deafening silence replaced the turbine's whine.

Pally hopped to the ground and strained at the leash to get to some tall grass at the side of the strip. He lifted his bum leg at it, a dreamy look of relief on his face. He didn't bother to find other spots to mark.

Crocetti was glad to see a portable restroom, "Buckman's Honey Pots" on the door, beyond the fuel truck. Keeping his Kegel muscles clamped down, he hurried to it with Pally in tow. The dog sniffed every square inch of the restroom floor. A dollop of hand sanitizer afterward zapped those germs.

A big-bellied man in a faded denim shirt, overalls, and a baseball cap inserted the hose's nozzle in the chopper's tank and started fuel flowing as Klindt looked on.

Crocetti walked over and stood beside Klindt. "From time to time I get hunches. I listen to them, because I usually regret it when I don't. I've got one now."

Klindt turned and looked at him. "Yeah?"

"Kardos is a tricky bastard. My hunch is whispering to me that he didn't head south from Chemult, that instead he doubled back and took Route 58 heading west. Lots of hiding places between here and Oakridge."

Klindt shrugged. "Far be it from me to doubt your hunch. Let's check it out."

Back in the air, Crocetti's own doubt began to creep in. Since he had a personal stake in finding Kelly, what if wishful thinking was affecting his hunches? They were committed either way. If it didn't pan out—he winced at the thought, since they were racing against time—they'd have no choice but to try elsewhere. In the meantime it was crucial that he stay frosty and focus on the search.

Klindt banked left when Route 58, the Willamette Highway, branched off to the northwest, cutting across flat, sandy terrain sparsely dotted with pine trees and scrub bushes. Nowhere to conceal a car, let alone a large motor coach. Two miles in, they came upon the first possibility, a Forestry Service road wide enough to accommodate the coach. They banked right and explored the accessible part before turning back to Route 58.

Railroad tracks and two county roads crossed the highway. They checked out the roads in both directions before continuing up 58. Further on they passed over a rustic lodge-style restaurant named the Homestead Inn, by the looks of it the kind of place that served down-home cooking and freshly baked pies.

"I love mom and pop restaurants," Klindt said, "Want to grab some coffee and a slice of pie? It's past noon and there's a place to set down."

Crocetti stroked his chin. On one hand, he hated to spend the time. On the other, he had to take a leak. Bad, now that he thought about it. Pally probably did, too. "Yeah, I guess we can stop for a few minutes."

Klindt made a U-turn and flew the short distance back. He set the chopper down in a graveled area at the northwest end of the restaurant, sending small chunks of gravel flying. Crocetti took Pally for a short walk before he and Klindt climbed the half-log steps to the entrance.

The Homestead Inn's interior decor was frontier rustic— rough-hewn wood, huge stone fireplace, and a dozen stuffed and mounted animal heads that presided over the dining room with glassy stares. Crocetti scowled. He didn't have any use for hunting for sport. When he was thirteen he went deer hunting with his father, at his father's insistence, and looked on in horror as the life drained out of a neck-shot doe, her liquid eyes full of pain. That finished it for him. Arm the animals with lethal weapons that could kill at a distance, and then it would be fair.

They found a table and ordered coffee and pie—fresh-out-of-the-oven Dutch apple with a scoop of vanilla—from a cute young brunette waitress wearing . . . yes, a gingham apron.

"I don't know, Doug," he said between bites, "we've been searching for over three hours with no luck. When I think about the odds against finding that damn black coach, I get a little depressed."

"Keep the faith," Klindt said. "We still got eight hours of daylight left. We found that coach once, didn't we?"

"Don't get me wrong, I'm not giving up. But I wish I had your optimism. It's like looking for a needle—"

A scrawny elderly man at the next table, his face baked brown by decades of desert sun, leaned over. "Excuse me, fellers," he said. "Don't mean to snoop in your business, but I jest couldn't hep overhearin that you been lookin for a black RV motor coach."

Crocetti looked at Klindt and back at the old guy. "That's right."

"Name's Casper, Casper Jempty." He stuck out his hand.

"Dan Crocetti." The man's hand felt like fragile twigs covered with parchment. "And this is Doug Klindt."

"You're the fellers what landed in that whirlybird. Mighty pleased to make your acquaintance."

"Likewise, Casper. So what about the black coach?"

"Wellsir, my double-wide's jest up the road. Got me a real clear view of folks passin by. I was settin out on the porch at five thirty, maybe a scosh earlier, jest killin time and waitin for this place to open up so's I could walk down here and have me some ham and eggs and hash browns for breakfast, like I do most days, unless it's rainin and then I drive my old Chevy. Anyways, I was settin there, and along come this big shiny black thing, passin like a battleship in the night, headin west to beat the band."

Crocetti's pulse quickened. "The coach we're looking for is all black, with dark-tinted windows."

"That's the one I seen, all right."

"And you say it was five thirty a.m. when you saw it?"

"Yeah, pret' near that.

"Casper Jempty, I am going to buy your lunch," Crocetti said. "You've been a tremendous help, so it's the least I can do."

"I thank you kindly, sonny. Glad I could be of hep."

Crocetti had the waitress add Casper's meal to their check and handed her his debit card. He saluted Casper before they went out the door. On the way to the helicopter he said, "I can't believe our luck."

Klindt grinned. "Feeling a bit more optimistic, are you?"

"We've got a handle on two things now: First, my hunch was on the money—we're on the right road. Second, we know approximately when Kardos passed by this point. And knowing that, we can work out how far from here he traveled before daybreak. Let's say it was five thirty when Casper saw the coach. That gives Kardos a little over forty-five minutes to find a place to hide. So given the road and the terrain, he's within thirty miles from here, give or take."

"That narrows it down quite a bit," Klindt said. "Let's go flying."

Back in the air, Crocetti consulted the map. "Thirty miles will take us into the mountains, past Crescent Lake and Odell Lake through McCredie Springs, as far as Oakridge."

"Right," Klindt said, "but he'll need some time to find a hiding place, you said."

"Yeah, so he probably won't try to make it as far as he can."

Klindt nodded. "We're going to be flying over a populated area between Odell Lake and Crescent Lake, so we'll gain some more altitude." He gave it more throttle and the craft began to climb.

"I still can't get over our luck," Crocetti said, "running into an old guy who just happened to be sitting on his porch when Kardos passed by. What if we hadn't landed there? What if Casper hadn't overheard us talking about the black coach? What are the chances against those events falling into place so perfectly? Must be a zillion to one."

"Fate. It was meant to happen."

"I don't believe in fate. It was just happenstance."

"Happenstance? Tell me, how do you explain your strong hunch that Kardos doubled back and took Route 58? Lucky guess?"

"You got me there. I don't have the slightest clue where my hunches come from."

"Exigent circumstances."

The unexpected word caught Crocetti by surprise. It must have shown on his face when he looked at Klindt.

"I'm only half an idiot," Klindt said.

Crocetti laughed. "Doug, there's nothing halfway about you. Talk about things falling into place—if I hadn't gotten hold of you I wouldn't have a chance in hell of finding Kelly."

"Fate, like I said."

"Whatever it was, I'm grateful for it."

After they descended back to five hundred feet, Klindt pointed. "Crescent Lake State Airport. Never landed there."

Shortly after that, Odell Lake on their left, Crocetti said, "Princess Creek Campground is right down there. I tried to camp there last year. Found out they had a thirty-two-foot limit on length, but mine's forty."

"Then we can eliminate it as a potential hiding place for the black coach—also a forty footer, you said."

"Kardos will pick a spot that's more secluded."

"There's plenty of secluded places up here."

That turned out to be an understatement. They lost count after the first three dozen possibilities, out-of-the-way places that could accommodate a forty-foot coach. Near Gold Lake Sno-Park they thought they'd hit the jackpot, but it turned out to be a big Winnebago with black and burgundy graphics on its side. It took several minutes for Crocetti's heart rate to return to normal.

Then five miles or so past Odell Lake, near Salt Creek Summit, a bright silvery glint off to the north caught Crocetti's eye. It was probably nothing, but he wanted to check it out nevertheless. He had Klindt bank hard to the right. The flash had come from a small clearing beside a narrow road labeled NF 5894 on the map.

"There's that son of a bitch," Klindt said, pointing.

And so it was. Looking as sinister as ever, the black coach was hunkered down next to the trees in a far corner of the clearing.

Jackpot.

36

Klindt set the helicopter down in the center of the clearing and killed the engine. Unless Kardos was in a coma he'd no doubt heard them arrive. It was entirely possible that he had a high-powered rifle's crosshairs trained on them at that very moment.

Crocetti reached around and grabbed the satchel. Klindt watched as he put on the shoulder rig and holstered the Colt, clipped the taser on his belt, stashed the flashlight, pepper spray, folding multitool, and lock picks in his jacket pockets. After hesitating, he slipped the UV light in his front pants pocket. Loaded for bear. Or a psychotic vampire wannabe.

He looked at Klindt. "If I'm not back in . . . twenty minutes, call the sheriff or state police. In fact, call them both."

Klindt snorted. "What the hell are you talking about? I'm going with you."

"Doug, I'm going alone. Kardos is a dangerous psycho. Stay here with Pally." The last thing he wanted was for Klindt to get killed or badly injured.

"Bullshit. I'm going with you, and that's all there is to it."

Crocetti sighed. "Do you happen to have a gun?"

"A flare gun. It'll discourage anybody."

"Got a flashlight? Kardos keeps it dark."

"I got something better than a flashlight—a lantern that will make it like daylight in there."

"Okay. Grab them and let's go."

The helicopter's door faced away from the coach, a good thing. After they got out, Pally jumped up from the blanket, wagging his tail.

"Pally," Crocetti said, "you have to stay here. We'll be back soon." Hopefully.

"What's the plan?" Klindt said after he closed the door.

"Kardos might be armed, so we can't just walk over there out in the open, exposed. We'll use the chopper for cover and head for those trees. Then we'll circle around to the coach. Ready? Single-file cover formation. I'll take the lead."

Until they reached the safety of the trees, a spot between Crocetti's shoulder blades tingled in anticipation of a bullet. True, he hadn't seen a rifle or other firearm inside Kardos' coach, but he hadn't had time to do a thorough search. For all he knew, Kardos could have had an armory stashed under his coffin. Approaching with caution would cost them only a few extra minutes and allow them to assess the situation.

Using the trees as cover they edged around the perimeter of the clearing. Crocetti ignored the knifelike complaints from his knee and ribs. A red squirrel on a log chittered at them as they passed; it sounded like a warning. Smart squirrel.

A sudden urge to urinate demanded his attention. Cursing his prostate, he relieved himself on a tree, hoping it would hold him for a while.

As they neared the black coach, adrenaline blunted Crocetti's pain while elevating his anxiety into the red zone. A disturbing possibility gnawed at him: What if Kelly wasn't in there? He shoved the thought aside and reached in his pocket for the lock picks. Then he turned to Klindt. "Cover me."

He crept up to the door and set to work. The adrenaline hindered. He dropped the picks and swore under his breath, willing himself to relax and focus. After several frustrating minutes he felt the mechanical click he'd been waiting for.

Before he opened the door he reached for the gun, thought better of it, palmed the pepper spray instead. He switched on the flashlight and motioned for Klindt to follow.

Inside, the by-now-familiar stench made his gorge rise. The look on Klindt's face in the interior's diffused light mirrored Crocetti's revulsion.

"Smells like something died in here," Klindt whispered.

Crocetti shushed him with an index finger across his lips.

Klindt switched on his lantern, bathing the salon in bright light. He gaped at the sumptuous Victorian appointments, which were even more elegant than Crocetti remembered. But he and Klindt were there for one purpose: to find Kelly. Flashlight in one hand and pepper spray in the other, he led the way aft, down the hallway.

He shined the flashlight into the bathroom. Empty.

The guest bedroom was further down the hallway, door closed. He hesitated with his hand on the doorknob. He hadn't prayed in earnest since he stopped attending mass at St. Ignatius after he turned thirteen, but he offered a brief, fervent prayer that she would be in there, alive and un-harmed. Then he took a deep breath and turned the knob.

The flashlight's beam found her huddled in the corner, eyes wide, mouth open to scream.

"Kelly, it's me," he whispered quickly.

She mouthed his name. Her eyes were rimmed in red with dark smudges underneath. Her wrists and ankles had been bound with windings of stout wire. Unwinding it would take too much time. He used the multitool's cutters to clip the wire quickly.

"Let's get out of here," he whispered.

She didn't need prodding. But being bound for so long had taken a toll, making her unsteady on her feet. With Crocetti supporting one arm and Klindt the other, they man-aged to get her out of the bedroom and down the hallway before they heard something approaching fast from behind. Something large.

"Oh, my dear God," Kelly said, her body going rigid, "it's him. Run!"

They ran and almost made it across the kitchen, a good ten feet short of the door.

The thing that emerged from the hallway into the light had the silhouette of a man, walked upright like a man, wore a man's clothes—but it was not a man, not by any conceivable definition.

"Holy Christ," Klindt said. "What the hell is that?"

Short fur covered the creature's face. It had pointed ears, flared nostrils, a bifurcated upper lip—split vertically, like an animal's—huge fangs, and feral claws. But the most chilling feature was its eyes, inhuman pools of blackest black, no white at all.

"That," Kelly said, her voice trembling, "is Kardos."

"*That's* Kardos?" Klindt said. "That . . . thing?"

"Don't look at his eyes. That's how he hypnotizes you."

Klindt raised the flare gun, but before he could fire, Kardos moved with blinding speed and knocked it out of his hand and then blocked the door, preventing their escape.

Crocetti gathered Kelly behind him.

With a claw-like finger, the creature pointed at Crocetti and said in a strangely sibilant growl, "*You. Come to me.*"

Unable to look away from those piercing obsidian eyes, Crocetti took an involuntary step toward Kardos, as though his leg had moved of its own volition.

Kelly grabbed his arm. "Dan!"

It jarred him out of it. Still clutching the pepper spray, he gave Kardos a three-second blast, square in the face. Kardos screeched and wiped his face with a sleeve, and then he hissed at Crocetti. Evidently, the spray would discourage bears, but not vampires. Kardos grabbed the front of Crocetti's jacket and hurled him against Klindt, knocking them both down. Kelly screamed.

Klindt got to his feet and charged Kardos, who swatted him away almost casually. Crocetti drew the taser and pulled the trigger. It made a loud percussive sound, followed by clicking. Kardos looked down at the darts in his abdomen, grabbed the wires, and yanked them out. "Neuromuscular incapacitation will immobilize any attacker," the salesclerk had said. Except vampires, apparently.

Kardos hissed and started toward Crocetti. Seeing no alternative, Crocetti drew the Colt and fired. Kardos kept coming. Crocetti fired five more times, emptying the cylinder. Kardos snatched the gun and bent the barrel downward. It was hardened steel; incredible strength would be required to bend it. Kardos dropped the gun and seized Crocetti, lifting him off his feet and holding him suspended by his armpits as though he were a child. Crocetti turned his head and held his breath, so as to avoid Kardos' putrid exhalations. Kardos growled, "*Sleep . . .*"

Kelly jostled him awake. He found he couldn't move his arms or legs. They'd been trussed up with wire. Kelly, beside him on the guest stateroom bed, was similarly immobilized, as was Klindt, still asleep next to her. Kelly jostled Klindt with her shoulder until he came to, blinking and shaking his head to clear it. Hard to say how long they had been unconscious, but the curtained window above them let in enough light to indicate it was still daylight. His ribs were killing him, but they were the least of his concerns.

"I been in a lot of tight spots," Klindt said, "but this takes the cake."

"Keep it down, Doug" Kelly whispered. "Kardos will sleep until nightfall if he's not disturbed."

"Incredible," Crocetti said, more to himself than to them. "The bastard's an honest-to-God vampire."

"And he was planning to 'turn' me, make me a vampire too, so I could live forever beside him," Kelly said.

Crocetti shuddered.

"Kardos hates what he's become, hates it," she said. "I saw him cry when he looked at the photographs on the wall out there. I couldn't help but feel sorry for him."

Crocetti snorted. "I can't help feeling sorry for his victims."

"Lately he's been stealing blood from blood banks so he could stop killing. It's not working. He hopes to find a doctor who specializes in rare diseases who can cure him."

"Call me a pessimist, but I've got a feeling he won't have much luck finding one."

"Then he'll go on killing. And hating himself for it."

"Tell you one thing, Kelly, that's not hypnosis he uses. It's something else, something a lot more powerful."

"Powerful enough to make me tell him about the tracking device. I didn't want to, but I couldn't stop myself."

"I wondered how he found that thing. He also made you tell him about the knife, the one I took away from Jughead, right?"

"Yes," Kelly said. "This whole thing is my fault. If I hadn't gone back for my purse after I forgot it, he wouldn't have caught me. It was after dark and I should have known better. He had me under his spell in two seconds. My mind went blank, like a zombie. I had to do whatever he said."

"Listen, don't beat yourself up over it." A sharp pain in his ribs made him catch his breath. "At least that brute didn't hurt you."

"Not physically, anyway. Kardos thinks I'm his beloved long-dead wife, Gabriella, reincarnated. He said the resemblance is uncanny. Looking at her in the photograph, I can kind of see it. With longer, darker hair and the right dress—"

"Here's my concern," Crocetti said, "Kardos feeds at night, right? Dinnertime is approaching, and Doug and I are on the menu. We can shoot the breeze until it gets dark, or we can try to figure a way out of this mess."

"Got any ideas?" Klindt said.

"One idea. In my right jacket pocket there's a multitool. I'll need to turn over on my stomach, and if Kelly can get her hands on the tool, she can clip the wire around my wrists and I'll take it from there."

"Let's do it," Kelly said.

He managed to flop over, receiving a stab of pain in his ribs in the process and wishing again he hadn't run out of oxycodone. "Okay, go for it."

After considerable squirming, Kelly slipped her hand in the pocket. "Got it."

"Good. It has wire clippers that fold out . . . no, that's the scissors . . . no, that's the pliers . . . there you go. Now if you can get to the wire around my wrists . . ."

"I'll do my best."

It required contortions on both their parts, but eventually their efforts were rewarded with a sharp snick. With luck it hadn't woke Kardos.

"One down," she said.

But it didn't loosen his wrists much. "Clip another one."

It took two more snicks before he felt the windings give way. He took the cutters from her and clipped the wire securing his ankles. He freed Kelly next and then Klindt.

He tiptoed to the door and listened. Nothing. He eased the door open and motioned for them to follow him. The trio crept down the hall single-file: Kelly, Klindt, Crocetti, holding his breath.

The creature was waiting for them in the salon.

Kelly screamed.

"*You would take my Gabriella from me?*" Kardos growled, pointing first to Crocetti and then Klindt, "*I will have your blood.*"

In a low voice, Crocetti said, "Doug, on the count of three we'll double-team him. Kelly, you make a break for the door. One . . . two . . . three!"

Bad idea. Kardos grabbed them, one six-footer in each arm, and hurled them across the salon. The hard landing knocked all the wind out of Crocetti. Breathing was painful. His formerly cracked ribs felt as though they might now be broken. And Kardos clearly intended to finish him off.

"Viktor," Kelly said, "please let them go. Please, I beg of you. For me?"

Kardos halted and seemed to consider her request. Then he said, "*No, Gabriella. They sought to destroy me.*"

"They were just defending themselves. They were afraid. Please, Viktor."

"*They must pay a blood debt for their foolishness.*" He started toward them.

It seemed wildly incongruous, given the situation, but Kelly had her phone in hand. A bit late to call 911.

Crocetti remembered the UV light in the front pocket of his pants. Everything else—pepper spray, taser, gun—had been about as effective as tossing popcorn, so he might as well try UV. He fished it out of his pocket and switched it on, and then he aimed the beam at Kardos' head.

The UV had an instantaneous and dramatic effect. Kardos screeched and shielded his face with his sleeved arms as he backed away.

Disregarding the painful protest from his ribs, Crocetti scrambled to his feet. He kept the beam on Kardos and motioned to Klindt to open the door. Smoke rose from Kardos' exposed claw-hands and the skin blistered. Kardos screeched again and started toward the hallway and safety. Crocetti circled around and blocked him. When Kardos dropped his arms, Crocetti aimed the beam at his eyes.

Kardos roared and lashed out, blind. Crocetti dodged the slashing claws and trained the light on his face and head, blistering the skin. A smell of burning meat mingled with the background stench. Crocetti maneuvered him in front of the open door and nodded to Klindt. He charged at Kardos and delivered a shoulder hit worthy of an NFL linebacker, knocking him through the doorway and out into the bright sunlight.

With a tortured screech that reverberated across the clearing, Kardos burst into flame. As they watched, stunned, from the doorway, in mere minutes Kardos became a vaguely man-shaped cinder, rising tendrils of smoke the only remaining movement.

They climbed down out of the coach.

"Jesus, that didn't take long," Klindt said. "What now?"

Kelly said, "Think it's time to call the State Police?"

Crocetti shook his head. "They'd never believe it."

"But you're an ex-cop."

"Wouldn't matter. We'd all probably get jammed up bad. Maybe even charged with murder."

"In that case, I vote no," Klindt said.

She handed her phone to Crocetti. "Press play."

He did. "I'll be damned," he said, watching the thirty-second video. "You caught the whole thing. Have a look at this, Doug."

"The video backs up our story," Kelly said. "They'd have to believe it after they saw it, wouldn't they?"

Crocetti considered it and then shook his head. "Nothing, not even that video, will convince them Kardos was a genuine vampire. I can hardly believe it myself. We'd end up suspects in his death, guaranteed. I don't know how you feel about that, but it doesn't appeal to me even a little bit."

"Me neither," Klindt said. "I got a flying business to run."

"So if we're not going to contact the Oregon State Police or FBI," Kelly said, "what do you suggest we do?"

"Collect any evidence that we were here and then get in the helicopter and fly the hell away. Eventually someone will find the coach and investigate."

The burnt thing that had once been Kardos had stopped smoking.

"We can't leave his body out here," Kelly said.

Klindt turned to her. "Why not?"

"We just can't, that's all."

"Okay," Crocetti said. "How about we carry it in there and lay it in the coffin?"

"That's perfect," she said.

Crocetti took the head and shoulders, Klindt the feet, and they lifted the charred corpse, taking care that it remained intact. It was as light as styrofoam. They carried it into the coach and laid it in the soil lining the coffin.

"If there are any worms in that dirt I hope they have a taste for charcoal," Crocetti said.

Klindt closed the lid.

"Smear the place you touched, to get rid of your fingerprints," Crocetti said. "Use the palm of your hand."

Out in the salon, Crocetti picked up the Colt with the bent barrel and holstered it. He'd keep it as a memento of his stubborn skepticism. He opened the freezer.

"Holy shit!" Klindt said. "How much is there?"

"Not sure. Let's count it."

He took off his jacket to use as a makeshift sack. Kelly held it while he loaded it with cash, bundles of ten thousand each, counting as he went. It soon got too heavy for Kelly to hold by herself, so Klindt gave her a hand.

"That makes three hundred thirty thousand," he said after he tossed the last packet in. "A hundred ten each. Doug, will a hundred ten grand cover today's helicopter charter?"

Klindt laughed. "Close enough."

"We're just going to take that money?" Kelly said.

Crocetti gave her a look. "Better us than whoever finds the coach."

He tied the sleeves together to close the sack and set it by the door. After he smeared the refrigerator handles he went back and smeared the guest stateroom's door handle.

Then he joined Kelly and Klindt in the salon and picked up the sack of money. "Let's get going. Make sure you don't leave anything behind."

Klindt snapped his fingers, bent down and retrieved the flare gun from under a chair, where it had slid after Kardos knocked it out of his hand. "Almost forgot this."

Crocetti smeared the door's inner and outer handles on the way out.

When they got back to the helicopter, Pally registered his displeasure at being left alone with a round of ear flapping. Then his tail vibrated with joy when he caught sight of Kelly. She picked him up and held him for a bit and then snapped the leash on his collar and took him for a short walk.

Ten minutes later they were climbing above the clearing, very glad to leave the horror behind.

37

Crocetti adjusted the water temperature and stepped in the motel's shower. After scrubbing his hair and body he stood under the hot spray for ten more minutes, letting it sooth the places that hurt. As he toweled off, it seemed to him the aches and pains might have diminished a bit.

He dressed and checked on Kelly before he left. She was snoring softly, butterfly wings beating against a silken drum. A couple hours' extra sleep would be good for her.

He drove through town to Bond Honda and buttonholed the service manager and told him to expect a flatbed truck to deliver the Fit. "What are the chances of putting my car at the head of your repair queue on this fine Monday morning?"

The man snorted. "We're awful busy. I would say you're looking at Wednesday at the soonest."

Crocetti laid a crisp hundred-dollar bill on the countertop. "I'm in kind of a hurry."

"You and everyone else." But the C-note disappeared into his pocket faster than the eye could follow. "If it gets here by two, we'll have it ready by ten tomorrow."

"Sir, it always warms my heart to encounter a man with understanding."

On the way back to the motel he stopped at Bi-Mart to pick up a prepaid cell phone. They were in a rack near the register. He selected one and paid for it with cash.

When he got back to the motel room, Kelly was in the bathroom blow-drying her hair, head tilted at an angle that hurt his neck just looking at it. The scent of soapy-clean girl wafted out into the room. He sat down and picked up the TV remote. In what struck him as macabre irony, the Monday Matinée Movie feature turned out to be John Carpenter's *Vampires*. Jack Crow, played by James Woods, was a vampire hunter seeking out and destroying creatures of the night. Crow and his team used a cable and winch to drag a vampire into the sunlight, whereupon it burst into flames.

"Been there, done that," Crocetti said and switched off the television.

"So," Kelly said, "what's the status on the car?"

"We can pick it up tomorrow at ten. Then we'll head out for John Day."

"It'll be good to get back." She picked up the disposable phone. "Why did you buy this? You've got a phone."

"That, my dear girl, is a burner. A must-have for making anonymous calls."

"You plan to call someone anonymously?"

"Not me, you. You're going to call the Willamette National Forest ranger station and ask them to check out the area at these geocoodinates." He gave her a Post-it with the lat-long. "Your name is Carolyn Pratt. You and your husband were camping in a little clearing just off NF 5894. You heard a hair-raising scream from inside the only other RV camping there, a fairly new all-black coach. You knocked to see if someone needed help, but nobody answered the door. It's been bothering you, so you decided to report it."

"Give me the number and I'll make the call."

It took him five minutes to find it with his phone.

She tapped in the number and drummed a muted cadence on the table top with her fingertips before she said, "Hello, my name is Carolyn Pratt. This might turn out to be nothing, but ..." She launched into the story, not deviating much from the scenario he'd suggested, other than adding a few embellishments.

Crocetti made a circle with his index finger and thumb.

"Thank you very much. That will ease my mind," she said into the phone. "And I would appreciate it if you'd call me back and let me know one way or the other." She recited the number embossed on the handset.

After she ended the call, he said, "Honey, you're ready for Hollywood. That was perfect."

"You're too kind. You do realize when the ranger enters the coach and discovers the thing in that coffin, he'll call the state police?"

"I'm counting on it."

Four hours passed before the new phone's ring jolted them from afternoon naps. Kelly answered it and listened for several minutes before thanking the caller and ending the call with a tap on the screen. She looked at Crocetti and shrugged. "The ranger found no coach in the clearing, black or otherwise, only tire tracks where a large coach had been parked."

Crocetti swore. "I knew I should have locked the door so it wouldn't be stolen. Somebody drove off with a million-dollar coach, marveling at his luck."

"With a crispy corpse in a coffin in the back bedroom."

"And an interior badly in need of fumigation."

"Anyway, it's not our problem."

"Good point." It was a loose end, though, and loose ends bugged him.

An hour later Kelly announced she was hungry and suggested they go out to dinner. "Let's go someplace nice and celebrate being alive."

"Steak and baked?"

"Surf and turf. And perhaps a margarita?"

"You weren't kidding about celebrating. Okay, I'm ready to go when you are."

They picked the Brickhouse downtown. It had a bar and a lively atmosphere. The hostess showed them to a table toward the back, well away from boisterous revelers. A waiter brought them margaritas. They clinked their glasses together.

"Too bad Doug isn't here to celebrate with us," Kelly said.

"If I know Doug, he's celebrating privately with a few cold ones," Crocetti said. "On the flight to back to Chemult he was like a kid on Christmas morning, excited to buy new paint, a refurbished interior, and state-of-the-art avionics for Bella with his share of the money."

"Nothing but the best for his baby."

"What are you going to do with your share?"

She shrugged. "I'll have a pension, so I won't need it to live on. I think I'll probably invest it."

"Planning to retire soon?"

"I'm going to put in my papers just as soon as we get back to Brookings. I made the decision last night."

"Then I guess we have two things to celebrate."

They clinked their glasses together again.

"Cleo cat will be glad to see me," she said. "A neighbor is caring for her while I'm away."

"I'd forgotten about your cat. I wonder how she and Pally would get along?"

"Let's introduce them and find out."

The waiter arrived and set their food in front of them. His steak was tender and tasty. Kelly made "ummm" sounds over her surf and turf.

Between bites he said, "What are your plans after you retire?"

"I haven't given it much thought."

He blurted it out before he had time to rein in the impulse: "Would you like to explore Route 66 with me?"

She put her fork down. "Route 66?"

"A slice of Americana. Interesting places to see, eccentric characters to meet, adventure to be had. You know—kicks."

"Kicks?"

"Like the song says, that's what you get on Route 66."

"Ah. Interesting places, you said. Such as?"

"Such as ... the famous Cadillac Ranch in Amarillo. Ten graffiti-covered Cadillac automobiles buried nose-down in a line facing the same way."

"Only semi-interesting. Keep going."

The Georgia O'Keeffe Museum in Santa Fe. The museum has over a thousand of her paintings."

"See, now that appeals to me. That would be interesting. And educational to boot."

"You like museums? The Will Rogers Memorial Museum in Claremore, Oklahoma also might appeal to you."

"Sure, I'd love to see that."

"I like museums, too, but I love the kitschy stuff—wigwam motels, dinosaur attractions, drive-in theaters, funky cafes, vintage gas stations—Americana."

"Drive-in theaters?"

"Among the last in the country."

"Tell you what. I'll explore Route 66 with you, but only if we can go to the drive-in."

"It's a promise."

"And only if Cleo and Pally get along with each other."

"Right."

"You know," she said, smiling broadly, "this really does feel like a celebration. Let's have another margarita."

On a cloudy Tuesday morning they downed a quick breakfast at Sargent's Cafe on Third and then picked up the Honda. The service manager told him they had replaced a bad fuel sensor. Kelly followed him to the local Excelsior Rent-a-Ride to drop off the Fusion. Then they hit the road, not a bit sorry to leave Bend behind.

They reached John Day a little after two. The 150-mile trip had taken exactly three hours.

His coach was a welcome sight. He parked the car and grabbed the satchel, heavy with money. Kelly took Pally's leash. He climbed the steps and unlocked the door.

Home.

"Back in a minute," he told Kelly. He went down the hall to the master stateroom and transferred the money from the satchel to the safe in the floor of the closet, hidden under the carpet. Two hundred twenty, his and Kelly's shares.

Kelly had changed into a white short-sleeve pullover shirt and tan shorts with sandals. Bruising where the wire had bound her wrists and ankles was the only visible remnant of her ordeal. "Pally is tickled to be home," she said.

"I'm pretty tickled myself. Wish I could stay here and relax. But I've got to go see Einhorn now and settle him down. I'm going to tell him I had to leave town to rescue a friend stranded in Bend after her wallet was stolen."

"Better take me with you. I can back up your story."

They drove to the police station on East Main, asked to see Einhorn. After they were seated in his office they took turns telling him the story. He listened silently, his face a mask.

"She couldn't buy a bus ticket with no money, so she called me and told me what happened. I jumped in the car and made it there in under three hours.

"Just as we were about to start back to John Day, my new car gave me a check-engine light. It was Sunday, so we had to stay over to get it fixed. I took it to Bond Honda on Monday and picked it up this morning. Here's the repair invoice." He handed it to Einhorn. "Then we drove to John Day, got here forty-five minutes ago. I thought I'd better check in with you first thing."

Einhorn handed back the invoice. "I wish you had advised me before you took off."

"In hindsight I should have, but I figured I could zip over there and be back before anyone even realized I was gone. I hadn't counted on having car trouble. So have you made any progress on the Blunt murder investigation?"

"We like Pruitt for it."

"What does he say?"

"He doesn't say much. He hanged himself in his cell night before last. Tore his pants into strips and made a rope."

Pruitt hadn't seemed like the suicidal type—too obsessed with muscles and tattoos and tanning, a form of self-love. But his demise had an upside: Now it wouldn't be necessary to come back to John Day to testify against him.

"So we're good?"

Einhorn nodded. "But trouble seems to follow you around, Crocetti, so do me a favor. Next time you have an urge to visit John Day, try Pendleton instead, okay?"

"I assure you, you've seen the last of me." Crocetti spoke with utmost sincerity. If he never saw John Day again it would be too soon.

On the way back to the RV park, Crocetti looked over at Kelly. "Hard to believe Pruitt hanged himself. Think Kardos gave him a subliminal suggestion with a timed release?"

"I wouldn't doubt it. I haven't told you all the things he could do. Unbelievable stuff."

"Well, I know one thing—I've had my fill of this part of Oregon. Unless you have some reason for sticking around I'd like to head back to Brookings."

Her laugh had an humorless edge. "Nothing would please me more." A minute later she said, "How's your shoulder?"

"My shoulder? My shoulder is fine. I wish the rest of me felt as good."

"In that case . . ." She punched his shoulder, but not hard enough to hurt much. "Slug bug green. No hit backs."

"Where?"

She pointed at an old Volkswagon parked across the street.

Crocetti threw up his hands in surrender. But the juvenile humor was a welcome sign, given what she'd been through.

38

The bedside clock's segmented blue numerals indicated 6:12. He got out of bed as stealthily as he could, trying not to wake Kelly, and padded out to the kitchen and flipped the switch on the coffee maker. Four minutes later he filled a cup and sat down to read the online *Oregonian* for Wednesday, October 26. A GOP congressman from Alabama was discovered to have a substantial financial interest in a Huntsville brothel. The congressman angrily told a *Washington Post* reporter he had thought it was just a modeling agency. The Flat Earth Consortium announced an expedition to the South Pole, beyond which, they said, is the edge of the gigantic disc that is the Earth. They were going to get photographic proof of it to humiliate the arrogant scientists who called them crackpots. In other news, more and more people were buying steel shipping containers and converting them into homes.

He'd just finished reading the letters to the editor when Kelly shuffled out, belting her bathrobe, eyes squeezed shut against the bright October morning. She dropped into a chair at the table. He poured her a cup of coffee and gave her a peck on the cheek.

"I used mouthwash," she said. "My breath is minty fresh."

"That's nice. Mine's not. More like the exhaust fan in a chicken processing plant."

"I'll hold my breath."

"All right, but don't say I didn't warn you." She didn't seem repulsed afterward, so either she was being kind or her sense of smell had gone haywire. "How did you sleep?"

"I had a strange, strange dream. I was in bad trouble with the IRS for tax evasion."

He gave her side eye. "Seriously?"

"When you declare money as income, you have to reveal its source. Doug can run his share through his flying business, but what are you and I going to do come April fifteenth?"

"I'll say my rich uncle Victor kicked the bucket and left it to me in his will. You got to admit, it's more plausible than 'I killed a vampire and took his cash.'"

"Much more plausible. Well then, I guess I could've had a rich aunt. Aunt Victoria. Batty old thing as I recall."

"Batty as a football bat."

They turned their heads toward a commotion from the salon. Kelly's cat, a Siamese Pally's size, was on top of the desk with Pally's stuffed vampire in her mouth. The dog was objecting. Loudly.

Kelly jumped up. "Cleo! That's Pally's. You've got your own toys. Now give it back."

The cat dropped the toy on the desktop, and it tumbled over the edge. Pally snatched it before it hit the floor.

She inclined her head in their direction. "They get along okay, pretty much. Don't you think?"

"Other than constantly teasing each other. Not that I don't prefer that to fighting. Yeah, they're okay."

"I'm glad."

"I'm relieved. I wasn't sure it would work out."

"Don't look now, but your pal Hopple just drove up. I'm going to go throw on some clothes."

Hopple walked in with a self-satisfied look on his face. "I just collared a car thief," he said. "Call came over the radio to be on the lookout for an Acura stolen in Bandon, and damned if I didn't spot the car in McDonald's parking lot fifteen minutes later. The skell was in it, chowing down on a Quarter Pounder. I took him into custody without a fuss."

"Nice work."

"Thanks, partner. Where's Kelly?"

"She's—"

Kelly appeared just then wearing jeans and a light green sweater with canvas boat shoes. "Hi, Alex."

"Hey, Kelly. How do you like retirement so far?"

"It's only been a few weeks, but so far, so good."

"When do you two plan to hit the road?"

"End of the month," Crocetti said. "Route 66 is calling. It promises adventure."

"I'm envious. I got five years to go before I put in my papers. Meg and I are talking about maybe buying a small trailer after that and doing some traveling ourselves."

"You'd have a ball. Beats the hell out of staying in motels."

"Partner, I been meaning to ask you ... I was surprised when you just up and quit looking for the vampire killer. You were on it like a pit bull on a butt steak at first. What gives?"

Crocetti and Kelly exchanged looks. "Well, it's like this. After Popejoy told me to back off I did some soul searching, and I decided he was right. It's better that I leave it to active duty law enforcement. Besides, Route 66 will be more fun."

"Well, the killings have stopped, at least in the Pacific Northwest. The vampire's taking a break or he moved on."

"Good news either way."

Hopple rose to his feet. "Gotta go write that arrest report. End of the month you're out of here, eh? Meg and I want you two to come over for dinner before you leave. Later, partner."

"Take care." Crocetti closed the door after him.

Kelly raised an eyebrow. "Soul searching, huh?"

He grimaced. "That sounded dumb, didn't it? But he bought it. He's a good guy. I wish I could tell him the whole story, but it's better we keep it between the three of us like we agreed."

"Your call."

"What time are we meeting Doug at the Pine Cone, was it five?"

"Six."

"It wouldn't hurt to reinforce our vow of silence."

"Three-way pinky swear?"

"And hope to die. By the way, Miss Buchanan, those sure are some tight jeans. They're like a second skin. Hopple's eyes bugged out when he saw you."

"These days the females of the species are wearing form-fitted jeans, or haven't you noticed?"

"I've noticed, but very few have a form like yours to fit in them."

Her head tilted to the side. "That could be taken a couple different ways."

"I meant it in the more flattering way."

"In that case . . ." She presented her mouth to be kissed.

He obliged.

The old woman was sitting outside her RV, tea service and tarot cards on the table in front of her. This time she wore a navy jogging suit with a white strip up the side. Her dark eyes watched them approach.

"This is Kelly Buchanan," Crocetti told her. "Hope it's okay that I brought her with me."

"Of course," she said. "Sit."

She poured them steaming cups of tea and began drawing cards from the deck and placing them face-up on the table in four vertical rows. She turned over a card. "It seems you have faced great danger. Your fortitude enabled you to escape what appeared to be certain doom."

On the money.

She turned over another card and looked up at him. "You have found another mate."

Kelly squeezed his arm. Right again.

The last card. "Your quest is not at an end. The matter is still unresolved."

Two out of three wasn't bad. "With all due respect, the matter has been resolved for all time."

"Yes?"

The teapot was empty by the time he finished telling her the whole story. She had him repeat the part about placing Kardos' charred corpse in the coffin.

"That explains it," she said.

"Explains what?"

"Why there was no death card. In this context it can only mean Kardos is still alive."

"Ma'am, with all due respect, the tarot must be mistaken. If you had seen what was left of him . . ."

The dark eyes closed a moment. "You do not understand something about vampires. Among a vampire's considerable powers is the ability of its body to regenerate. That is why your bullets had no effect. Kardos' body healed almost instantaneously. You had a choice of three methods to destroy him permanently—a wooden stake through the heart, decapitation, or scattering his ashes to the wind. Instead, you laid him in a coffin lined with soil from his native Romania, which would expedite the regeneration process."

Kelly's hand flew to her mouth.

Crocetti tried to swallow, but his mouth and throat were dry. He couldn't recall reading anything about scattering a vampire's ashes.

"I had fervently hoped that you would destroy Kardos the Night Traveler. For two centuries, wherever he has gone, he has left untold misery behind."

"There haven't been any killings since."

"That you know of."

She had him there. Still, it was difficult to believe that anything on earth could survive incineration. It seemed flat impossible that anything could be regenerated from a cinder. In spite of her perfect record so far, maybe she had to be wrong about that, and Kardos' blackened corpse was lying in a ditch, dumped there by whoever hijacked his coach.

"Well," he said, "on that depressing note, we'll be on our way. Thank you for everything."

"I'm very honored to have met a phuri dai," Kelly said.

The old woman bowed her head.

They walked back to the car in silence. After they got in, she turned to him. "Well?"

"Kelly, it just doesn't seem possible Kardos' body could regenerate. You saw that thing. It was a cinder, nothing but ash. It would take a supernatural force to regenerate from that, and I still don't believe in the supernatural."

"Skeptic to the bitter end, eh?"

"I've grudgingly accepted the idea that vampires are part of the natural world, perhaps resulting from an unknown virus. But I'm certain there's nothing supernatural about them."

"At least the killings have stopped, according to Hopple."

"Then let us relax and proceed on the assumption that the Night Traveler remained a crispy critter. What do you say?"

"Okay. I just hope you're right."

He spotted the headline while scanning page three of the paper edition of the *Oregonian* he'd bought at the Circle K. The article rated only three column-inches at the bottom of the page.

RV Park Murders Mystify Mounties

RCMP Forensic investigators are collecting evidence after a Regina man was found murdered Tuesday at a Red Deer, Alberta RV park. It was the third murder to take place in an RV park in the past six weeks; the first was in Fort MacLeod, the second in High River.

When asked if the murders were connected, RCMP spokesman Sgt. Nigel Preston said, "That is yet to be determined." But unnamed sources said that all three victims died under "mysterious circumstances involving massive loss of blood."

The name of the latest victim is being withheld pending notification of next of kin. The investigation is ongoing, Preston said.

Crocetti put the paper down and stared out the window for a long time, seeing but not registering the scene outside, some old geezer unhitching his fifth-wheel.

Kelly came over and stood beside him. "Pretty quiet there, mister."

He handed her the paper and pointed to the article.

She sat down across from him to read it and then she got up again. "Do you think it's him?"

"It's tough to reconcile with my scientific understanding, but I've got a strong hunch it is. He crossed over into Canada and he's working his way north."

Crocetti considered giving the RCMP a call. He thought about it for all of three seconds. They'd just dismiss him as a crank. Or if they did believe him, having no idea how to overcome Kardos, they'd get themselves killed. He went to the closet and got the items he'd ordered from a specialty company and set them on the table.

Kelly pointed. "What are those things?"

"UV lights. Ten times more powerful than the one I used against Kardos and almost as compact."

Kelly nodded. "What do you plan to do with them?"

He stood and faced her, his palms on top of her shoulders. "Ever been to Canada?"

"No. And I have no plans to go."

"I don't blame you." He opened the refrigerator, got a beer, and returned to his chair. "I wouldn't go if I had a choice in the matter."

She sat down. "You really feel you have to, huh? I mean really and truly?"

"It's October twenty-sixth. We witnessed Kardos burn to a crisp on August twenty-eighth. In the two months since, I've been thinking about all the people spared grisly deaths at Kardos' hand. No telling how many that would be, but I was damn proud that I helped prevent it. Now we learn Kardos is alive and on another rampage, this time in Canada. And for me what started out as a contest, a matching of wits, has now become an obligation.

"If you can find somebody else with the knowledge and experience necessary to go up against Kardos then I'll gladly step aside. As things stand, I'm it, baby." He picked up a UV light. "I'm the only vampire hunter available."

Kelly was quiet for a long while. Finally she said, "How do you plan to find him? Canada's a huge country."

"Without the tracking device I guess I'll have to depend on hunches and luck."

"Well . . . there might be another way to find him."

"Such as?"

"Me."

"I don't understand."

She looked out the window. "I haven't talked very much about what happened to me while I was held captive. I've been trying to come to terms with it. I was raped. Not physically, psychically. Again and again, Kardos entered my consciousness and forced my body to respond sexually. I was powerless to resist. And I could hear him inside my mind, whispering, 'My Gabriella, my love.' Afterward, I felt dirty, as though my own body betrayed me."

"He never violated you in a physical sense, never laid a hand on you?"

"It was only mental. Psychic rape. But in some ways . . . in some ways it was more invasive."

"God," he said. "I'm so sorry."

"It's my own fault. I keep thinking, if only I hadn't gone back for my purse, he never would have caught me."

"And if only I had known about scattering his ashes, he wouldn't be on a killing spree now. Let's not dwell on past mistakes, honey. Now what did you mean about another way to find him?"

"I'm getting to that. The sexual assault was made possible by a psychic link, some sort of mental connection. I could sense him and vice versa. He knew when I was thirsty or I needed to use the bathroom, and I felt his ravenous hunger and how the blood in his refrigerator—which he warmed in the oven before he fed, by the way—only partially satisfied him.

"After he died—or appeared to—the psychic link weakened. But it didn't go away entirely. I thought it was some sort of residual effect, like an echo, and assumed it would dissipate. Instead, starting when we got back to John Day, it became stronger. I pushed it down, willing it to leave me. When I dropped my guard, though, there it was, growing stronger by the day. I thought I was going crazy. Post-traumatic stress disorder or something. But now it makes sense.

"I am a psychic tracking receiver. Right now the signal's faint, because Kardos is so far away. But it would increase in strength if he were closer. I can home in on him as though he had a tracking device, one he can't remove.

"So, my errant knight, you're the only person with the knowledge and experience necessary to defeat Kardos, and I'm the only person who can locate him. And like you, I can't refuse, not and live with myself. Besides, the son of a bitch violated me. I want revenge."

"Boy, you are one tough broad, Kelly Buchanan."

"I don't feel tough. I feel scared."

"That makes two of us."

Crocetti got another beer and sat down on the sofa. Pally jumped up and licked his face. Crocetti hugged him. "You're a good boy," he said, tousling the animal's fur.

"You know," Kelly said, "there was a time, not too long ago, when a dog licking your face would have filled you with horror. And I haven't seen you use hand sanitizer in quite a while, come to think of it. Don't tell me you no longer have germophobia?"

"I don't know. Maybe." He wiped his cheek with his hand. "I'm not feeling all that much anxiety about it these days. Funny."

She sat down next to him and rested her head on his shoulder and sighed. "I was really looking forward to seeing Route 66."

"We'll get there, honey, we'll get there. Promise."

After several minutes of silence she said, "Hey, as vampire hunters, shouldn't we have uniforms?"

He laughed. "We'll pick them up on the way. I'm thinking epaulets."

"And maybe gold braid?"

"But of course."

"Should we invite Doug to join the party?"

"Definitely."

And so, at the Pine Cone later, over the first round of beer, Crocetti turned to Klindt and broached the subject. "Ever done any flying in Canada, Doug?"

"Nope. Why do you ask?"

Crocetti took a long pull on his beer before he answered. "There's been an unexpected development . . ."

39

Under an overcast November sky, the helicopter hovered above a grove of western Alberta pine trees. The thick boughs concealed everything underneath. Including, according to Kelly, a black coach.

"It's—*he's* right below us," she said. "I'm certain of it."

"Now to find a decent landing spot," Klindt said. He tapped the screen of the new state-of-the-art, do-everything GPS in the center of the instrument panel, and it displayed a closeup satellite view of their present location. He pointed at the screen. "There's a treeless area over here that looks like it might do. Let's check it out, boys and girls."

The spot was large enough, but barely. The rotor blades had only about a yard of clearance, but Klindt set the chopper down like it was no big deal. After the turbine's whine died, they climbed out. Crocetti opened the satchel and handed one of the new UV flashlights to Klindt and gave the one he used before on Kardos to Kelly. The satchel contained three sharpened oak stakes, a mallet, a machete, and the lock picks. The taser and pepper spray were in the bottom desk drawer back home next to the Colt with the bent barrel.

He looked up at them. "Everybody ready?"

"Just a sec," Klindt said and climbed into the cockpit. He reached behind the back seat and came out holding an AR-15 with a 30-round magazine. "A little insurance."

"Bring it along if you want, but bullets are ineffective against a creature that heals instantly."

Klindt shrugged and slung the rifle over his shoulder and grabbed his lantern. "Christ on a Ritz cracker it's cold."

Kelly had the look of someone listening hard, and then she said, "Kardos knows we're coming. He's waiting for us. I can sense it."

"A psychic connection tends to put a serious crimp in the element of surprise," Crocetti said.

Klindt pointed to an opening in the trees. "This way."

Twenty yards into the woods they encountered dense underbrush. It thinned out, and eighty yards further on they came upon the black coach. It lurked in the shadows under a thick canopy of pines, practically invisible.

The coach's steps were fully extended, like an invitation. Before reaching into the satchel for the lock picks, Crocetti tried the door handle. It wasn't locked. He glanced back at his fellow vampire hunters. Kelly was chewing her lower lip, face white. Klindt was clutching the AR-15, jaw set. Crocetti eased the door open.

Several seconds passed before a baritone voice spoke from the shadows within. "Please come in, good people. I assure you, no harm will befall you." Thick Eastern European accent.

By the interior's dim light, Crocetti could make out a dark shape. He paused, his thumb on the UV switch. "A bit dark in there for my friends and me."

"You may bring a lantern if you lower the brightness. My eyes are sensitive to light."

Crocetti turned around. "Well, good people, should we accept his cordial invitation?"

"Considering it took us two days to find him," Klindt said, "it wouldn't make much sense to fall back now."

"I agree," Kelly said, "even though my better judgment is telling me I'm stark raving mad."

They climbed the stairs and stepped inside, ready to bolt back through the doorway at the first provocation. Klindt adjusted his lantern's brightness level to that of a 15-watt bulb.

The stench of decay was less objectionable, masked by an insistent pine fragrance. A can of room deodorizer was on the counter. Beside it, a tin of Altoids. Crocetti almost smiled.

"Please . . . sit."

They sat on a royal blue velvet divan, Kelly in the center on Crocetti's left, Klindt on the other end, gripping the AR-15.

Their host sat facing them on a high-backed chair covered in red satin. In human form, Kardos appeared to be a tall man in his mid-thirties with a predilection for all-black clothes—odd attire for an RV traveler but appropriate for his features: Gaunt, but not emaciated, skin so pallid it had a translucent quality. Thick black hair, combed straight back. Thin-lipped, with a bit of an overbite. A patrician nose. Heavy black eyebrows. Most arresting of all, large eyes, dark as obsidian, that bespoke a great sadness, or seemed to.

Sartorial differences aside, the man sitting before them and the man in the the old photograph on the wall were one and the same person, without question. However, the photo couldn't capture his presence. It made the hair stand up on the back of Crocetti's neck, like an electrical field.

Kardos regarded them silently for long seconds. Finally he said, "We keep encountering each other, Mr. Crocetti."

For a moment Crocetti wondered how Kardos had learned his name, and then he remembered the monogrammed cane. "Seems like it," he said.

"One would suspect our encounters are not accidental."

More dry humor from the sad-eyed vampire, but Crocetti didn't feel much like laughing. "Why did you invite us in?"

"I must apologize for my lack of hospitality," Kardos said. "I have no refreshments to offer you. Except chilled blood."

"We're good." Crocetti leaned forward. "Speaking of blood, if you have a refrigerator full, why have you resumed killing people?"

Kardos smiled sadly. "Alas, stored blood retains almost no life force." He sighed. "If I am to live, I must have fresh blood. Unfortunately, that means I must kill. For the past fifty years I have . . . regretted the necessity."

"Not as much as your victims." Crocetti sat back. "Have you kept count of the people you've killed for their blood?"

Kardos closed his eyes and took a long, slow breath before he answered. "Do you know how old I am?"

Crocetti nodded. "You are two hundred and ten years old. You were born in Bucharest in eighteen oh seven, the son of a prince. At age thirty-seven you became a vampire. You came to America by steamship, in eighteen eighty-seven."

"Impressive, Mr. Crocetti."

"I can't take credit. The information came straight from the phuri dai."

"Ah yes, the phuri dai. How many people, you ask? I have fed on the blood of five thousand eight hundred forty-two."

It seemed impossibly high, but a quick calculation showed the figure was plausible. "Good Lord," Crocetti said.

"The Lord had no part in it. The Lord has forsaken me."

Crocetti tried again. "Are you going to tell us why you invited us in?"

Kardos' gaze slid to Kelly and his eyes filled. "I wanted to see her one last time." He blinked the tears away. "Do you believe in reincarnation, Daniel Crocetti?"

Crocetti caught himself before he shook his head. "I won't say it's impossible." Not any longer.

The pupils in Kardos' eyes enlarged as he stared at Kelly.

She stiffened suddenly. "Viktor, no . . . please stop. I don't want you to do that, not ever again. Please . . ."

Crocetti raised the UV flashlight, his finger on the switch. "Stop it, Kardos. Now."

Kardos raised his hands. "As you wish." He rose from the chair. The top of his head came within eight inches of touching the ceiling, which made him around six four. He went over to the photographs on the wall and looked at them for long moments. When he turned away his cheeks were wet. "My wife, my sweet daughter, everyone I loved, everyone I knew— gone. But I live on. And on, condemned to an eternity of loneliness, an eternity of feeding on the blood of innocents, an eternity of . . . this."

Short, fine black fur appeared on his face and neck. His nose and mouth reshaped into a muzzle with large flared nostrils. His ears grew pointed and fingernails became claws. His upper canine teeth elongated, becoming enormous needle-sharp fangs.

"*See*?" His voice had changed to a sibilant growl. He took a step toward them. "*Look upon the last of the royal Kardos line. Look upon an abomination.*"

Crocetti didn't care to have a closer look. He raised the UV light again. "Don't come any nearer."

The thing that was Kardos halted and growled, "*You need not worry. I mean you no harm.*"

But Klindt, visibly shaken, accidentally unleashed a burst of UV toward Kardos, who wrapped a wine-red velvet curtain around his body, protecting his head.

"I did not mean to frighten you," Kardos said from within the shroud, his voice back to baritone. "I am resuming my . . . other form." Thirty seconds later he let go of the curtain.

"Incredible, how quickly you can switch back and forth," Crocetti said.

"The result of two centuries' practice." He sat down again.

"You regret having killed innocent people for their blood, three of them recently. Are you going to go on killing?"

"No." He'd said it with finality. "Killing to feed is necessary for a vampire's survival. The urge is too powerful to resist. I have tried and failed. And that brings me to the main reason why I have invited you in." He paused for several seconds. "I want . . . I want you to kill me."

Crocetti glanced at Kelly and Klindt. Their faces mirrored his perplexity. "What was that again?"

"I do not wish to live any longer if I have to go on as I have. Only death will bring me peace. I look to you to provide it."

"But Viktor," Kelly said, "you told me you hoped to find a doctor who could cure you."

"A foolish hope. I have come to realize that medical science will not be my salvation." Kardos pointed to the satchel at Crocetti's feet. "Show me what you have brought to kill me."

Crocetti opened the bag and dumped out the machete, mallet, and wooden stakes onto the salon's deep green carpet.

"The machete will not be needed," Kardos said. "A stake through the heart will suffice."

Crocetti leaned forward. "Let me get this straight. You want one of us to kill you."

"Precisely."

Crocetti looked at Kelly. Color had drained from her face.

"First, however," Kardos said, "a few details." He stood and walked over to an ornately carved antique desk and returned with a stack of documents, which he handed to Crocetti.

The first document, addressed "To whom it may concern," had been created by hand with a quill; the writing looked like calligraphy. It said: "I cannot go on any longer. I have therefore elected to kill myself. Viktor Kardos." Short and to the point.

"It will ensure that you are not charged with murder," Kardos said, "if they find out you were here."

The next document was thicker and bound. Handwritten on the cover: "Last Will and Testament." Crocetti opened it and scanned the precise calligraphic script. One sentence jumped out: "Whereas I have no next of kin, I bequeath all my worldly possessions to Kelly Lauren Buchanan as sole heir." Kelly's Brookings address followed, no doubt obtained via the psychic connection.

At Kelly's sharp intake of breath next to his ear, Crocetti realized she had been reading over his shoulder.

The section that enumerated Kardos' worldly possessions listed his coach and its contents, his Fort Lauderdale home and its contents, and all monies in an account at Credit Suisse in Zurich. Undoubtedly a confidential numbered account. The will had been notarized two days ago, apparently by a notary public who worked nights.

Kardos took the documents from Crocetti and put them on the desk. "With that matter out of the way, let us proceed."

Crocetti had more questions he'd like to ask Kardos, such as whether he made Pruitt hang himself in jail, but they were relatively unimportant. "What do you want me to do?"

Kardos stretched out on his back on the floor of the salon. "Now you must drive a stake into my heart. Afterward, turn my body over to make it look as though I fell upon the stake. When you are a safe distance from here, telephone the police anonymously and tell them you saw my body through the window."

Crocetti stared at him. "Are you sure you want go through with this? It's going to be painful."

"The pain will be as nothing compared to the agony of my loneliness and self-hatred."

"Well . . . as long as you're sure." Crocetti looked at Kelly and Klindt. They sat silently, eyes wide.

Crocetti picked up the mallet and a stake and knelt beside Kardos. Once he had the stake's sharp point positioned just to the left of Kardos' sternum, he raised the mallet . . . and froze.

Kardos sorrowful eyes, overflowing with tears, were on Kelly. "Goodbye, my Gabriella," he whispered. "Goodbye, my love."

Kelly snuffled and reached in her pocket for a tissue and dabbed at her eyes with it.

Crocetti raised the mallet again. And then lowered it. "I can't," he said. "I can't do it." True, he had maneuvered Kardos outside to be incinerated in the sunlight, but that had been different. It was self-defense. This was assisted suicide. It felt uncomfortably close to cold-blooded murder.

"You must," Kardos said. "If you do not, I will kill again. And the blood will be on your hands."

Crocetti shook his head. "I'm sorry."

Kardos got to his feet and snatched the stake out of Crocetti's hands, and as the three of them watched in frozen horror, he fell forward on it, impaling himself with such force the stake's point tented the back of his coat. His arms and legs spasmed for several seconds and then were still. In death, Kardos' body seemed to shrink.

The shocked silence was broken by Kelly blowing her nose. "So terribly tragic," she said between sobs.

"Poor bastard," Klindt said.

Crocetti swallowed. However you looked at it, Kardos was a tragic figure. Faced with a choice between killing or dying, he chose to die. In the end he took the honorable course—too late, unfortunately, for his five thousand-plus victims. Crocetti turned to his companions. "We should get out of here."

"I'm all for that," Klindt said. "The sooner the better."

Crocetti stepped over Kardos' body to get to the antique desk. The will and suicide note lay on top, easily found by police. He opened the top drawer. It contained three items: two keys with tags labeled "Coach, spare" in precise script, and a red leather-bound book, its cover blank. Inside was a numbered list of dates, names, and places. The first entry was "5-4-1844, Andrei Bodescu, Ploiesti RO." He flipped to the last page. The final entry was number 5842: "11-15-2017, William Dalton, Red Deer AB CA." The Ostrows' two entries were five lines above it, followed by forest ranger Vern Lachlin's.

"What's in the book?" Kelly said.

"It's a listing of his victims. Every last one." He slipped the book in the satchel and grabbed one of the keys. Then he gathered up the items on the carpet and tossed them in the satchel, minus one wooden stake, and followed Kelly and Klindt out the door and locked it with the spare key.

When they got to the helicopter, Crocetti used the burner to phone the Royal Canadian Mounted Police and report suspicious circumstances at the coach's location. Then he crushed the phone under his heel and hurled it into the woods.

Alone with their thoughts, the trio didn't talk much on the flight back to Brookings. Crocetti tried to imagine the investigators' reactions when they found Kardos with a stake through his heart, a refrigerator full of blood, and an ebony coffin in the master stateroom. It would make for lively conversation in the Mounties' squad room.

When they were ten miles out, Kelly broke the silence. "Dan, do you think they'll probate Kardos' will right away? It would be nice to see Route 66 with you before I have to deal with all that inheritance stuff."

Crocetti shrugged. "If you have to attend to those things first, Route 66 will wait. We have all the time in the world."

She sighed. "When I read the part of the will naming me Kardos' sole beneficiary, I almost fell over. I mean, why me? I didn't want anything from him."

"Who else was he going to leave it to? After all, you were the reincarnation of his beloved Gabriella."

"Please don't make fun of that. He was so . . . smitten with me. Through our mind link I felt his loneliness and yearning for his lost lost love. And lost humanity. You saw his tears as he looked up at me from the floor?"

"They're the reason I couldn't drive the stake in his chest. I share your compassion for the miserable son of a bitch."

"Anyway," she said, "I didn't want anything from him."

Klindt leaned over. "I'll take whatever part of that fortune you don't want, Kelly."

Crocetti smiled to himself. She might be singing another tune after the probate. Kardos hadn't had a numbered account in a Swiss bank for his spare change.

Brookings was a welcome sight. He'd decided to make the friendly coastal town his home base instead of Newport, the other candidate. The helicopter made a pass over the Plush Horse. Crocetti pointed out his coach to Klindt. On approach to the airport he spotted the little Honda, its red paint once again unblemished, below in the parking area.

When the turbine's whine had diminished to a wheeze, they gathered up their stuff and climbed out of the craft. The sky darkened; rain was on the way, plenty of it.

"I don't know about you, boys and girls," Klindt said, "but I'm going to need some time to process . . . well, everything."

"Tell me about it," Crocetti said.

Kelly nodded, her face solemn.

A shuddering jaw-creaker of a yawn took over Crocetti's entire body. Thoughts of Kelly snuggled beside him in the king-size bed in his coach's master stateroom shoved all other considerations aside, including sad-eyed vampires.

He put an arm around Kelly. "Let's go home."

40

Toward the end of the first day of spring, an orange sun skimmed the ocean's horizon as they motored south on California Route 1, the Pacific Coast Highway. A late start from Brookings loused up their plan to make it to Santa Monica, the western terminus of Route 66, in a single day's drive. Not a problem. Kelly had called and reserved a spot at Osiris RV Resort in San Simian, fifty miles ahead. Seventy-five per night. The "Resort" in the name gave them license to charge fees that would make a stickup man blush.

"What a view," Kelly said, looking out her side window. "I love the Monterey Peninsula. Daryl and I were talking about moving here from Sacramento." She looked over at him. "I hope you don't mind me talking about Daryl."

"Not at all. Daryl and Alison shared a big part of our lives. It wouldn't be right to redact them."

"Redact . . . there you go again with the vocabulary. But I agree, totally."

"Change of subject," Crocetti said. "Are you feeling like an heiress yet?"

"Not so much. I can't get my head around the concept of having enough money to do or buy anything I wish. Literally anything."

"So what do you wish to do or buy?"

"I wish . . . to start a non-profit foundation."

"Excuse me?"

"Last week I was thumbing through Kardos' book, reading the names of his victims. That night, as I was drifting off to sleep, I had an incredible idea. The Kardos Foundation. It would have a single purpose—to track down his victims' next-of-kin and make restitution. What do you think?"

"The Kardos Foundation." He nodded. "It's genius."

"I would have been crushed if you had hated the idea."

"It will be an ambitious undertaking, though. For a setup like that, you'll need a battalion of researchers, investigators, accountants, administrators, and lawyers."

"Details, details. I just think it's the right thing to do with the money from Kardos' estate."

"I agree. And he'd probably approve."

"I'm certain of it. When we get back I'm going to find some experienced, competent people who can make it happen. You and I and Doug can be on the board of directors."

Crocetti grinned. "I can't get over Doug's reaction when you told him you were giving him Kardos' coach—he looked like he was going to pass out. That rig cost a cool million new, not including the coffin. Very generous, Kelly."

"He earned it. And I forgot to tell you—I sold the coffin to Meecham Funeral Home." She was quiet for a while and then she said, "After we're finished exploring Route 66, I think I'm going to use a small portion of my new wealth for something totally selfish."

"Oh?"

"I want to buy or build a small beach house for us, one with a killer ocean view. It will have a deck and lots of glass. Our home base in Brookings."

"You're just full of genius ideas, lady."

"Want to hear another one? I would like to see to it that every animal shelter in Oregon becomes a no-kill shelter. If that works out, we'll look at other states."

"Another ambitious undertaking. But well worth doing."

"Also, I'm going to have the rip in my truck's back seat repaired."

He chuckled. "Worth billions, and you're going to have your truck's upholstery fixed. Why not get a new truck?"

"The one I've got is just fine."

He pretended to talk into a handheld recorder. "The heiress is a peculiar woman . . ."

"Enough with the heiress stuff. Aside from our beach house, those billions shall be designated for restitution and philanthropic endeavors."

". . . but she's a very special one."

He had read about a woman in Corpus Christi who won a $548-million-dollar Powerball jackpot. She and her husband went on a spending spree—a mansion, a penthouse condo in Dallas, matching Bentleys, a Cessna Citation, and a yacht. A year and a half later they were broke.

Kelly seemed lost in thought, her lovely profile framed by a sunset of purples and pinks. He had resigned himself to being alone for the rest of his days, unable to conceive of being with any other woman after Alison . . . but now the thought of life without Kelly was unbearable—even though he missed Alison and always would.

He felt a wet tongue on his arm. Pally stood at his elbow, tail wagging, tongue lolling, eyes imploring. Crocetti stroked his soft fur and scratched the spot above his tail the way he liked. The thought of life without Pally was also unbearable, he'd come to realize. After his furry partner returned to his bed, Crocetti reached for the hand sanitizer. Empty bottle. He would refill it when he got a chance, no hurry.

A bit later they stopped at a rest area between Monterey and Big Sur. A VW Beetle trailing blue smoke chugged past.

He punched Kelly's upper arm. "Slug bug yellow."

She walloped him back twice as hard. "You forgot to say no hit backs."

"I forgot on purpose," Crocetti lied.

THE END

ABOUT THE AUTHOR

Carter McKnight is at present touring the country in a motor coach, accompanied by a small canine companion. When not writing spine-tingling horror in the coach's office-like parlor, McKnight enjoys exploring places that are well off the beaten path, always on the lookout for intriguing locales for future horror-thriller novels.

BEFORE YOU GO …

If you enjoyed *Night Traveler*, please consider letting your friends know through Facebook, Twitter, or word of mouth. And if you're so inclined, Carter McKnight would be honored indeed if you would leave a review. Here's a link to the book's Amazon page:

https://www.amazon.com/dp/0986395757